NEVER TELL THEM

A PSYCHOLOGICAL SUSPENSE THRILLER

N. L. HINKENS

This is a work of fiction. Names, characters, organizations, places, events and incidents are either products of the author's imagination or are used fictitiously. For more information about the author, please visit **www.normahinkens.com**

Text copyright @ 2021 Norma Hinkens

Published by Dunecadia Publishing, California

ISBN: 978-1-947890-28-2

Cover by: **www.derangeddoctordesign.com**

Editing by: **www.jeanette-morris.com/first-impressions-writing**

1

G lancing up at a commotion outside her kitchen's bay window, Sonia caught sight of a small U-Haul truck attempting to back into the driveway of the vacant house that bordered her back yard. She scrubbed distractedly at the congealed remnants of the previous evening's lasagna, now welded to the white porcelain casserole dish she had cooked it in, as her eyes lit on the lean, dark-haired man emerging from the moving truck. She had spotted him at the house several times over the past month, but he had yet to stop by and introduce himself. One of Celia's estranged sons, no doubt.

Abandoning the dish to a much-needed soaking, she shook the suds from her hands and watched as the man staggered inside hefting an unwieldy box. Folding her arms across her chest, she let out a disgruntled humph. Her elderly neighbor had only been dead six weeks and, as Sonia had predicted, the scavengers had descended.

She inserted another capsule into her Nespresso, vowing it would be her last shot of caffeine for the day, before retreating to the family room to update her mother on the new arrival to the neighborhood. After Sonia had divorced her husband, Finn, seven years ago, her widowed mother sold her house in Raleigh and moved in to help defray the cost of the mortgage and to care for Jessica, Sonia and Finn's eight-year-old daughter. Stationed overseas in some classified location, Finn hadn't darkened the door of the house since their acrimonious divorce, and only called his daughter on the rare occasion—usually with some lame excuse about why he hadn't sent her a gift for Christmas or a card for her birthday.

"The vultures have landed," Sonia announced, sinking down on her favorite nail-head-tufted gray couch next to Evelyn, her mother, who was glued to the local morning news on TV. Her recent hip surgery had put a temporary halt to her customary morning walks around the neighborhood to glean the local gossip.

Evelyn blinked at her in confusion. "What's that, dear?"

"I said the vultures have landed."

Evelyn frowned. "You mean the cardinals? I saw five or six of them at the feeder earlier."

Sonia let out a snort of laughter. "I'm not talking about birds."

"Then, I have no idea what you're rambling on about." Evelyn eyed the mug in Sonia's hand with a disapproving air. "How much coffee have you had this morning?"

Sonia shrugged good-naturedly. "Enough to call it a serious hobby. Back to the vultures—I'm talking about Celia's missing-in-action offspring."

A glimmer of curiosity flickered in Evelyn's eyes. She glanced uncertainly at the television before muting it and giving Sonia her full attention. "Are they at the house?"

Sonia gave a teasing nod. "A U-Haul truck just pulled in."

"Then they must be moving in—or maybe they're here to pick stuff up." Evelyn sniffed in indignation. "I'd like to give those boys a piece of my mind for neglecting their mother all these years." She frowned, rubbing a thumb over her gnarled fingers. "Still, I suppose we should take something over, for Celia's sake. I could whip up some of my French Toast muffins. Not that—"

"Whoa! Slow down, Mom! You're getting ahead of yourself." Sonia took a quick sip of coffee, and wrapped her fingers around her mug. "Here's what I do know. I saw a small U-Haul backing into the driveway, so I *assume* someone's moving in, although they can't have brought much."

"They won't need it. All Celia's furniture is still there." Evelyn cocked her head to one side. "Did you get a good look at them?"

"*Him*, not them," Sonia corrected. "Only one guy got out of the truck. I watched him carry a box inside. Tall, dark-haired. That's about all I could make out through the kitchen window. I think it's the same guy who stopped by a couple of times already."

Evelyn quirked an eyebrow. "Maybe you should fix yourself up and go over there."

Sonia shot her mother a reproving look. "Seriously? You're trying to pair me up with the jerk who neglected his mother for years on end? A minute ago, you wanted to give him a tongue lashing."

Evelyn pulled her wrinkled lips into an exaggerated grimace. "I might still do that, after I introduce myself."

Sonia gestured with her chin at the television. "Any news I need to know about?"

Evelyn reached for the remote and turned the volume back up. "Only the same depressing tidbits—break-ins, robberies, and what the weather's planning to unleash on us next. Oh, and it's the five-year-anniversary of that missing local girl—Katie Lambert. Such a sad story. You remember her, right? Her mother died of cancer when she was young; her father raised her. He committed suicide after she'd been missing for two years—couldn't take it anymore."

"Ugh, don't remind me." Sonia shuddered. "This is why I don't watch the news anymore. It puts a damper on the rest of the day. How about you go bake some muffins for our new neighbor instead?"

"So now you're warming up to the idea of taking a peace offering over, are you?" Evelyn turned off the television and got to her feet with a grunt. "Admit it, you're just as curious about him as I am."

"Nobody's as nosy as you are, Mom. I'm willing to extend a neighborly introduction, as long as you promise not to rip into him right away for being missing in action all these years. As far as we're concerned, Celia was a sweet lady, but we don't know her sons' side of the story."

Evelyn patted her ash blonde pixie bob. "She constantly made excuses for them—they were always too busy with their careers and the like to visit. It's a crying shame. I think one of her boys used to call her now and again, but neither of them ever came to visit in all the years she lived here."

Sonia shrugged. "They must have had their reasons."

Evelyn drew her thin brows together. "Or maybe they're ungrateful louts, plain and simple—here to cash in on her estate now that she's gone."

"Guess we'll find out." Sonia drained the last of her coffee. "Why don't you start baking and I'll take the muffins over as a gesture of goodwill. Test the waters, so to speak."

. . .

A LITTLE OVER AN HOUR LATER, Sonia stepped onto the back porch of Celia's house and rapped on the screen door, shivering in her cotton shirt in the morning breeze. To appease her mother, she'd taken the trouble of getting dressed and pulling a comb through her unruly, dirty blonde waves. More often than not, she spent the day in her pajamas working on room layouts or mood boards for her home-based interior design business. When presenting proposals to potential clients, however, she always struck the right note with a clean, polished look that complemented the modern farmhouse designs she was known for. For the reconnaissance muffin mission, she'd kept it casual, opting for a loose-fitting, long-sleeved, white Henley shirt and a pair of skinny jeans with just enough perfectly positioned fraying holes not to look ridiculous for a woman in her late thirties.

She shifted impatiently from one ankle-boot-clad foot to the other, balancing the platter of her mother's freshly baked muffins in her left hand, the tantalizing aroma of sugar and cinnamon wafting into the spring air. Several cardinals were flitting around the bird feeder in the yard. Jessica had been diligent about keeping it full of seed ever since Celia's passing. But her son might not be so keen on the idea of greeting the neighbor kid bright and early every morning. He was taking his sweet time answering the door, but Sonia was reluctant to knock again in case he was knee-deep in boxes and deliberately ignoring the bell. She could always try again later after she picked up Jessica from school.

Just as she was about to head back home, the door swung open. Sonia took a step backward, blinking in surprise. The dark-haired man she'd seen emerging from the U-Haul stood in the hallway, a whimpering child wriggling doggedly in his arms. He set him down on the floor, and the little boy promptly stuck his thumb in his mouth and backed away, staring wide-eyed at Sonia. He looked to be about three or four-years-old, pale-faced, with a head of dark curls.

"Hi, I'm Sonia Masterton," she said in a breezy tone. "My mother and daughter and I live in the bungalow that backs up to your yard. I saw the moving truck and wanted to welcome you to the neighborhood. My mother, Evelyn, was a good friend of Celia's. She sent you over some muffins. We're terribly sorry for your loss."

A nerve twitched in the man's neck, but his face remained expressionless. "Thank you."

Sonia arched a questioning brow. "So, are you Ray, or Tom?" she prompted, in a tone designed to highlight his rudeness at failing to introduce himself.

He cleared his throat, his gaze flitting briefly over her shoulder and back. "Uh ... I'm Ray, Celia's oldest."

Sonia leaned over and ruffled the boy's curls. "And what's your name, little man?" He flinched under her touch, backing farther away, a look of panic in his eyes.

"It's okay, buddy," Sonia said, straightening up. "New house, and a strange woman asking him questions—no wonder he looks scared."

"That's ... my son—Henry," Ray said. "He's tired. It's his nap time."

"Well hello, Henry," Sonia said, softening her tone. "I have a daughter called Jessica, and I know she's going to be very excited to meet you when she gets home from school. Would you like to come over and play later on?"

Henry lifted his head a fraction and glanced mistrustfully at Ray. He pulled out his thumb, his eyes skimming to

Sonia and then back to his father, as if teetering on the verge of answering.

"Perhaps another day," Ray said brusquely. "This has been a rough transition for Henry. His mother—my wife—passed away shortly before Celia."

A dismayed gasp slipped through Sonia's lips. "I'm ... so sorry to hear that. I had no idea. Celia never mentioned you were married, or that she had a grandson."

Ray fidgeted with the door handle, as though itching to close it. "We weren't in contact much over the years. She didn't know about Henry."

"Oh, I see. Well, family dynamics aren't easy," Sonia offered, feeling flustered at the minefield she'd inadvertently steered the conversation into. "I'm not in touch with Jessica's father much either." She bit her lip, kicking herself for volunteering information that was none of Ray's business.

An uncomfortable silence fell between them, broken only by the intermittent trills of the birds nearby.

As though sensing the tension in the air, Henry began sniffling again.

"Poor little guy!" Sonia exclaimed. "He must be exhausted."

Ray swooped him up, his face reddening when Henry began screaming and pounding his tiny fists on his father's chest.

"I'll leave you to it," Sonia said, directing a meaningful look at Henry. "I'm sure you have plenty to do, unpacking and sorting through boxes."

"Yes, it's overwhelming," Ray responded in a harried tone.

Sonia gave a sympathetic nod. "If you need any help, weeding things out or rearranging furniture, I'm an interior designer by trade." Raising her voice to make herself heard over Henry's wailing, she held the muffins aloft, "I can set these in the kitchen for you, if you want."

Ray gave a tight smile, reaching out a hand for the muffins, all the while struggling to keep Henry in a precarious grip. "Thanks, no need. I'll make sure and get your plate back to you."

"Don't worry about it. Jessica can pick it up later," Sonia replied. "She'll want to meet Henry anyway."

She waved an awkward goodbye and turned to go, exhaling a sigh of relief as she made her way back across the adjoining lawns. All in all, it had been an uncomfortable encounter. Ray had been evasive when it came to her questions. She'd basically had to pull the answers out of him. And Celia's grandson had been a jaw-dropping twist. Wait until her mother heard about that!

She frowned to herself, rubbing her arms briskly as she quickened her step. Was she reading too much into things, or had Henry seemed frightened of his father? And why on earth was there a price tag hanging from the kid's sweater? Something felt off about the situation. Ray had been in an awful hurry to get rid of her—a little too eager for someone with nothing to hide.

2

E velyn was busy wiping down the polished concrete kitchen counters and putting away her baking supplies when Sonia got home. She looked pointedly at her daughter as she wrung out the sponge in the sink. "Well, what's the scoop?"

Sonia pulled out the rattan-and-walnut bar stool at the kitchen island and slid onto it. "He's aloof. I got the impression he couldn't wait for me to leave."

Evelyn put a hand on her hip, a testy look on her face. "Did he at least thank you for the muffins? Maybe his highness thinks I should have made a bigger effort for the long-lost son. Which of them was it anyway—Ray or Tom?"

"Ray, the older one." Sonia reached for an apple from the white marble fruit bowl and twisted it coyly in her hand. "To tell you the truth, I don't think he noticed what was on the plate I handed him. He was too busy trying to restrain his child."

Evelyn's lips flapped open and closed several times before she spluttered, "Child? What child? Celia never mentioned anything about a grandchild."

Sonia munched on a bite of apple, savoring the rare opportunity to relay some juicy news. "Ray has a little boy—he looks to be about three or four. His name's Henry."

Evelyn gave an annoyed shake of her head and began rubbing a cloth vigorously over the gleaming countertop. "I can't believe it. Why would Celia keep something like that from me all these years? I mean, she adored Jessica. She always said there was nothing she would have loved more than a grandchild of her own."

"That's the sad part. Ray said she didn't know about Henry. Apparently, she didn't know Ray was married either. He told me his wife passed away recently too."

"What?" Evelyn gasped, her papery skin contorting in shock.

"Crazy, isn't it?" Sonia shook her head. "Regardless of how neglectful he was of his mother, that's a rough hand to be dealt all at once."

Evelyn gave a dismissive grunt and resumed wiping. "It's that little boy my heart bleeds for. Let's hope, for his sake, Ray's a better father than he was a son."

"He didn't look like he was coping too well with the whole single parent thing. Henry was extremely upset, kicking and screaming, and Ray didn't have a clue how to calm him down. He seemed more embarrassed that I was witnessing the situation than anything."

Evelyn smoothed a hand over her wispy bob. "Well, if he was always working, as Celia claimed, I imagine his wife did most of the childcare. Henry may not have spent much time with his father up until now. No surprise Ray's struggling to figure things out. Sounds like he neglected all his relationships."

"Maybe. Henry acted like he didn't want to be anywhere

near him. You'd think if he'd just lost his mother, he wouldn't want his dad to put him down."

Evelyn gave a small shrug. "Children are unpredictable. I'm sure Henry's confused about all the changes in his life."

"That's true," Sonia conceded. "But it made me uncomfortable. Right when I was leaving, I noticed a price tag hanging from Henry's sweater. Don't you think that's weird?"

Evelyn let out a snort. "It proves my point. Ray's a neglectful father. I'm guessing he has no idea what boxes he put Henry's clothes in. He probably took him shopping and forgot to pull the tag off."

Sonia got to her feet. "Yeah, sounds like something I would do. Anyway, I need to get to work picking out window treatments for a renovation project. I'll be in my office if you need me."

BY 3:00 P.M., Sonia was in the carpool lane outside Broad River Elementary School waiting for Jessica to emerge. She'd managed to finish the design she'd been working on for the young couple who was planning on remodeling the 1970's house they'd bought as a starter home. But Sonia hadn't been entirely focused on her work. Her thoughts kept wandering to her new neighbor—although, he hadn't actually confirmed he was moving in. In fact, the more she thought about it, the more she realized how little she'd learned about him. She'd done most of the talking—something she was good at—filling in the gaps in the conversation with the details of her life in a bid to exude a welcoming aura. To say Ray hadn't reciprocated was an understatement.

"Mom! Look what I painted today!" Jessica cried, as she

clambered into the car trailing her backpack behind her and waving a sheet of paper in Sonia's face.

"Wow! That's beautiful!" Sonia exclaimed, admiring the lifelike robin her artistic daughter had drawn.

"It's for Grandma," Jessica said matter-of-factly, fastening her seatbelt. "She misses seeing all the birds on her morning walks."

"That's thoughtful of you," Sonia said. "It won't be too much longer before she's back cruising around the neighborhood again. Speaking of which, we have a new neighbor—two new neighbors, in fact."

"Who?" Jessica asked, her freckled nose pressed to the window as she waved goodbye to one of her school friends.

"You know Mrs. Jenkins who passed away—it's her son, Ray, and her grandson, Henry."

Jessica's eyes widened. "I never knew she had a grandson. Is he going to my school?"

"Henry's only a little guy," Sonia explained. "Three or four, I'm guessing. I told him we'd invite him over to play later."

"I *love* little kids. Maybe I can babysit him sometime." Jessica furrowed her brow. "Do you think he likes to play with Legos? I can teach him how to build a fort and ... "

Sonia settled in for the fifteen-minute-drive home, offering intermittent responses as Jessica prattled on about the upcoming playdate—all the while wondering why Ray Jenkins had hidden Henry's existence from his mother. There was obviously more to the story, and she intended to get to the bottom of it.

AFTER A QUICK SNACK of apple slices and peanut butter at the kitchen counter, Jessica began bouncing up and down in anticipation of meeting Henry. "Can he come over now, Mom, *please*?"

"We can invite him, but he may not be able to play today," Sonia warned her.

"Are you sure it's a good idea to go back over there again?" Evelyn muttered, pursing her lips as she cleared away Jessica's plate. "Maybe you should give them some time to settle in."

Sonia shrugged. The fearful look in Henry's eyes as he'd gazed up at his father nagged at her. "What's the worst that can happen—he says no?"

For the second time that day, Sonia found herself standing on her neighbor's porch, about to engage the new inhabitant. This time she'd brought Jessica along as an olive branch of sorts. With a bit of luck she'd go across better than the muffins had.

The door opened and Ray stared out at them. His steel-gray eyes shifted from Sonia to Jessica and then back, revealing nothing.

"Jessica was wondering if Henry would like to come over and play," Sonia said, hitching her lips up into a smile. "I thought maybe it would give you a chance to unpack."

Ray's face clouded over. "Henry's ... napping."

Sonia raised amused brows at the banging noise coming from inside the house. "Sounds like somebody's awake now."

Seconds later, Henry appeared in the hallway clutching a pair of pot lids. He stopped dead in his tracks, his attention drawn at once to Jessica.

Before Sonia could intervene, Jessica ducked under Ray's arm and darted down the dark wallpapered hallway to greet Henry, enveloping him, pot lids and all, in an exuberant hug.

Ray peered nervously over his shoulder as the kids disappeared into Celia's old guest bedroom.

Sonia gave an apologetic chuckle. "Sorry! Jessica's used to running in and out of the house. Celia always gave her free rein. I worried about your mother leaving the door unlocked all the time—she had her purse stolen once, but even that wasn't enough to convince her to change her ways."

Ray's lips twitched into a flicker of a smile. "Uh, actually … I'm glad you stopped by. I wanted to ask you a favor." He hesitated, folding and then unfolding his arms awkwardly. "The thing is, I've signed Henry up to start at the local preschool and I have to list someone as an emergency contact. I work from home, so I don't anticipate them needing to call on anyone, but I was wondering if I could put your name down, just to satisfy the school's requirements. I realize it's an imposition, but I don't know anyone else in the neighborhood, yet."

"Of course, no problem at all," Sonia responded. "I work from home too, so my schedule's flexible. And Jessica will be delighted to have someone to play with."

Ray gave a grateful nod. "Thank you."

They glanced up as the kids came barreling back down the hallway hand-in-hand.

"Henry wants to come to our house to play," Jessica announced.

Sonia pinned a questioning look on Ray. "Is that all right with you? You're welcome to come over too, of course."

Ray rubbed a hand over his jaw, debating with himself. "Um, I think I'll unpack the rest of our stuff. It's difficult to get anything done with a young child underfoot."

"Tell me about it." Sonia chuckled. "We'll bring Henry back over in an hour or two."

She waved goodbye and followed the kids across the lawn to her house. Judging by the grip Henry had of Jessica's hand, he had no intention of letting go anytime soon. He seemed more comfortable walking off with a virtual stranger than he was with his own father. And that bothered Sonia.

"Well, hello there, you must be Henry!" Evelyn exclaimed, setting aside the sage green shawl she was knitting when Jessica brought him into the family room. She smiled warmly at him, her eyes twinkling. "Did you like my muffins?"

After a moment's reflection, he gave a tentative nod. Sonia got the impression he didn't know what she was talking about.

"I'm going to show Henry my toys," Jessica said, giving his hand a tug.

"Trust Jessica to win his heart," Evelyn said, reaching for her knitting as the kids tore out of the room. "She has him wrapped around her little finger already."

Sonia wrinkled her brow. "He reminds me of someone."

"Celia, no doubt," Evelyn replied with a disgruntled sigh. "That son of hers is a right piece of work for keeping something so precious from her."

"Ray was a little friendlier this time around," Sonia said. "He asked if he could put my name down as an emergency contact for Henry's preschool."

Evelyn twisted her lips, her needles picking up speed. "That just tells me he can turn on the charm when he needs something."

"Maybe." Sonia glanced at her watch. "I need to take

care of some emails while those two are occupied. Can I get you anything before I disappear into my office?"

Evelyn shot her a scolding look. "Stop fussing, dear. It's been five weeks since I went under the knife. I can get around perfectly fine."

LATER THAT AFTERNOON, Sonia and Jessica walked Henry back over to his house. Halfway there, Sonia noticed he had one of Jessica's favorite stuffed toys under his arm. She contemplated bringing it up but decided against it. Upsetting Henry before she delivered him back to his father was hardly the way to win Ray's confidence. Jessica could always ask for the bear back later.

"Thanks for letting Henry come over," Sonia said when Ray opened the door to them. "The kids had a great time together."

Ray frowned down at Henry. "That's not your bear. You need to give it back."

Henry's bottom lip began to tremble.

Sonia opened her mouth to intervene, but Jessica beat her to it. "I gave it to him. He can keep it."

"That's ... very kind of you," Ray replied in a hesitant tone. "If you're sure—" He trailed off, raising his brows at Sonia, who nodded in approval.

"See you tomorrow, Henry," Jessica chirped, letting go of his hand and bending over to hug him.

A solitary tear trickled down his pale face.

Sonia winced as though she'd taken a punch, the feeling in her gut that something was terribly wrong clamoring for her attention.

"Thanks again," Ray said, swiftly scooping Henry up in his arms. He gave a curt nod and shut the door on them.

"That was nice of you to give Henry your bear," Sonia said, as she and Jessica walked back home. "I know Fudge was your favorite. Aren't you going to miss him when you go to bed tonight?"

Jessica looked pensive. "Henry needs him more than me. He's not allowed any toys of his own."

3

"Did you have fun playing with Henry today?" Evelyn asked when they sat down to dinner that evening.

Jessica nodded, a forkful of chicken halfway to her mouth. "Uh-huh. He liked my Legos but he wasn't very good at building stuff. I had to help him."

"Did he talk to you much?" Sonia asked.

"Nope. He mostly nods and points."

Evelyn doused her dinner vigorously with pepper. "Poor little mite just lost his mother. He's still traumatized."

Jessica puckered her brow. "What does traum—what does that word mean?"

"It means he misses his mom," Sonia said.

Jessica gave a pensive nod. "He didn't want to go home. He crawled under my bed and kept saying, *I want my mommy. I want my mommy.*"

Sonia raised her brows a fraction, exchanging a furtive look across the table with Evelyn. It troubled her to hear that Henry's plea for his mother had been triggered at the thought of returning home to Ray.

"Maybe you can invite Henry over to play again soon," Evelyn said, patting Jessica on the hand. "He really likes you."

"It was good of you to take him under your wing, sweetie," Sonia added. "I know sometimes little kids can be annoying when they go through all your stuff."

"Henry's not annoying! He's cute!" Jessica said. "I wish I could have a little brother. Can he have a sleepover, Mom?"

"It's a bit early for that. I know he's missing his mother, and he likes being with you, but we need to support his relationship with his dad too."

Jessica took a gulp of her milk and set the glass down with a thunk. "Mom, you should tell his dad to buy him some toys. He only has one little Matchbox truck."

"I'm sure he has plenty of toys, Jess," Sonia soothed. " They're probably in a box somewhere. Maybe his dad got them out this afternoon while Henry was over here."

Jessica shook her head. "He doesn't even have any stuffed animals to sleep with."

"Not to worry. I bet the next time you go over there his bedroom will be all set up with his toys," Evelyn chimed in.

"Speaking of bed, it's time you washed up and got your jammies on," Sonia said. She got to her feet and began clearing the table, trying to quash the lingering feeling that something was off about the relationship between Ray and Henry. Ray had totally overreacted when he saw Henry with Jessica's bear. Was he really not allowed any toys? As she scraped the dishes into the garbage disposal, she mulled over all the little things that were bugging her: Ray's close-lipped conversation, the fear in Henry's eyes, his aversion to his father, the price tag hanging from his sweater, Jessica's insistence that he had no toys, even the nagging suspicion that Henry looked vaguely familiar—what did it all mean, if anything?

She wanted to give Ray the benefit of the doubt. His world had been turned upside down, after all, with the loss of his wife and his mother. He had to be under a lot of stress, coupled with the recent move. It wasn't all that surprising that he and his son were floundering in their efforts to find a new normal in their relationship with one another. She sighed as she set the dishwasher to run. She'd invite them over for dinner next week and try to get to know Ray Jenkins a little better. If they were to be neighbors, she needed to be sure she could trust him. And as things stood, she didn't.

It took several attempts before Ray finally committed to dinner the following Friday. Sonia settled on cooking a pot roast, carrots and mashed potatoes, figuring it was something Henry would eat. Evelyn hadn't been too thrilled at the prospect of entertaining Ray, but despite her misgivings, her curiosity about him won out. She had even deigned to make her famous brownies and homemade ice cream for dessert.

When the doorbell rang, Sonia stiffened momentarily, before reminding herself that the simplest explanation was usually the right one. Ray might hold his cards close to his chest, but it was highly unlikely he was a serial killer—more likely a lost soul struggling to cope with the double whammy of losing his wife and mother within weeks of each other and facing the unenviable challenge of raising his young son alone.

Sonia pasted a smile on her lips before pulling open the door. "Welcome!"

"Thank you," Ray replied, tugging Henry after him as he

stepped through the door, clutching her platter in his other hand.

Henry peered around his legs, a hopeful expression on his face.

"Someone's been waiting very patiently for you to get here, Henry," Sonia said, ushering him and Ray into the kitchen.

Jessica jumped to her feet and ran to squeeze Henry, before dragging him off to play with the Lego town she'd spent the afternoon assembling on his behalf.

"So, Ray, are you all settled into your mother's place?" Evelyn inquired, her prickly tone conveying her distaste for him.

"More or less. I didn't have much to unpack." He fidgeted with the sleeve of his shirt as if feeling the need to explain himself further. "I ... thought it best for Henry to have a fresh start away from the home he associates with his mother."

"And where's that?" Evelyn asked.

"Richmond, Virginia," Ray said. "I've—we've been living there for the past ten years."

"It must be overwhelming having to deal with so much loss at once," Sonia said.

Ray gave a stiff nod. "It's been ... difficult."

"Can I offer you something to drink?" Sonia asked. "Glass of wine, sparkling cider, water? Sorry I don't have any beer. My ex was a big beer drinker. Uh—" She trailed off, painfully aware that she was prattling on again.

"Sparkling cider sounds great," Ray said. He glanced nervously over his shoulder as Sonia opened a bottle of Martinelli's. "Do you think we should check on the kids?"

Evelyn threw him a sharp look as she set three glasses down on the counter. "I'm sure Jessica won't let Henry out of her sight. But if it makes you feel any better, I'll peek in on them."

A look of relief flitted across Ray's face. "That would be great. It's just that ... with everything that's happened, Henry's ... not himself. He cries himself to sleep every night."

Sonia tutted sympathetically as she poured the drinks.

"It's kind of you to invite us over," Ray said hesitantly, once Evelyn had shuffled out of the kitchen. "I sense your mother doesn't have a very high opinion of me—Celia being her friend and all. She probably thinks I'm a right heel for never visiting my mother."

"It's none of our business," Sonia replied, avoiding eye contact as she lifted a cast iron pot out of the oven. "Celia was a sweet neighbor, but every family has their issues."

Ray took a gulp of his drink. "My father was extremely abusive to me and my brother, Tom."

Sonia bit her lip. "That's awful. Did ... Celia know?"

"Yes, she refused to leave him." He traced his fingertips over his jaw. "She was too scared of him to do the right thing. She lied to Child Protective Services when a teacher reported our bruises." Ray paused, his forehead rumpling as if revisiting the betrayal. "When I left home at sixteen, I was a broken kid. It took me years to recover. My father suffered a heart attack and died a few months after I left. But, I vowed I'd never return home. I couldn't bear the thought of ever setting eyes on my mother again, or even hearing her voice—it just ... triggered everything."

"I'm so sorry," Sonia choked out, tossing the potholders on the counter and reaching for her glass. A pang of guilt hit when she saw the wretched expression etched on Ray's face. Surely no one could fake that kind of pain. Perhaps she'd been too quick to judge him. She had no idea what it was like to be raised by an abusive parent, but she did know something about the toll abuse took on the soul. "I can understand why you wouldn't want to visit your mother under those circumstances." She hesitated before adding, "My ex-husband was abusive. And a liar too. There's nothing I hate more than being lied to. Thankfully, I have a very supportive mother. I couldn't have gone through my divorce without her."

"You're lucky to have her. I'm sure she's a big help with Jessica."

Sonia swallowed a mouthful of sparkling cider, twisting the stem of her glass between her fingers. "Do you mind if I ask what happened to your wife?"

Ray dropped his gaze. "She had ... stomach cancer—stage four. By the time they discovered it, it was too late."

Sonia blew out a heavy breath. "That's so sad. You really have been through the ringer."

"The hardest part is figuring out how to raise a four-year-old alone. Anyway, I didn't mean to start the evening out on such a downer. I just thought you deserved an explanation." Ray tweaked a grin and raised his glass. "Here's to not being victims anymore."

"Is dinner ready?" Jessica cried out, as she burst into the room. "Henry's hungry."

"Yes, all set," Sonia replied, setting down her glass and kicking into gear. "Go get Grandma and Henry."

She placed the Mikasa stoneware serving dishes in the center of the table as everyone took their places. "Ray, you're the guest, so dig in. I'll leave you to make a plate for Henry."

"The table looks amazing," Ray said, running an admiring eye over the rustic floral centerpiece and pillar candlesticks. "You have such an artful touch. Your clients must love you."

Sonia unfolded her linen napkin, fighting to keep her expression neutral when she saw the overly generous helping of food Ray dished out for Henry. Was he actually that clueless about how much a four-year-old could eat? Maybe her mother was right, and he hadn't spent much time at home with Henry before his wife passed away.

Evelyn raised her brows, a pinched expression on her face. "Make sure to leave room for my brownies and ice cream."

"My grandma makes the best brownies," Jessica said, turning to Henry. "Do you like brownies?"

Henry stared at her, his mouth full of potato. After a long moment, he gave an indifferent shrug.

"How about homemade ice cream?" Jessica persisted.

Henry looked as if he was about to shrug again, but Ray spoke up for him. "Henry loves ice cream." He lowered his voice before adding, "He ... wasn't allowed to eat it very often."

AFTER THE KIDS had gobbled up their dessert and scampered off to play, Sonia got up to make some coffee.

Evelyn pinned a penetrating gaze on Ray. "So, can we expect to see something of your brother now too?"

A tiny furrow formed on Ray's brow. "I'm not in contact with him either. To be honest, I have no idea where he lives." He scratched the back of his neck. "Actually, I was going to ask you if he had ever shown up here."

"Not that we know of," Evelyn replied, glancing at Sonia for confirmation.

Ray gave a defeated nod. "I figured as much. Our mother left the estate to the two of us, but I don't know how to get a hold of him."

"I believe your brother kept in touch with Celia," Evelyn said, in a mildly reproving tone. "I overheard her talking to a man on the phone one time and she said it was Tom—that he used to call her every other month or so."

Sonia caught her eye and gave a subtle shake of her head as she carried the coffee over to the table. She hadn't had a chance to fill her in on what Ray had shared about his abusive childhood, and why he had cut off all contact with his mother.

"You might be right," Ray went on, "I think she was sending him money every month. I've been going through her bank statements, and she was transferring several thousand dollars out of it on a regular basis. I closed her account so maybe Tom will show up now that his funding's been cut off."

"Do you have any idea what he's been doing all these years?" Evelyn asked.

Ray shook his head. "No. He left home shortly after I did, didn't tell anyone where he was going—he was only fifteen. I was planning on letting him come live with me, even though I only had a small studio apartment at the time, but I never got the chance." He sipped his coffee and glanced around appreciatively. "Your home is beautiful. You have a great eye, Sonia."

She smiled as she reached for her coffee. "Thank you. I love designing interiors."

"What is it you do for work, Ray?" Evelyn asked. "I understand you work from home too."

"I'm a freelance journalist." He gave a sheepish grin. "Better with the written word than making small talk."

Evelyn arched a brow. "That must be where Henry gets it from. He's a man of few words too."

Ray's expression darkened. He set his coffee cup on the

side table and got to his feet. "It's late. I should get Henry off to bed."

"Of course," Sonia said. "I'll round up the kids."

After a few tense minutes of cajoling at the door, Henry accompanied Ray home with the promise of another play date soon. Sonia closed the door on them with a sigh of relief and retreated to the kitchen to help her mother load the dishwasher.

"I think that went well, don't you?" Sonia ventured.

Evelyn pursed her lips. "I still can't forgive him for neglecting Celia all these years."

"About that, Mom, he has his reasons, as it turns out." Sonia leaned back, gripping the edge of the countertop. "His father was abusive to him and his brother. It must have been pretty bad because CPS was involved. He said Celia refused to leave and lied to the authorities to cover up what was happening. Ray and his brother left home before they turned eighteen. He was too traumatized to reach out to his mother again. To be fair, he does seem like the sensitive sort now that we've got to know him a little better."

Evelyn eyed her skeptically, digesting the information. "Celia never mentioned anything about abuse. She did say her husband was a drinker. He died young, early fifties I think."

"Alcoholism and abuse often go hand-in-hand. I'm leaning toward believing Ray. He got pretty choked up when he was telling me about it," Sonia said, reaching for a tea towel.

"Talking about abuse, did you hear him say Henry wasn't allowed to eat much ice cream?" Evelyn tutted indignantly. "What was that all about? I don't think the poor kid got to eat any of my French Toast muffins either. He looked at me like he didn't know what I was talking about when I asked him if he liked them."

"Some parents are stricter on sugar intake than others," Sonia pointed out. "It's hardly a crime."

"I still think he's a neglectful father," Evelyn huffed. "Did you see how much food he piled on Henry's plate? He's clueless. Something's not right about him."

Suddenly aware of eyes on them, Sonia spun around to see Jessica standing in the doorway, silently observing them.

"Hey, sweetie!" she said brightly. "Did you get your room tidied up?"

Jessica gave an uncertain nod. "What's not right about Ray, Grandma?"

"Nothing at all," Sonia cut in. "Grandma and I were just laughing about the amount of food Henry's dad put on his plate."

Jessica blinked solemnly at them. "He's not Henry's real dad."

4

Ray sank into a rickety, spindle-back chair at the oak kitchen table and rested his head on his arms—drained after another long evening spent trying to coax Henry to go to sleep. It was the same arduous process night after night, and things weren't improving. Exhausted from crying, the child had finally nodded off, clutching Fudge—the bear Jessica had given him. Ray had been touched by her kind gesture, despite his reluctance to accept it. He was grateful Henry had made a connection with someone, even if it was only a child. Jessica's mother, Sonia, had been equally warm and welcoming of them, which was problematic. She and her mother asked a lot of questions. Too many questions.

At first, Ray had declined Sonia's dinner invitation, but he'd felt obligated after she'd agreed to serve as the emergency contact for Henry's preschool. He cracked his knuckles recalling the pinched face of Trish Miller, the principal of Small Steps, as she'd walked him through the parent orientation. Trish was a stickler for procedure, which presented another conundrum. He hadn't figured out how he was going to pull this off, yet. But Booneville was a small town, and, hopefully, he could find a way around the regulations. If it wasn't for the fact that he had to work, he wouldn't have bothered signing Henry up for school at all for the short time they would be in North Carolina.

His plan had been to keep to himself while he worked out his next move, but Sonia was one of those persistent women with an uncanny ability to disarm his defenses before he realized what had happened. Besides, with Jessica running freely in and out of his house as though Celia's open-door policy was still in play, he hadn't had much choice but to interact with his new neighbors.

Over dinner, he'd felt compelled to open up to some degree, at least to explain his absence all these years. Too much secrecy on his end would only add to their suspicions. The odds were already stacked against him. Sonia's mother, Evelyn, had made it clear by her barbed remarks what she thought of adult children who neglected their elderly parents—reappearing to reap the benefits when they were gone. But, in her defense, Evelyn didn't know about his troubled childhood. She had no concept of anything other than a healthy relationship with her own child. She was everything a mother should be: compassionate, caring, and available—emotionally and physically. She was also comfortable in her own skin, the type of woman who would fight tooth and nail for her child.

Celia, on the other hand, had been frightened of her own shadow. She had kowtowed to every one of her abusive husband's unreasonable demands until she'd been stripped of any sense of self. Their dangerous and dysfunctional relationship had destroyed her children in more ways than she knew. Ray could understand why his mother had done what she'd done, but he couldn't forgive her for it. Not when it led to the merciless abuse he and Tom had suffered at their father's hands. What he'd done to them should have been enough to drive the weakest mouse to summon the courage to leave—flee barefoot if that's what it took. The abuse hadn't been limited to physical beatings; it was far worse than Ray had hinted at to Sonia—something he didn't care to vocalize to another human being. It still chilled him to the bone every time he recalled being denied food or compelled to take cold showers as punishment for the smallest infractions. For more serious offenses, their father sometimes made them sleep in the dog pen in the garage overnight and humiliated them by forcing them to pee in the cat litter box. Ray and Tom had endured the kind of abuse that destroyed the soul of a child, and some people never came back from that dark place.

Instead of protecting them when they'd told their mother what was happening, she'd believed their father's lies—*pretended* to believe them. Fear was a powerful paralytic agent. At sixteen, Ray had finally run away from home. Before he left, he'd promised fifteen-year-old Tom he would come back for him as soon as he found them a place to live. He hadn't wanted to take Tom with him initially, knowing they would be sleeping rough on the streets, exposed to a whole new set of dangers for which they were ill-prepared. But he never got the opportunity to return for him. Tom bolted a few short weeks after Ray, disappearing in the middle of the night, giving no indication to anyone where he was heading or what his plans were, if any. Ray had spent the next few years agonizing over his brother's fate, knowing how broken he was inside and fearing the worst—that he would end up dying in a gutter somewhere.

After years of intensive therapy, Ray had eventually managed to climb out of the dark hole he'd been in. He graduated from college with a degree in journalism and established a career for himself that he enjoyed—all the while wondering if Tom had been fortunate enough to find his place in the world too. At one point, Ray had even hired a reputable private investigator to try and track his brother down, but, despite months of extensive searching, she'd been unable to find any trace of him—no online presence, no address, no phone number, no history with law enforcement, no record of death. Ray had been forced to come to one of two conclusions: either Tom had died a John Doe, or he was living in isolation off the grid somewhere.

As young boys, they had both been fascinated by shows about surviving alone in Alaska or living a self-sufficient life as a prepper in some remote region. Maybe it was the idealized adventure the lifestyle promised, or maybe it was simply the relief of knowing you were completely safe from the people who had hurt you.

Ray grimaced, rubbing a scar on his knuckles that he'd earned from the buckle on his father's belt. Up until a few weeks ago, he'd given up any hope of finding out what had become of Tom. It was ironic that their mother's death had finally given him the answer he'd so desperately sought. But now that he had it, he wished the secret had stayed buried. His hope had always been that Tom had managed to create a life for himself where he was happy. He'd never for one minute suspected anything like the horror of what his brother had become. If he was right that the monthly transfers from their mother's bank account had being going into Tom's account, then she'd unwittingly been funding a dark, secret life.

Ray stared at the untouched plate of food he'd reheated in the microwave earlier. Could he really pull this off? He blew out a weary breath. What choice did he have but to keep going? He had Henry to think of. The boy had no one else left in his life but him.

Rising from the table, Ray tossed his dinner in the trash and retreated to the family room. He leaned against the doorframe and surveyed the room cluttered with antique nesting tables, velvet storage ottomans, and an endless array of knickknacks and lace doilies scattered over every surface. Perhaps it was true that the lonelier a person got, the more they surrounded themselves with stuff they clung to. Even the air in the room was a level of stale that suggested the window hadn't been opened in a decade. It was going to take a ton of work to clear the place out to sell it. At least it wasn't his childhood home he'd inherited. He wouldn't have been able to handle going back to the house that held so many horrific memories.

Flopping down on the beige couch, he folded his hands behind his head as exhaustion clawed at him, his eyes scratchy from lack of sleep. But the thought of letting go made his blood run cold. The nightmares had returned— more terrifying than ever. Plunging him to depths of despair only previously hinted at, causing him to wake up, night after night, soaked in sweat and screaming. Only this time it wasn't his father igniting the fear inside him—it was Tom.

He couldn't stay in this house for long. He couldn't risk his neighbors discovering any more about him than he had already divulged. He would take a couple of months, at most, to figure out a more sustainable, long-term plan for himself and Henry, and then he would put the house up for sale and disappear. Moving here had been somewhat irra- tional, but he'd had to act quickly. This had been the only real option open to him at short notice. He couldn't have returned to his home in Richmond under the circum- stances. What he really needed was a place to settle down where no one knew him, or anything about his past—unlike Sonia Masterton and her mother, both of whom displayed a disturbing affinity for sniffing out things best kept buried.

He reached for the musty, pin-tuck cushion behind his head and punched it, wriggling onto his side to get more comfortable. As he lay there, listening for any indication that Henry was on the move, he mulled over his next steps, his eyes growing increasingly heavy.

HE WOKE WITH A START, bolting upright on the couch, not knowing for a moment where he was. His eyes bulged at the sight of Henry standing in the darkened doorway, staring at him. In his right hand, he clutched the toy truck Ray had bought him at a Target store on the way here.

"What are you doing out of bed, Henry?" he asked, struggling to keep the irritation from creeping into his voice. "It's time to go to sleep." He rubbed a sleeve across his sweaty forehead as he got to his feet, resigning himself to repeating the process of putting Henry to bed for what probably wouldn't be the last time that night.

Henry stuck his thumb in his mouth, before trotting back down the hallway to his bedroom. Ray followed him and lifted him into bed, tucking the covers in around him. "How about you set your truck on the nightstand," he said.

Henry let out a whimper, hugging the toy to his chest.

Ray was too weary to entertain another meltdown. He kissed Henry gently on the forehead. "All right, you hold onto it. Good night, Henry."

He didn't respond, his luminous brown eyes fixed on the ceiling above. Ray turned off the overhead light, leaving the room bathed in the soft glow from the rotating nightlight he had purchased after realizing Henry was never going to be able to sleep in complete darkness.

He hesitated in the hallway, peering around the door to make sure Henry stayed in bed this time. Groaning inwardly, he watched him wriggle out from beneath the duvet and slide his feet to the floor with a dull thunk, his truck firmly in his grasp. He crawled over to the outlet where the nightlight was plugged in and watched it, slack-jawed, the light reflecting shadows of galloping horses across his face with each rotation.

After a few minutes, he turned his attention to his truck, pushing it back-and-forth across the floor as he sang softly to himself. Ray strained to pick up the words.

"Ne-ver ... tell ... them. Ne-ver ... tell ... them."

5

Sonia shrugged off her coat and tossed her keys and purse onto the kitchen counter. She had just finished overseeing the final touches of a kitchen installation for a young professional couple who were expecting the arrival of twin daughters any day now. Timing had been critical, under the circumstances, and Sonia was proud of what she'd managed to pull off for them, despite the rush and their limited budget. Their emotional reaction —dissolving into tears in each other's arms at the big reveal —had been worth the long hours she'd put in to hit all the right notes on their ambitious wish list.

Hunger pangs gnawing, she pulled open the refrigerator door and assessed her options for lunch. After settling on a turkey-and-arugula sandwich, she made her way into the family room and sat down in front of the television, scrolling through the menu for something mindless to watch while she ate. An hour of relaxation was in order before she tackled the invoices and emails stacking up in her office. Her mother had gone to visit a friend and Sonia had promised to pick her up when she made the school run at three. Until then, she had the house to herself.

Her thoughts inevitably drifted to her reclusive, new neighbor. Despite extending several more invitations to dinner, and attempting to set up another playdate for Henry, she hadn't seen much of him in the past week or two, other than a fleeting glance as he hurried in and out to his car. It seemed he wanted nothing to do with them now that the obligatory introductions were behind him. Maybe her mother was right—he was only interested in them when he needed something.

Her suspicions that he was hiding something had gone into overdrive the night Jessica dropped the bombshell about Ray not being Henry's real dad. After some prodding, Sonia had managed to dig a little more information out of Jessica.

"I asked Henry what his favorite thing to do with his dad was," Jessica explained. "But he just ignored me and kept on playing with blocks. Then I asked him, *do you like flying kites, how about going to the park, do you watch movies together*—things like that. That's when he said it."

"Said what?" Sonia asked. "Can you remember Henry's exact words?"

Jessica furrowed her brow. "He said, *he's not my real dad.* Only he said *weal* instead of *real.*"

Sonia replayed the conversation in her head as she took another bite of her sandwich. Henry had clammed up after that, despite Jessica's attempts to find out more. Sonia had talked it over with her mother later in the day, and they'd come to the conclusion that Henry might be adopted. Perhaps the adoption had only just been finalized when Ray's wife passed away. It would make sense on several levels. It would explain why Henry had seemed so traumatized when they'd first met him, and why he didn't display any affection for his father. If Ray's wife had been the one to push for the adoption, Ray might even resent Henry now that he was stuck with a child he hadn't really wanted to begin with, and certainly hadn't planned on raising alone.

Sonia was halfway through her sandwich when her phone rang. An unknown number, but a local one, popped up on the screen. Anticipating a new client, she hurriedly swallowed the bite of turkey in her mouth and wiped her lips on a napkin. "Good afternoon, Masterton Designs."

"Uh, yes, hello, is this Sonia Masterton?"

"It is," Sonia replied, hurrying into her office to retrieve her appointment book. "How can I help you?"

"This is Trish Miller, the principal from Small Steps Preschool." There was a brief pause before she continued, " Ray Jenkins hasn't shown up to pick up his son from school today and your name's listed as the emergency contact. Is there any chance you could come and get Henry now?"

The hairs on the back of Sonia's neck tingled. Her thoughts catapulted in several directions at once. Was Ray simply running late? Or had he actually forgotten to pick Henry up? Maybe Evelyn was right about him being a negligent father. She gripped the phone in her hand tighter, a foreboding feeling creeping over her. Surely, he hadn't taken off again—bailed on his own kid. It might have been justified when he was sixteen, but he had responsibilities beyond himself now, no matter how broken he was over his wife's death. She gritted her teeth, anger welling up inside. Whatever the case, Henry had suffered enough already. He didn't deserve to be stranded at his preschool watching all the other kids go home one-by-one until he was left alone with the principal.

"I'm on my way," Sonia said, gathering up her purse and

keys as she sprang to her feet. She hurried out to the garage
and retrieved Jessica's old booster seat from the wire
shelving at the back. It was covered in dust and she had no
idea if it was suitable for Henry's height and weight, but it
would have to suffice for now.

Her fingers clenched the steering wheel like a vice as
she drove to the preschool. What was she supposed to tell
Henry? As little as possible would be best. She didn't want
him worrying that he'd been abandoned by his dad, on
top of losing his mother. Sonia glanced at the clock on the
dash. It was almost time to pick up Jessica. She might as
well drive over to Broad River Elementary after she got
Henry and wait rather than going home first. Besides, it
would be a lot easier to keep Henry calm with Jessica in
the car. She chewed on her lip as she went over what to
tell the kids. Something simple—Ray had an appointment
and had asked her to pick up Henry. Curiosity ran in Jessica's genes, but hopefully she'd be too consumed with her
plans for Henry for the rest of the afternoon to press for
details.

Her mother, on the other hand, was another matter. She
would see straight through her if she tried to fob her off
with a lie. Sonia would have to explain the situation to her
before picking her up. After dialing her mother's number,
she tapped her fingers impatiently on the steering wheel.
Evelyn wasn't the best with technology, not to mention the
fact that half the time her phone was on silent or buried at
the bottom of her cavernous purse. She might even have left
it behind at the house that morning. Sonia wracked her
brains trying to remember if she'd reminded her mother to
take her phone with her.

"Hello, dear," Evelyn said, sounding flustered when she
finally answered the call. "I hope you haven't been trying to

get a hold of me. Mary and I were sitting out in the garden. I totally lost track of time. Are you on your way?"

"No ... I mean, yes. But I need to pick Jessica up first ... and Henry."

"Henry?" Evelyn echoed in a puzzled tone. "Where is he?"

"The principal from Small Steps called me. Apparently, Ray forgot to pick Henry up."

"See, what did I tell you?" Evelyn ranted. "He's irresponsible. How could he forget to pick up his four-year-old?"

"Look, we can talk about this later," Sonia answered, picturing her mother's lips clamped in a disapproving line. "I just wanted to give you a head's up so you don't say anything in front of the kids."

There was a long pause before Evelyn spoke, voicing Sonia's own fear. "You don't think he's ... disappeared again, do you?"

"We can't jump to any conclusions, yet," Sonia cautioned her. "There could be a perfectly simple explanation. It's possible Ray might even be at the school by the time I get there. Either way, I'll swing by and pick you up afterward." She ended the call, rolling her knotted shoulders to ease the tension. She hoped for everyone's sake that Ray was at the school by the time she arrived. What was she supposed to do if he didn't show up at all?

Henry was seated at a small desk in the school office coloring a picture of a long-eared puppy when Sonia arrived.

The principal, a small-framed woman with a tight, chestnut bun, got to her feet, relief flooding her face. "You must be Sonia, I'm Trish. Henry's been waiting very patiently for you, haven't you, Henry?" After checking Sonia's ID and showing her where to sign him out, the principal escorted them both out to the car. She stood to one side observing as Sonia strapped Henry in, her eagle eye taking in the dusty booster seat. When Sonia closed the back door, Trish laid a hand on her arm and cleared her throat in a hesitant manner. "I hate to trouble you any further, but perhaps you could remind Mr. Jenkins that he needs to bring in Henry's birth certificate and immunization records on Monday. I realize circumstances have been difficult for him, with the recent deaths of his wife and mother. He mentioned he's been going through boxes trying to find where he put certain documents. I let the paperwork slide for the first week, but, as you can appreciate, there are procedures I'm obligated to follow. I'm afraid Henry won't be able to return to school on Monday unless we have all the necessary documentation in hand."

Sonia gave a wary nod, her pulse thundering in her ears—little red flags fluttering in her head again. No matter which way she looked at it, there were too many pieces that didn't fit together. Her brain was blaring a warning at her that something was wrong. Jessica's words haunted her, *he's not Henry's real dad.*

She wasn't even sure if she should take Henry home with her. Maybe she should call the police. If Ray really had disappeared, she couldn't be responsible for a traumatized four-year-old who barely spoke and cried himself to sleep every night.

Trish glanced at her watch. "My apologies, I have to dash. I have a parent meeting in a few minutes. Thanks for coming so promptly to fetch Henry." Before Sonia had a chance to respond, Trish turned on her sensible heels and marched briskly back inside the school.

Sonia took a deep breath and climbed into her car. She

glanced in the rearview mirror as she pulled away from the curb. "Did you have a fun day at school, Henry?"

He stared back at her, wide-eyed and solemn, offering nothing in response.

Sonia took a steadying breath, determined not to give up at the first try. She eyed the dried-up paint in his hair and took another stab at it. "Were you painting today?"

After a moment or two, he gave a nod so slight she half-suspected she might have imagined it. "What did you paint?" she asked, restraining herself from offering up multiple possible answers as she had a bad habit of doing when a conversation lagged.

"Mommy." His voice was little more than a whisper. He stuck his thumb in his mouth and turned his head to gaze out the window.

Tears scalded Sonia's eyes as she turned down the street to Jessica's school. She wanted nothing more than to pull over, take Henry in her arms and squeeze him tight. But that might make matters worse. He didn't trust her, yet. He might think she was trying to replace his mother. While they waited in the car line, she made several more attempts to engage him in conversation before eventually giving up. She loosed a sigh of relief when the bell rang and kids began spilling out into the yard, their laughter replacing the silence she had tried to fill with her various Spotify playlists.

Moments later, Jessica yanked the car door open, squealing with delight when she spotted Henry. She scrambled in next to him and leaned over to tickle him. "You're sitting in my old car seat! What a big boy you are!"

Henry pulled out his shriveled thumb and gave her a crooked smile.

"Is he coming to our house to play?" Jessica asked, wrestling with her seatbelt.

"Yes, but first we have to pick up Grandma. She went to visit her friend, Mary."

"Can we feed the goldfish in her pond, please Mom?"

"Some other day, Jess," Sonia replied. "We need to get home—Henry's dad will be back soon."

"Where is he?"

"He ... has an appointment." Sonia plastered a smile on her face. "So, what do you kids want for a snack when we get home?"

She glanced in the rearview mirror as Jessica whispered something in Henry's ear. He let out a shy chuckle followed by a nod.

"Milk and chocolate chip cookies, please," Jessica announced.

"You got it," Sonia said. "I'm pretty sure we have some in the freezer."

Evelyn was ready and waiting with her coat buttoned when Sonia arrived. She clambered into the passenger seat with a grunt and turned around to greet Jessica and Henry. "Isn't this fun, kids? Another playdate."

"Yup," Jessica said, kicking the back of the seat in her excitement. "Mom said we could have chocolate chip cookies and milk for snack today."

"Much better than apple slices and peanut butter," Evelyn said with a wink. She turned to Sonia, arching a brow. "How was your day, dear?"

"Great," Sonia replied, immediately launching into a rundown of the kitchen installation. As she talked, she cast the occasional glance in the rearview mirror at Jessica and Henry who were huddled together, giggling—playing some game Jessica had made up. Sonia lowered her voice. "The principal at Small Steps said Ray hasn't submitted all of Henry's paperwork."

Evelyn gave a small shrug, peering in the mirror on the visor as she patted her hair into place. "There's so much red tape involved in sending a kid to school these days. In my day, all you had to do was show up with your lunch pail."

"He hasn't turned in Henry's birth certificate." Sonia shot her mother a meaningful look. "What if he doesn't have one?"

6

A s soon as Jessica and Henry were out of earshot, Sonia and Evelyn sat down at the kitchen table with a pot of Moroccan mint tea to discuss the situation.

"I had a bad feeling about him from the minute I set eyes on him," Evelyn mumbled with a disgruntled humph. " How could he be this irresponsible?"

Sonia braced her elbows on the table. "The more pressing question is where is he?"

"What are you going to do if he doesn't return by this evening? You'll have to keep Henry overnight."

"I can't think about that yet," Sonia said, pulling out her phone and dialing Ray's number for the umpteenth time. "I'm going to keep trying until he answers."

Not unexpectedly, her call went straight to voicemail. She set down her phone on the table with an exasperated sigh, staring at it as if she could will Ray into responding.

Her mother tutted her disapproval. "You're wasting your time. You've already left him several messages. He'll get back with you when he's ready."

"When he's *ready*?" Sonia angled a brow. "What does that mean?"

Evelyn shrugged. "Maybe he's caught up in some story or other. He's a journalist, isn't he?"

"Yes, but not an investigative journalist. He works from home writing freelance articles for magazines, or something along those lines." Sonia dragged a hand through her hair. "My gut tells me this isn't about work. He seemed so overwhelmed by Henry, without his wife here to help. Maybe he cracked—couldn't take the pressure."

Evelyn blew on her tea, looking pensive. "Do you think he planned this after meeting us? Perhaps that's why he asked you to be Henry's emergency contact for preschool."

"It's possible, I suppose. He might have decided to take the easy way out when he saw how well Jessica and Henry got along." Sonia let out a beleaguered sigh. "They say grief does strange things to people."

Evelyn nodded, a faraway look in her eyes. "Poor little Henry. Celia would be turning in her grave if she knew her son had abandoned her only grandchild."

"We don't know that's what happened. I'm going to give it until dinner," Sonia said. "If he hasn't gotten in touch by then, I'm calling the police."

"You can't do that!" Evelyn threw her a horrified look. "They'll have Child Protective Services pick Henry up. We can't let them take Celia's grandchild."

"Mom, we don't have a choice. We can't just keep him. We have a duty to inform the authorities."

Evelyn blinked, her face beset with concern. "We can keep him overnight, since you're listed as his emergency contact at the school. If Ray hasn't returned by morning, we'll call the police then."

Sonia picked at a broken nail, her mind spinning. She

shouldn't have been so quick to agree to serve as Henry's emergency contact. She'd sensed something was off about the whole situation from the very beginning, but she'd ignored her instincts in a misguided attempt to be hospitable, for Celia's sake. But Celia wasn't here anymore. Ray was a stranger. She should have been more cautious about letting him into her life. Draining her tea, she pushed her chair out from the table. "I'm going over to Ray's place— to make sure he's not there. Can you keep an eye on the kids for a few minutes?"

"Of course he isn't there," Evelyn said in a testy tone. " His truck's gone."

Sonia shrugged. "Doesn't mean he's not home. What if his truck broke down, or he's having it serviced or something? He might have taken an Uber home and fallen asleep. Or tripped on Celia's clutter and knocked himself out. He might need medical attention for all we know. But I can't just sit here and keep dialing his number all afternoon."

Evelyn pursed her lips, reaching for their mugs as she got to her feet. "Be careful. If he opens the door, don't go inside, whatever you do. I don't trust him. And take your phone with you."

Sonia winked as she exited the kitchen. "Now who's fussing?"

SHE RAPPED on Ray's back door multiple times, but no one answered. Gingerly, she crept around to the side of the house and peered through the family room window. To her surprise, it looked exactly as it had when Celia lived there. She'd expected Ray to have moved things around, or perhaps even to have gotten rid of some of his mother's belongings. But it didn't look as if he'd put his personal stamp on his new abode in any shape or form.

Sonia continued on around the house and squinted through Celia's bedroom window next. The same faded floral comforter covered the queen sleigh bed, the same dancing china figurines graced the top of the dresser—nothing about the room indicated it had a new male occupant. Sonia moved on to the guest bedroom, tenting her fingers over her eyes to peer through the smeared glass. Jessica had told her this was Henry's bedroom, but nothing suggested a child was sleeping in it. A row of moving boxes was stacked along the bottom of the bed, and Sonia could make out several Target bags lying on the floor next to them. What on earth had Ray been doing all this time if he hadn't even bothered to unpack Henry's things?

She froze at the sound of a vehicle pulling into the driveway. Finally, he'd returned! She gritted her teeth as she stepped out of the planter she was standing in. He'd better have a good explanation for his absence. Hurrying around the house to greet him, she came to an abrupt halt at the sight of a squad car parked in place of Ray's gray Toyota Tacoma pickup. Her eyes traveled to the front door where a thickset policeman stood, one hand on his holster. He dipped his head at her, as if to reassure her he didn't consider her a threat, before striding over to her.

"Afternoon, ma'am. I'm Officer Reed with the Fannin County Sheriff's Office. Do you live here?"

"I ... no ... I'm a neighbor." She gestured at her house with a flick of her wrist, confusion flooding her brain. Was she in some kind of trouble? Had someone seen her peeking in the windows and mistaken her for a burglar? She immediately dismissed the irrational thought. The police couldn't possibly have gotten here that quickly. The officer had to be here for some other reason. And then it hit her. This must concern Ray. Her heart clattered in her chest. "Is ... everything all right?"

A furrow of concern formed on the officer's forehead. " I'm trying to reach Ray Jenkins' next-of-kin."

Sonia clapped a hand to her mouth. *Next-of-kin.* Was Ray dead? Her legs quivered. How would she ever break the news to Henry? The poor child had been through so much already. "I ... don't understand."

"I'm afraid there's been an accident."

Sonia rested a hand on the fence to steady herself. "What ... what kind of an accident?"

"Mr. Jenkins wrecked his truck. He's been transported to the hospital. I'm trying to contact his family."

"He doesn't really have any family." Sonia sucked in a labored breath, trying to collect her thoughts. "This is his mother's house. She passed away recently—shortly after he lost his wife to cancer. He has a younger brother, but he hasn't seen him in over twenty years. There's really only his son, Henry."

The officer adjusted his stance. "Do you know where I might find him?"

Sonia squeezed her hands nervously. "He's with me. I picked him up from school when Ray didn't show up."

Officer Reed pulled out a pad. "What's your name, ma'am?"

"Sonia Masterton."

"Phone number and address?"

Sonia reeled off her details, still trying to process the situation.

"If you like, I can talk to his son for you," Officer Reed offered.

Sonia swallowed the hard knot in her throat. "He's only four-years-old."

The officer's expression softened. "Are you able to care for him for now? Otherwise, I can radio for someone from child welfare to pick him up."

Sonia flinched. He meant no harm, but he made it sound like he was talking about a stray dog. Evelyn and Jessica would be outraged if she didn't agree to take Henry in. But this was a huge responsibility. Henry was so young, and vulnerable. She chewed on her lip, plagued by guilt at how she'd spent the afternoon fuming at Ray. She'd been quick to rush to judgment, believing the worst of him. All this time, he'd been lying in a hospital bed, injured, possibly needing surgery for all she knew. How could she refuse to help him? She gestured to her house. "If you want to come in for a few minutes, we can discuss it."

Evelyn looked up in alarm when Sonia walked into the family room followed by a police officer.

"Ray's been in an accident," Sonia blurted out as they sat down. "Officer Reed came to notify Ray's next-of-kin. I explained to him that it's only Henry."

Evelyn's eyes darted frantically between Sonia and the officer. "Is he ... dead?"

"No, he survived the accident," Officer Reed volunteered. "The only information I have from the paramedics is that he sustained a head injury. His truck was totaled. Based on the tire marks, it's possible he swerved to avoid another vehicle. We found his phone in the wreckage, but it's shattered."

Evelyn's hands fluttered to her throat. "That's awful! What hospital is he in?"

Officer Reed pulled out his notebook and consulted it. "He was taken to Fannin Regional."

"Henry can stay here with us, of course, until his father is released," Evelyn said, shooting a fierce look Sonia's way.

"Absolutely," Sonia agreed. "Is Ray able to have visitors?"

"You'll have to check with the hospital." Officer Reed produced a card from his pocket and handed it to her. "Feel free to call me if you have any questions I can help with."

Sonia slipped the card into her pocket and escorted the officer to the door, a knot of worry twisting in her stomach. On the spur of the moment, she'd volunteered to take Henry in without knowing the full extent of Ray's injuries. What if he ended up in rehab for weeks on end?As much as she felt sorry for Henry, she couldn't afford to invest that amount of time in a small child. She had a business to run. It would be next to impossible to get any work done at home with all the interruptions that would ensue. And her mother couldn't be expected to care for a four-year-old, not while she was still recovering from hip surgery. The principal of Small Steps had made it clear that the boy couldn't return to school without the proper documentation, which meant Sonia would be stuck trying to figure out childcare.

Her best option was to go straight to the hospital and get a full report on Ray's condition. Perhaps she'd be allowed to see him for a few minutes. If he was able to talk, she could ask him where the paperwork was for Henry's preschool. Celia always kept a spare key for the house buried in the planter by the back door. With Ray's permission, she could go inside and look for Henry's records—this was her opportunity to find out what was going on, once and for all.

She pulled on her coat and slung her purse over her shoulder before sticking her head into the family room. "I'm going to the hospital, Mom. Please don't mention the accident to the kids. Just tell them Ray said Henry could spend the night. I'll let you know as soon as I find out anything."

Her thoughts were scattered as she sped toward Fannin Regional Hospital, incurring the indignant blare of a horn from a driver she cut off. Speeding was not a smart move, especially given her current state of mind, but she was desperate for details about Ray's accident. A head injury was a vague diagnosis. Did that mean he had a concussion, or was he brain dead? The skin on the back of her neck prickled as her thoughts continued to spiral downward. What if Ray succumbed to his injuries? Images of raising Henry until he was eighteen flashed to mind. She couldn't take that on—not even for Celia's sake.

Then again, it might be the best thing that could happen to Henry. She couldn't shake the feeling that he was in danger from the stranger next door.

7

After checking in at the registration desk in the hospital lobby, Sonia took the elevator up to the third floor where Ray's room was located. She hesitated in the hallway outside his door for a moment or two, watching as a young nurse fussed around his bedside. To Sonia's surprise, Ray's eyes were open, and he appeared to be conversing in low tones with the nurse. Feeling somewhat less anxious about the gravity of the situation, she knocked gently on the door and entered. "Hey Ray, how are you doing?"

His head jerked in her direction, his eyes sweeping her face like a searchlight. He studied her with a blank expression for an uncomfortable moment before turning to the nurse, his brows hunched together.

The nurse glided discreetly over to where Sonia stood. "I'm afraid he doesn't recognize you," she said in a hushed tone. "He sustained some head trauma in the accident—a nasty concussion. The doctor should be around shortly. He can give you more details about his condition. Are you his wife?"

Sonia shook her head. "No. I'm Sonia Masterton, his next-door neighbor. I'm looking after his son." She shot a furtive glance at Ray and then whispered, "His wife passed away recently."

The nurse pouted her lips. "That's so sad to hear. He's not had it easy, has he? It's fortunate he has you to help him out. Make sure you address him by name when you're talking to him, it helps anchor him." She walked back over to the bed and tucked in the sheets. "Anything else I can get you, Ray? Would you like some more water?"

He turned his head, wincing as he eyed the half-full disposable plastic cup and straw on his bedside table. "I'm good for now, thanks."

"You have a visitor, Ray. Your neighbor is here to see you," the nurse said in an encouraging tone. "I'll be back to check on you later." She flashed a grin at Sonia as she breezed out of the room.

Gulping a breath, Sonia approached the bed with a trepidatious air. "Hi there, Ray. I'm Sonia Masterton, your next-door neighbor. I live in the bungalow that backs up to your mother's old house."

Ray lifted a hand to his cheek and scratched it, a flicker of a frown traversing his forehead.

"Your mother's name was Celia Jenkins," Sonia went on, sitting down in the chair next to the bed. "She passed away recently. You moved into her house a couple of weeks ago."

Ray twisted the sheet between his fingers in an agitated fashion. "I'm ... sorry. I don't remember any of this—or you."

"It's okay," Sonia said, trying to mask her dismay. "I know this must be difficult for you—the shock of it and all. Henry's fine, so you don't need to worry about him."

Ray threw her a baffled look, as he attempted to adjust his pillows. "Who's Henry?"

Sonia trapped the startled gasp that almost fell from her lips. It was clear from Ray's tone that he had absolutely no recollection of his son. How was that possible? She couldn't imagine forgetting who Jessica was. It was a truly terrifying prospect to think a concussion could make you forget you were a parent.

Despite her misgivings about Ray, she leaned forward and laid a reassuring hand on his arm. "Henry's your four-year-old son. Don't you remember? He came over to play with my daughter, Jessica. She gave him her teddy bear, Fudge, to take home."

A haunted look crossed Ray's features. "Are you ... sure I have a son?"

"Positive!" Sonia pulled out her phone and scrolled through to a picture she'd taken of Henry playing with Jessica's blocks. "Look, here he is!"

Ray gave a dubious shake of his head. "I don't remember him at all."

"I can bring him along to visit you tomorrow, if you like," Sonia suggested.

"If you think it won't scare him." Ray gestured to his IV. "Seeing me ... like this."

"I think he'll be fine. That reminds me, I need to pop over to your house to pick up some clothes for Henry. Your mom kept a key in the planter out back. Would you mind if I grabbed his PJ's and some of his favorite toys?"

Ray sighed and leaned his head back against the pillow, staring morosely up at the ceiling. "Of course. I'm sorry I can't be of more help. I can't remember what the house looks like, let alone what planter you're talking about."

"Is it just short-term memory loss you're experiencing?" Sonia asked. "Do you remember anything further back—what about your brother, Tom?"

Ray's brows shot up in surprise. "I have a brother?"

"Yes. You haven't been in contact with him in years. But you mentioned that your mother's been sending him money. Maybe you can track him down through his bank account."

"Maybe," Ray said, the frustration in his voice matching the defeat in his eyes.

Sonia shifted position, the vinyl chair squeaking in the awkward silence that fell between them. "Do you recall the accident at all?" she ventured.

Ray shook his head. "I had no idea where I was when I woke up. I don't remember how I got here either." His frown grew deeper. "To tell you the truth, I didn't even know my name until they showed me my driver's license."

"I'm sure it's only a temporary memory loss," Sonia soothed. "The nurse said the doctor will be making his rounds shortly. He'll be able to tell you more."

As if on cue, a knock on the door interrupted them and a tall, gray-haired man with a shiny bald spot stepped into the room, one hand tucked into the pocket of his white coat. He nodded to Sonia as he approached the bed. "Good afternoon, Ray. I'm Doctor Robinson. You might not remember me. I treated you when you were brought in. How are you feeling?"

Ray frowned. "Bruised, and confused," he answered after a long pause. "My head hurts, and I can't remember anything before waking up in here."

"I know it's distressing, but your symptoms are not uncommon after a concussion," Doctor Robinson explained. "Your CT scan looks good. You can expect the memory loss to resolve itself within the next few days. We'll need to run some more tests tomorrow, but if everything checks out, I see no reason why we can't discharge you."

"What if he doesn't have his memory back by then?" Sonia cut in.

The doctor smiled at her. "That's where you come in. Ray will need someone to keep a close eye on him for the next few days."

"Oh, I'm not his wife, she's—" Sonia caught herself, her cheeks flushing. Now was not the time to break the news to Ray that his wife was dead too. "I'm his next-door neighbor." She pressed her lips together, suppressing the panic welling up inside. Why was all of this falling on her shoulders? She couldn't possibly care for a virtual stranger with severe memory loss, not to mention his traumatized four-year-old son, especially with the gnawing suspicions she had that something was amiss. Not that that was of any relevance to the doctor—it was the police she should be talking to.

Doctor Robinson rubbed his chin thoughtfully. "Does Ray have any family nearby?"

"Only his four-year-old son. I'm looking after him, for now."

The doctor drew his wiry, gray brows together. "It will be important for Ray to be with his son over the next few days. It will help speed his recovery."

"How long before my memory returns?" Ray interjected.

"It's impossible to predict," Doctor Robinson replied. "It might be a day or two. Or it could take a couple of weeks."

Sonia locked eyes with Ray. She couldn't say for sure what she saw in them. Bewilderment? A plea for help? Or was he fooling them? He seemed genuinely flummoxed at the situation he found himself in, but could it all be an act? Beads of sweat formed along her hairline. She couldn't invite a stranger into her home. He might be a serial killer for all she knew. At the very least, he was a negligent son and an emotionally distant father—and he was hiding something, that much she was sure of. A dull throbbing began in her temples.

"You don't have to decide how to handle this just now," Doctor Robinson said, breaking into her thoughts. "If you're not in a position to help out, we can find an alternative solution."

Sonia gave a dismissive nod. "Thanks, we'll talk it over."

The doctor took out his penlight and checked Ray's eyes, and a few other vitals, before taking his leave. "Like I said, we'll run some more tests in the morning. I'll be back to check on you again once I have the results."

Alone in the room with Ray, Sonia felt obligated to explain herself. "I didn't mean I wouldn't help you. It's just that ... I have my mother living with me and she's recovering from hip surgery, and I run my interior design business from home and Jessica has after school activities and—"

"I wouldn't dream of imposing on you. I'm sure I'll be perfectly capable of looking after myself by tomorrow," Ray responded, his eyelids fluttering closed.

Sonia got to her feet. "I should let you get some rest."

"Henry," Ray muttered, so softly Sonia almost missed it. "How old did you say he was?"

"He's four," she replied, a smile breaking out across her face. "Just the cutest little thing with dimples and dark curls." She waited for Ray to respond, but he said nothing. Was he already asleep, or did he want to hear more about his son? What would she tell him? It would be disingenuous to say that Henry was going to be excited to see him again when she knew he wouldn't. Instead, she turned and tiptoed toward the door.

"Thank you ... for taking care of my son," Ray called after her.

She threw him a parting smile and hurried out of the room.

Safely back in her car in the hospital parking lot, Sonia rested her head on the steering wheel and released a tired breath. Of all the scenarios she'd imagined regarding her mysterious neighbor, this was not one of them. Up until the accident, he'd kept her at a distance, dodging questions, acting secretive, and dropping strange comments about Henry. Now, apparently, he had no recollection of any of that. In fact, he'd quite happily given her permission to enter his home and retrieve whatever she needed for Henry. Her heart begin to beat a little faster. This was her chance to find out more about the real Ray Jenkins.

It wasn't that she wanted to snoop around, but she needed to reassure herself that he was who he said he was, and that everything was above board with Henry—especially in light of the worrisome anomalies she'd picked up on. She owed it to her mother and daughter to make sure they were safe with Ray living next door. Her mind made up, she put the car in gear and pulled out of the hospital parking lot. If nothing else, finding Henry's birth certificate —or even adoption papers—would put her mind at rest.

Twenty minutes later, Sonia pulled into Ray's driveway and switched off her car. She had debated talking her plan over with her mother but decided against it. She'd wait and see what she found out first. If it could be avoided, she'd rather not admit to snooping around in Ray's house. Evelyn would never approve of her going through Celia's things.

After climbing out of the car, Sonia threw a hasty glance over her shoulder. Despite having Ray's permission to pick up a few necessities, she felt somewhat guilt-ridden at the liberties she was about to take. She walked around to the back of the house and picked up a broken piece of terracotta to dig through the dirt in the planter with. Halfway down, she found the Ziploc bag with the spare house key. Good old Celia, dependable as the day was long. Unexpected tears stung her eyes. It was so unfair that Celia had been denied the chance to meet her grandchild. It wasn't that Sonia didn't believe Ray had been telling the truth about his abusive childhood, but she couldn't help feeling there was more to the story.

She pushed the key into the lock and jiggled it until it turned. Inhaling a shallow breath, she stepped inside the house and cast a glance around, not knowing exactly what she expected to find. Apart from the moving boxes, there was nothing to indicate that Ray and Henry were living here. As she'd observed through the windows, the place looked just like Celia had left it. The same faded landscape prints hung askew on the walls, the same rose-colored glass dish sat on the console table in the hallway, the same frayed runner covered the worn, walnut floor. Steeling herself to see this through, she padded down the hallway and tentatively pushed open the door to the guest bedroom. She would gather up what she needed for Henry first, and then take a gander around the rest of the house.

Frowning, she took in the quilted mauve Jacquard duvet and antique dresser topped by a pair of dusty, glass candlesticks—trying to make sense of it. Granted, Ray had only been living here a relatively short time, but why had he not made any attempt to transform the space into a child's room? Opening the closet door, she peered in at Celia's collection of winter coats, wrinkling her nose at the pungent odor of mothballs. Evidently, Ray hadn't been able to bring himself to go through his mother's belongings. One-by-one, she pulled open the dresser drawers, but there was no sign of Henry's clothes anywhere.

Eying the cardboard boxes at the bottom of the bed, she made her way over to them. Maybe Ray hadn't unpacked his son's things. The first box she opened was chockfull of books—none of them children's books. She carefully closed the flaps back up and checked the remaining boxes, which contained mostly files and office equipment. Lifting out one of the folders, she flicked through it, glancing at the magazine articles inside. This must be some of Ray's work. It seemed odd that he hadn't set up his office yet.

Feeling increasingly uneasy, she reached for a Target bag peeking out from behind one of the boxes. She dumped the contents out on the bed and stared at the items in bewilderment. Was this the extent of Henry's wardrobe: four pairs of pants, six long-sleeved tops, two pairs of pajamas, a ten-pack of superhero underwear and several pairs of socks?

Fear fingered its way up her spine as she eyed the receipt. Why was all of Henry's clothing brand new with tags?

8

S onia hurriedly stuffed Henry's clothing back into the plastic bag, her mind racing to make sense of what she'd discovered. Half-dreading what she might come upon next, she reached for another bag peeking out from beneath the bed and rooted around inside it. An Avengers toothbrush, a tube of Crest Kid's Cavity Protection Toothpaste, Velcro Spiderman tennis shoes, a pair of jeans, and a familiar-looking blue T-shirt. Frowning, she pulled it out and examined it more closely. Henry had worn it to dinner at her house—she remembered him dribbling ice cream all over the baby dinosaur on the front of it. It had evidently been washed since, so why hadn't Ray put it away in the closet or a drawer, afterward? What was the logic in putting it back in a Target bag and shoving it under the bed? These weren't the actions of someone who was moving in— more like the behavior of someone who was prepared to pick up and leave at a moment's notice.

She slid an unsettled gaze around the guest room, a disturbing thought pushing to the forefront of her mind. Had Ray been lying to her about his wife? What if Henry's mother wasn't dead at all? Could Ray have abducted his son in the throes of a nasty divorce? It wasn't beyond the realm of possibility. Kids were abducted by non-custodial parents all the time. Considering how much Henry missed his mother, and how unattached he was to his father, the shoe seemed to fit. It would also explain why Ray had arrived at Celia's house with none of Henry's clothes or toys, other than what he'd purchased in a Target shopping spree. Gritting her teeth, Sonia got to her feet with a new resolve. She could justify snooping around if it meant rescuing an abducted child. The first thing she needed to figure out was whether Ray's wife was really dead.

Her chilled skin prickled as she pushed open the door to Celia's old bedroom, half-expecting a larger-than-life Ray to step out from the shadows and accost her, even though logic assured her she'd left him lying in a hospital bed. She inhaled a ragged breath as she picked her way across the floor. Celia's pink, fluffy slippers jutted out from beneath the unmade bed. A pile of miscellaneous coins and crumpled receipts sat atop the oak nightstand, next to a laptop. She lifted the lid and took a quick peek, but, as she'd suspected, it was password protected. Heart hammering, she reached for the receipts and uncurled them one-by-one: innocuous supplies from a local hardware store, a receipt for gas, and a coupon from a local pizza restaurant—nothing of consequence.

Next, she opened the drawer in the nightstand and poked around inside it. Like most of the other items in the room, the contents of the drawer had Celia's stamp all over them; a crocheted coaster, a scented sleep mask, a book of poems by Robert Frost—even a birthday card Jessica had made for her two years ago. Sonia grimaced as she closed the drawer, realizing too late that she should have worn gloves. She ran a critical eye over the rest of the room. Judging by what she'd seen so far, it was unlikely she would find any of Ray's belongings in the closet or the dresser. The moving boxes neatly stacked at the bottom of the bed were her best bet.

To her disappointment, the first box was stuffed to the brim with wrinkled sweatshirts and workout gear. She rummaged half-heartedly through it before closing it back up and moving on. The next box contained a miscellaneous assortment of men's clothing. Opening the final box, she jerked backward on her heels, the odor of sweaty sneakers assailing her senses. Curling her lip in disgust, she closed the box back up and got to her feet, defeated. She still knew next to nothing about Ray or his past, other than what he'd told her—a version she harbored mounting doubts about.

Determined not to give up on her quest to uncover any secrets Ray might be hiding, she made her way over to the closet and slid open the mirrored door. There was always a chance he he'd stashed some personal items inside. A black, canvas backpack on the floor caught her eye—modern and masculine. Definitely out of place in this old lady haven of fluff and bric-a-brac. After throwing a glance over her shoulder to reassure herself she was alone, Sonia swiftly unzipped the bag and viewed the contents: men's jeans, boots, and a flannel shirt—in addition to a few basic toiletries, and a fancy-looking GPS.

She closed the bag back up and then, as an afterthought, slipped her fingers into the zippered front pouch. Pulling out a map, she carefully spread it out on the floor in front of her. A yellow highlighter marked a trail into the Blue Ridge mountains, and a set of coordinates was neatly printed in blue ink along the edge of the map. A campsite, most likely. She snapped a quick picture of the coordinates to check them out later, then folded the map back up and returned it to the pouch. Other than surmising that Ray Jenkins liked to hike or camp, she still hadn't learned anything of consequence about the man, or his presumed dead wife. Frustrated, she set about putting everything back the way she'd found it. Maybe Ray actually had lost his memory, but she wasn't taking any chances. If he'd lied in the past, he might be lying now too.

As she shoved the bag back into the closet, she caught a glimpse of several dilapidated women's shoeboxes on the shelf above the clothing rack. The lid was propped open on one of them and she could see some papers sticking out. She had yet to find any documentation pertaining to Henry, or Ray's wife, but maybe she could learn something about Ray from his mother's records. *Forgive me, Celia*, she mouthed as she reached for the box. Fingering through it, she quickly realized it was full of old bank statements. Ray had mentioned something about his mother transferring several thousand dollars each month to an account he suspected was his brother Tom's. Curious, Sonia scanned the transactions on the most recent statement. The sum of $4500 stuck out like a sore thumb in comparison to the other much smaller amounts that Celia withdrew on a regular basis. Sonia leafed through several more statements. They all showed the same transfer on the fifteenth of each month. Apparently, Ray had been telling the truth about something.

She eyed the remaining shoeboxes, but a ghostly sense of claustrophobia was building, closing off her airways. She needed to get out of this house—the place smelled of dust, damp, death, and too many buried secrets. Skin prickling, she jammed the statements back into the overflowing shoebox and replaced the lid. She had crossed a line by prying into Celia's personal finances. This was between Celia and Tom. It had nothing to do with Sonia's quest to get to the bottom of Ray's evasiveness and his strange relationship with his son. She glanced at her watch. Her mother would be wondering where she was by now. Time to wrap up her search and get back home.

As she turned to leave, a sound startled her. Her heart leapt into her throat. Was that the back door opening? Surely Ray couldn't have been discharged from the hospital already. Had he left of his own accord? All her fears about her mysterious neighbor came rushing back with a vengeance. What if he really had faked his memory loss? But to what purpose? And then another thought struck. What if this was Ray's younger brother, Tom? It was possible the lawyer who'd settled Celia's affairs had managed to track him down. Or maybe the police had got a hold of him. Either way, it would be hard to explain what she was doing in his mother's bedroom.

Silently, she got to her feet and tip-toed toward the open door, freezing at the thud of footsteps. Seconds later, Jessica burst into the room. "Mom! What are you doing?" Her eyes darted behind Sonia as if looking for someone. "Why are you in Ray's bedroom? Is he here?"

Sonia shook her head vehemently, trying to collect her thoughts. "No, sweetie. He's away on business. He asked me to pick up some stuff for Henry." Her heart lurched in her chest. "Where is Henry?"

"He's napping. I went out to the garden to play on the tire swing, and I saw your car. Why'd you park here?"

"I thought it would be easier to throw everything in the car rather than carry it across the lawn," Sonia said breezily. "Let's go grab Henry's stuff."

"You've been here for ages," Jessica said, following her

down the hallway to Henry's room. "What were you doing this whole time?"

Sonia thought for a moment, wishing for the umpteenth time that her daughter hadn't inherited her grandmother's keen nose for information. She hated lying to her. Jessica got enough of that from Finn: lies about when he was going to call her, what he was sending her for her birthday, and when he was coming home on leave—none of which ever materialized. "I was just sitting here thinking about Celia. It's kind of sad without her."

Jessica nodded, looking pensive. "I miss her too. I'm sad for Henry that he doesn't have a grandma. But he can share mine."

Sonia flashed her a grateful smile. "That's very sweet of you, Jess. All right, help me pick out some clothes for him."

After deliberating over the meager choices, Jessica made a clumsy attempt to fold Henry's clothes, and then shoved them into one of the bags. "I told you he doesn't have any toys," she said, her eyes zig-zagging around the room. "Now do you believe me?"

"They're probably still at his old house," Sonia said dismissively, following Jessica down the hallway to the front door. She cast a darting glance into the family room as they went by and then hesitated. "Why don't you take this bag and run on home? I need to look for some paperwork for Henry's preschool. Tell Grandma not to start dinner. I'll order Chinese tonight."

"Yeah! My favorite!" Jessica chirped, skipping out the door, swinging the Target bag with Henry's clothes in it.

Sonia waited until she was sure her daughter wasn't going to come running back to tell her something else she'd forgotten about, before slipping into the family room. The gloomy space sported a mismatched assortment of relics from the past: faded couches with sagging seat cushions, a small, squat TV, yellowing net curtains, a dome clock that chimed out time like a melancholic countdown to death itself, and enough dust in the air to mimic a double helix on a sunny day. Sonia wandered over to the bookshelf in the entertainment center to the left of the TV and glanced through some of the titles. Celia had always had a penchant for romance novels—maybe it was to compensate for the abusive relationship she had endured.

Sonia was about to leave when she spotted some faux-leather photo albums in the cubby directly below the television. She reached for one and flipped it open, eying the pictures curiously. Most of them were black and white. Judging by the clothing and hairstyles, she guessed they were from Celia's childhood. She skimmed through the album and then returned it to the shelf and grabbed another one. This one contained color photos, and someone had meticulously logged notes and dates next to each one; *Tom's first birthday, Tom and Ray at Outer Banks Beach, Ray's first lost tooth.* On and on it went. The carefully catalogued childhoods of two sons Celia had obviously adored. Whether or not there was any truth to Ray's tales of an abusive father, there was no evidence in the photo albums that he had ever been in his sons' lives. Either Ray was lying about that, or Celia had taken care to erase any trace of him.

Sonia thumbed through to the final page, studying the expression on Ray's face in the photo—the resigned look of a broken young man, just as he'd described. His brother, Tom, stood next to him, a whole head shorter, a hint of rebellion simmering in his eyes. Ray must have been about fifteen-years-old when it was taken—right before he left home. There were no more photos in the album after that. Perhaps Celia hadn't had the heart to continue photographing Tom alone, or maybe Tom had refused to be the subject of any more staged photos hiding an ugly secret. Because if Ray was telling the truth, this entire album was a lie. Their abusive father had been in the background on every one of these occasions, the dark underside to the happy life Celia had tried to portray.

Sonia snapped the album shut, her heart pounding in her chest. She understood only too well the desire to weave a fantasy over a brutal reality. She'd tried to do the same thing at first with Finn. It was easy for Ray to judge Celia for being too weak to leave. But would Sonia have had the fortitude to leave if she hadn't had the unconditional support of her mother?

She replaced the album on the shelf and cast one last searching glance around the room. A folded-up page of newspaper lying on the end table caught her eye. She reached for it, straightened it out, and read the headline:

Five Years After Katie Lambert's Disappearance.

9

Sonia folded the newspaper article back up, her thoughts suddenly firing in an entirely new direction. Ray had told her he was a freelance journalist —was he working on a story about abductions? He might even be a private investigator posing as a journalist— looking into the disappearance of Katie Lambert. She traced her fingertips across her forehead considering the idea. He could be using his mother's house as a temporary base, with no intention of moving in long-term. That would explain why he hadn't unpacked.

Sonia racked her brain trying to remember more of the details surrounding Katie Lambert's disappearance. It was hard to separate the facts from the gossip and speculation that had spread like wildfire at the time and continued unabated over the years. Sonia remembered Katie as a friendly girl with a mischievous grin and one too many ear piercings, who had worked in a local coffee shop in Booneville on the weekends. Her father was a successful contractor, and everyone in town knew the family. His suicide in the wake of Katie's disappearance had shocked

the close-knit community to its core—some even specu-
lating that he was involved and had killed himself out of
guilt. Sonia frowned as she stared down at the article in her
hand. If Ray was investigating the story, he wasn't going to
get much information by hiding away from everyone like a
recluse. It didn't make sense.

Her muddled thoughts drifted to Henry. Whatever Ray's
real reason for being here, his odd relationship with his son
troubled Sonia more than anything. She set the newspaper
article back down on the end table, positioning it as she'd
found it. It was time to go home and check on Henry. After
all, she was the one who'd been entrusted with his care
while Ray was incapacitated. She couldn't depend on her
elderly mother or her eight-year-old daughter to keep him
safe. Although exactly what danger he was in, and from
whom, remained to be seen.

After locking the back door, Sonia replaced the key in
the planter and pulled her car into her own driveway.

"We'd almost given up on you. I was just about to make
the kids some grilled cheese sandwiches," Evelyn chided,
the minute Sonia walked into the kitchen. "How's the
patient?"

"Doing surprisingly well. No apparent physical injuries,
other than bruises," Sonia replied, pulling open the junk
drawer where she kept the takeout menus for local restau-
rants. "He has a concussion, but he's perfectly coherent—
other than the fact that he can't remember anything from
before the accident. He didn't know who I was, and he didn't
remember he had a son. His doctor doesn't seem overly
concerned. He's optimistic it will resolve itself in a matter of
days."

"Well, that's a relief," Evelyn said. "I was fretting about
having to give Henry more bad news. He's suffered enough

as it is." Her piercing gaze locked with Sonia's as she pulled out a chair and sat down at the farmhouse kitchen table. " Jessica said you were over at Celia's house."

Sonia gave a vague nod as she scoured the menu options. "I asked Ray if it would be all right to pick up some overnight things for Henry."

Evelyn tilted a quizzical brow. "Was Jessica right about Henry not having any toys?"

Sonia hesitated, deliberating whether to share her findings with her mother. She didn't want to alarm her unnecessarily, but she could use a second opinion on what she'd discovered. "Yeah, but it gets worse. Let me call in this order and then I'll fill you in."

After she hung up, she slumped down in a chair next to her mother. "Are the kids okay?"

"They're fine." Evelyn said. "Although they wolfed down a few extra cookies this afternoon. That little Henry acts like he's never tasted sugar before."

Sonia pulled her hair back from her face and twisted it thoughtfully. "I can't help wondering if Ray's wife is really dead. I mean, what if they were getting divorced and Ray abducted Henry or something? He hasn't unpacked a single thing in the house. He hasn't even hung up his clothes in the closet."

Evelyn blinked a few times. "I ... don't understand. I thought Ray was unpacking that afternoon Henry came over to play."

Sonia grimaced. "He lied about that. He's living out of moving boxes and plastic bags, almost as though he wants to be prepared to bolt at a moment's notice. He also has a backpack with a change of clothes and a map of the mountains in it. I suppose it could be for hiking, but it looks more like something you'd put a laptop in. And I have no idea where any of Henry's stuff is. The only clothes Ray has for him are some items he purchased at Target."

Evelyn was quiet for a moment. "Maybe Henry's things are still at their old house."

"But why would he leave his son's stuff behind—important things like his birth certificate?"

Evelyn hesitated, a perturbed look on her face. "I don't know—it's all very strange."

"Yes, it is. And that's what worries me." Sonia shot a darting glance in the direction of the door as the kids ran by, chasing each other and shrieking. Lowering her voice, she continued. "I found something peculiar in the family room."

Evelyn reached for the pearls around her throat, twisting them nervously. "Were you snooping around in Celia's house?"

"It wasn't trespassing, if that's what you're worried about. Ray gave me permission to go in there, remember?"

"To pick up Henry's things, not to poke around," Evelyn huffed. "If Ray abducted his son, then the whole house is a crime scene. You shouldn't have touched anything—"

"Relax!" Sonia cut in, patting her mother's arm. "You're getting ahead of yourself. I'm just bouncing my wild theories off you for a little perspective."

Evelyn pursed her lips. "What did you find that was so odd?"

"It was a newspaper article from the local paper—the story they ran recently on the five-year anniversary of Katie Lambert's disappearance. Remember you were watching it on the news a couple of weeks ago?"

A befuddled expression flitted across Evelyn's face. "Why's that so odd? Ray's a journalist, isn't he?"

Sonia shrugged. "Honestly, I don't know what to think. I don't even know if he's really a journalist. Maybe he's a private investigator. The family could have hired him to look into Katie's disappearance. It would explain why he keeps his distance—he's probably treating everyone as a potential suspect."

Evelyn looked doubtful. "Who would have hired him? Katie's parents are dead, and her grandparents are in a memory care facility. I can't imagine them engaging an investigator to look into her disappearance."

Sonia picked at her finger. "What if he was reading up on Katie's story because he has a personal interest in child abduction? What if Henry's mother—"

She broke off at the sound of the doorbell. "That's our food. Don't say anything in front of the kids. And don't bring up the accident either. The last thing I want to do is traumatize Henry any further by telling him his dad doesn't remember who he is."

Seated around the kitchen table, Sonia divvied up the cartons of Chinese food. Henry stared wide-eyed at the orange chicken, fried rice, and egg roll she set on the plate in front of him.

Picking up on his hesitancy, Jessica leaned over. "It's yummy," she said encouragingly. "Just eat it like this." She proceeded to pick up her egg roll and demonstrate, making increasingly exaggerated sounds of enjoyment until Henry started giggling. Sonia and Evelyn exchanged cautious smiles. With enough prodding from Jessica, he was starting to open up. It was almost as if she gave him the permission he needed to be a child.

As she chewed her food, Sonia thought back to the night Ray had come over for dinner and the strange comment he had made about Henry not being allowed to eat much ice cream. Perhaps his wife had restricted Henry's sugar intake. Some parents had a bit of a phobia when it came to letting their kids eat sugar. But there had been such an air of sadness in Ray's expression when he'd said it that it made her think there was more to it than that. Had his wife deprived Henry of toys too? But if that was the case, why did he miss her so much?

"I talked to your dad today, Henry," Sonia said, smiling at him. "He said you could stay with us for a few days."

"For real?" Jessica spluttered, choking on a mouthful of rice. "Yeah! This is going to be so much fun. I always wanted a little brother or sister." She jumped up from the table and hugged Henry before resuming her seat. "We can build a blanket fort and I can read Henry stories."

"That's a great idea," Sonia agreed. She turned to Henry. "Do you like reading stories with your dad?"

He stopped munching his egg roll and stared across the table at her. After a beat of silence, he gave a dejected shake of his head.

Sonia let him swallow his food before trying again, "What kinds of things do you and your dad like to do together?"

Henry threw a distressed look Jessica's way before giving a barely perceptible shrug of his shoulders.

"Do you like to go swimming with him?" Jessica asked in a helpful tone.

Henry shook his head.

"How about watching movies?" Jessica persisted.

After thinking about it for a moment, he gave a tentative nod.

"We love watching movies too," Sonia said. "What's your favorite movie, Henry?"

His gaze roved around the table searching each face in turn, as if seeking the answer, before his eyes welled up with tears. "I miss ... my... mommy."

"Oh, sweetie!" Sonia said, rising from her seat and reaching over to pick him up. She settled him in her lap and rocked him gently back-and-forth for several minutes as he sniffled pitifully. "I know you miss your mommy. Did you used to watch movies with her?"

Henry scooted up in her lap and rubbed his eyes with the backs of his hands. "No," he hiccupped. "We ... we played ball."

Sonia caught her breath. Henry had talked a little to Jessica off and on, but this was the first thing he had ever shared directly with her. She kissed the top of his head as she thought of how best to respond. She didn't want to say anything that he might perceive as criticism of his mother—it sounded as if she'd been as strict about television and movies as she had been about sugar. "Playing ball is fun too. I love being outside in the fresh air."

"Not outside," Henry said, furrowing his dark brows. "In our room."

Sonia exchanged a perplexed look with Evelyn. "You mean, in your house?"

Henry studied her face, before nodding in agreement.

Not for the first time, Sonia got the feeling he was giving her the answers he thought she wanted. It was almost as if he was afraid to say the wrong thing. She was no child welfare professional, but her motherly instincts told her Henry had been taught to live in fear. But of whom? And by whom? His father, or his mother? Had Ray abducted Henry to get him out of an abusive situation—or an overly controlling one? But then why did Henry seem so disconnected to Ray?

"What did you play with your mom when she got sick?" Jessica asked, resting her chin in her hands and blinking innocently across at him.

Alarmed at the direction the conversation was taking, Sonia tried to catch her daughter's eye. She shot Evelyn an urgent plea for help, but her mother merely shrugged in response. No doubt, she was all too eager to hear everything Henry had to say now that he was talking.

"She not got sick," Henry said in a scolding tone.

"What happened to her then?" Jessica prodded.

Sonia groaned inwardly, fearing the worst—that Henry would clam up again, or burst into tears and be inconsolable for the rest of the evening. But, to her surprise, he remained composed. He seemed to handle Jessica's blunt line of questioning better than even the most innocuous interaction with adults.

"He hurted her." His little voice was unwavering and insistent. He turned to Sonia, put his small hands around her neck, and gave a quick squeeze. "Like this."

10

Sonia shrank back from the unexpected pressure of Henry's hot, little hands around her throat. "Who are you talking about, Henry?" she asked in a subdued tone. "Who hurt your Mommy?"

His body turned rigid, as if it had suddenly dawned on him what he'd let slip. Silently, he slid down from her lap and trotted back to his seat.

"Did your daddy do it?" Jessica whispered loudly to him, eyes wide with fascination.

Henry clutched his spoon, his gaze fixed firmly on the fried rice on his plate.

Jessica made a couple more attempts to drag an answer out of him, before Sonia's glaring daggers silenced her. There was a reason Henry had abruptly stopped talking. The fear in his face had been unmistakable. It would be wrong of them to push him for more details. Was it his dad he was frightened of? Had he witnessed his mother being abused? Sonia's throat pulsed as she pictured an enraged Ray with his hands locked around his wife's neck, tightening his grip as their young son looked on. The food churned in her stomach. She'd suspected all along that something was off, but after Henry's disturbing revelation, she could no longer brush it aside. As a concerned citizen, she should pick up the phone and report this to the police. But what exactly would she tell them? Henry was only four years old —the authorities wouldn't take what he said at face value without any evidence. And what if it wasn't Ray he was talking about? Maybe his mother had a boyfriend who had hurt her, and that was why Ray was hiding out here, using his wife's cancer as a cover story. It was understandable that he would be willing to do anything to protect Henry after what he'd gone through in his own childhood.

Sonia chewed on her lip, briefly meeting her mother's anxious gaze before glancing away again. For several minutes they continued pushing their food around their plates in silence, before Sonia cleared her throat. "Okay kids, run along and play while Grandma and I clean up the kitchen. We can watch a movie together after that."

"You're shaking like a leaf," Evelyn muttered, the minute the kids hightailed it out of the kitchen. "Are you all right?"

Sonia leaned over the sink, feeling as if she was about to throw up everything she'd just eaten. "It brings back bad memories, that's all." Snapping out of it, she turned to her mother. "But, this isn't about me. Do you think I should report what Henry said to the authorities?"

Evelyn set down the tumblers she was holding with a sigh. "It might come to that, but we should think this through carefully. With Ray in the state he's in, Child Protective Services will put Henry in a foster home until they get to the bottom of things. I can't bear the thought of Celia's grandson winding up in the system—that never ends well."

"What choice do we have? We can't control what they end up doing with him." Sonia folded her arms in front of her. "It's not like we can foster him. I have a business to run, and you have your hands full already helping out with Jessica."

Evelyn rolled her eyes. "I'm not naïve enough to think I can run after a four-year-old at my age. I just meant we have to be sure of our facts. Neglected children sometimes say things to get the attention they crave. We need to figure out if Henry's telling the truth, and who he's talking about. The police are going to need more information —evidence."

"Whoever he was talking about, it's obvious he's afraid of him," Sonia replied. "If it's Ray, we need to act before he's discharged from the hospital. We can't risk him taking off with Henry in the middle of the night. If he finds out Henry's been saying things, he might load up his truck and disappear with him."

Evelyn rubbed a mottled hand over her brow. "Who else could he have been talking about?"

Sonia shrugged. "I don't know. What if Ray's wife was having an affair? Maybe her boyfriend was violent. He could have been the one who put his hands around her throat. Ray might have abducted Henry to keep him safe. His own horrific childhood would be enough to drive him to do something this drastic."

"If that's the case, we need to help Ray," Evelyn said, a worried tone in her voice. "If he can't remember anything, then he won't remember why he took Henry away from his wife in the first place. She might take advantage of the situation to get him back."

The trill of Sonia's phone cut into their conversation. "I'd better get that," she said, hurriedly drying her hands. "It could be the hospital. I gave them my number in case they needed to get a hold of me." She reached for her phone which she'd left plugged in on the counter. "Hello, Masterton Design."

"It's me," a gruff voice answered.

Sonia's heart sank like a lead weight. Finn's voice sounded distant and gravelly, as if he'd been drinking. The last thing she wanted to do was put Jessica on the phone with him when he was belligerent, but she would be devastated if she found out her father had called and Sonia hadn't let her know. No doubt he was calling to apologize for missing Jessica's eighth birthday last month. He'd have the same old excuse as always—he'd been off on some classified mission in some dangerous part of the globe and unable to call home.

Fighting to keep her frustration in check, she said in a clipped tone, "I'll fetch Jessica." Without waiting for his response, she set her phone on the counter and mouthed to her mother, *it's Finn.*

Evelyn flattened her lips and turned away to begin loading the dishwasher. She didn't approve of Sonia allowing Jessica to talk to her father at all. But Sonia knew that one day her daughter might hold that against her. She was of the firm opinion that Jess would realize herself before too long what an utter waste of time her relationship with her father was—if you could even call it a relationship.

Giddy at the news that her dad was on the phone, Jessica skipped her way down the hall to the kitchen, face aglow. Sonia followed close behind holding Henry by the hand. She sat him down at the kitchen table and gave him a cookie, then made a show of wiping down the counters while unobtrusively trying to listen in on the conversation between Jessica and Finn. Jessica always got upset if she put the phone on speaker, or made it obvious she was listening in, so she was stuck with a one-sided conversation.

"Grandma made me a chocolate cake for my birthday with raspberries on top ... uh-huh ... uh-huh. I got an "A" for my art project ... yup ... I know ... when are you coming home on leave? No, not really ... Mrs. Jenkins died and some new people moved in. Well—" She broke off and shot a furtive glance Sonia's way before darting to the door. "I need some privacy," she called over her shoulder.

Sonia bit back her frustration, deciding against going after her. It would only make Jessica dig in her heels. Instead, she pulled out a broom and began sweeping the floor while her mother sat down next to Henry and tried to engage him in conversation. He answered in monosyllables, his expression wary and watchful, as if waiting on the fallout from what he'd said earlier.

Minutes later, Jessica came running back into the kitchen. "Mom! Dad wants to talk to you. It's important."

Sonia leaned the broom against the counter, forcing herself to bite back a scathing retort: *nothing you say is important, Finn, I can't stand the sound of your voice, I can't wait for when Jessica's old enough to see through your pathetic lies.* Restraining herself, she held out a hand for the phone and pressed it to her ear. "What's up, Finn? I have work to do."

"What's all this about some weirdo moving in next door?"

Sonia squeezed her eyes shut. She should have warned Jessica not to mention Ray. Of course Finn would make a stink about it, just to make her life difficult.

"If you're referring to Celia's son, he's a single dad with a four-year-old. That hardly qualifies him as a weirdo."

"Jessica says he's weird. His kid isn't allowed any toys. What kind of a loser doesn't buy his kid any toys? He never gets to play outside, or watch movies, or eat sugar. You think that's normal? Sounds more like some twisted form of punishment by psycho-dad."

Sonia's fingers curled into a fist. Finn was one to talk. For the first couple of years after their divorce, she had purchased gifts on his behalf to give to Jessica on her birthday and at Christmas, but the reimbursement Finn promised never came. She had long since given up on the charade—it was better Jessica knew the truth. "Look, this is none of your business," she spat back. "I have no desire to discuss the merits of the next-door neighbor's parenting style with you of all people. If that's all you wanted to gripe about, I need to get back to work."

"Don't you dare hang up on me! I'm not done talking." Finn thundered into the phone. "One call to my superior and I'll have CPS knocking down your door to investigate why you're letting our daughter go over to that whacko's house, unsupervised. Trust me, the army will side with me that you're an unfit mother and get Jess out of there pronto. And then you can fight me in the courts for custody."

A bead of sweat trickled down the back of Sonia's neck. Even from thousands of miles away, Finn was trying to trigger the same old fears in her. But she wasn't the same person he'd bullied years ago. "Don't be ridiculous! You're talking about Celia's son, not some stranger. Besides, Jess isn't going over there unsupervised. Henry comes over here to play."

"That's not what she told me," Finn fired back. "She's been in and out of that house half a dozen times when he was home and you weren't there, so don't lie to me." His voice sank to a threatening snarl. "You know I don't like it when you lie to me."

Sonia grabbed the phone tighter, blood pounding in her temples.

"And where is the creep, anyway?" Finn asked. "Why's his kid staying at your place?"

"He rolled his truck—he's in hospital."

"Bummer! Too bad he made it."

"Look, what do you want, Finn? I've got better things to do than stand here and argue with you all night."

"I'm worried about Jess," Finn went on, his voice softening. "She told me what Henry said about his dad choking his mom."

The knot in Sonia's stomach tightened. "He didn't say it was Ray. We don't know who he was talking about. For all we know, his mother might have an abusive boyfriend. Maybe Ray's just trying to protect his son."

"Or maybe you're protecting him! I'm not buying it. Jess says he's weird, and if Jess says he's weird, I believe her. And if you were half the mother you should be, you'd believe our daughter too! He's a psycho!" Finn yelled, his fleeting attempt to remain calm wilting in a heartbeat. He lowered his voice to a familiar menacing growl. "Don't think for one minute that if anything happens to Jess, I won't come after you."

11

Sonia lay on her back in bed staring out at the moonlight spilling over the lawn. The truth of the matter was, Finn was right. She might have put Jessica in danger. For all she knew, Ray could be dangerous —violent even. It was reasonable to think that Finn, with his counter-intelligence training, had picked up on some warning signs from the snippets Jess had told him. Until she got to the bottom of things, she would have to forbid her daughter from going over to Ray's on her own anymore— even to fetch Henry.

Groaning in frustration, Sonia fluffed up her pillow for the umpteenth time and rolled onto her other side. Why did Finn have to pick today of all days to call their daughter? If he'd called a month ago on her birthday, like he'd promised, Ray wouldn't even have entered into the conversation. She hadn't had the heart to reprimand Jessica for telling her dad about their new neighbor. In retrospect, she should have thought to warn her not to bring it up. Finn's threat to have her investigated by the army likely amounted to little more than hot air—he had no real interest in taking responsibility for Jessica himself. Still, it had been a timely warning that she needed to be more careful. She wouldn't put it past Finn to try and stir up trouble purely for his own sadistic amusement.

Abandoning all attempts to fall back asleep, she clambered out of bed shortly before 5:00 a.m. Figuring she might as well get some work done while the house was quiet, she brewed a double espresso and sat down at her rustic wood desk in her office. Deep into a design concept presentation for potential new clients, she suddenly became aware of a presence in the room with her. Swiveling in her seat, she spotted Henry standing in the doorway, silently watching her. She let out a surprised yelp, her hand jerking to her throat. "You scared me, buddy," she said, with a flustered laugh. "Is Jessica still sleeping?"

Henry nodded and began pushing his toy truck up and down the doorframe.

Sonia waved him over. "Come here and sit next to me. You can watch me while I work."

After a moment's hesitation, he ambled over and climbed up into the swivel office chair that Jessica sometimes used for her art projects. Sonia spun him around a couple of times, relieved to see a smile break out on his face.

"What is you doing?" he asked, before plugging his mouth with his thumb.

Sonia tilted her foam board so he could see. "I'm designing a bedroom for a sixteen-year-old girl. She's getting all new furniture, retro lighting, teal-and-white bedding, and bamboo window shades. Do you like it?"

He shook his head and pulled his thumb back out with a plopping sound. "It's yucky."

Sonia laughed. "I can design you a fun boy's bedroom, if you like. What was your bedroom like in your old house?"

"Bad."

Sonia smiled. "Too many pillows, like this one, huh?"

"No. We didn't got pillows—" He broke off, his face quickly closing over.

"It's okay, Henry," Sonia said gently. "You can tell me."

He dropped his head and stared forlornly down at his feet.

"You're not going to get in trouble, sweetie."

A tear tracked down his cheek. "But ... he said ... he said ..."

Sonia held her breath. "What did he say?"

"He said, *never tell them*."

Sonia fought to keep her breathing steady. "Who, Henry? Who said that?"

"My ... my ... my dad," he sniveled.

Sonia tucked her pencil behind her ear and slid an arm around his shoulders. "It's all right. You're safe here, I promise. I won't let anyone hurt you."

Fueled up on caffeine, her mind was racing a million miles an hour. She had made him a promise now. There was no going back. If Ray Jenkins was a danger to his son, she had to find a way to keep Henry away from him.

A COLD CHILL crept over her as she rode the elevator up to the third floor of the hospital later that afternoon. It was time to confront Ray about a few things. She'd gone back on her word about bringing Henry with her to visit, but her promise to keep him safe had canceled out that possibility, for now. Before she left for the hospital, she'd retrieved the newspaper article from Ray's house and stashed it in her purse. It had been bugging her ever since she'd stumbled across it. She needed to ask him about it—that, and the unsettling things Henry had told her. It was time to try and jog Ray's memory before he came home to claim his son.

Taking a deep breath, Sonia painted on a smile before she knocked on the door to his room and stepped inside. "Hi Ray, how's it going today?"

A tiny frown flickered across his forehead. "I'm ... sorry, you ... look familiar, but I've forgotten your name."

"Sonia Masterton, I'm your neighbor. I was—"

"Of course! You were here yesterday." Ray adjusted his pillows and sat up a little straighter in his bed. "It's everything before the accident I can't recall."

Sonia pulled a chair over next to his bed and perched on the end of it, looking intently at him. "Do you remember what we talked about yesterday?"

Ray grimaced. "You said my mother passed away recently."

"Yes, her name was Celia. My mom and I were very fond of her—as was my eight-year-old daughter, Jessica. She was always over at her house—baking cookies or painting with her on the back deck." She took a quick steadying breath before continuing. "Do you remember who else we talked about?"

Ray scrubbed a hand across his jaw, his features tightening. "My son." His voice was low and gravelly, infused with some emotion Sonia couldn't pinpoint. Anger? Sadness? Frustration?

"Where is he?" He blinked accusingly at Sonia. "You said you were going to bring him with you today."

She sighed. "I did, and I'm sorry. It was premature of me to make you that promise. There are ... some things we need to talk about first."

"Like what?" Ray demanded, clearly irritated. "If you're trying to tell me you don't think I'm capable of looking after my own son because I have a concussion, you're wrong. The doctor assures me I'll have my memory back in another day or two." He frowned. "How is he ... Henry? Is he missing me?"

Sonia swallowed the ball of uneasiness bobbing in her throat. She couldn't lie to him, but she didn't want to plunge a knife in his heart either. "He's fine. Jess has been doing a great job of keeping him distracted. I haven't told him about your accident. I said you were working. I didn't want to traumatize him any further."

"Any further? What do you mean?" Ray's eyes widened. "Was Henry in the truck when I wrecked?"

Sonia raised her palms to calm him. "No! Nothing like that. He was at preschool when it happened. He's perfectly fine." She chewed on her lip wondering if she should just come out with it. How would he react when he learned that the mother of his child—his wife—had passed away recently too? Part of her felt bad for breaking it to him like this. She should have discussed it with his doctor first to make sure the shock of it wouldn't worsen his condition. But it was too late for that now. She'd dug herself in too deep.

Besides, this might be the only chance she'd get to wheedle some answers out of him before he realized he'd said something he wasn't supposed to. If he had lied about his wife dying of cancer, she needed to know. "Ray, this is going to be difficult for you to hear, but there's something else I need to tell you. Your wife passed away too. Henry really misses his mom. He talks about her all the time."

Ray's brows tugged inward as he digested her words. When he spoke, there was a tremor in his voice. "Was she ... in the truck with me?"

"No. She passed away before the accident. She had stomach cancer."

Ray's head dropped, his hand clenching into a fist on the sheet. After a few moments of silence, he lifted his head, his gaze trained on Sonia. He looked gutted and ashen—like an old rag someone had wrung out and tossed aside. "Did you ... know my wife? It's just that ... I can't remember what she looked like."

Sonia's eyes prickled with tears. "I'm sorry, I never met her. I don't even know her name. You must have photos of her." As the words left her lips, she realized it was another anomaly that didn't make sense. If Ray's wife had died of cancer as he'd claimed, why didn't he have a single picture of her anywhere in the house? Surely Henry must have a photo of his mother—stashed under his pillow, perhaps. She made a mental note to ask him about it when she got home.

"I don't understand," Ray said, scratching the back of his hand in an agitated fashion. "You must have known my wife if you live next door."

"The thing is, Ray, you just moved here a few weeks ago. You inherited the house when your mother passed away. You thought it would be best for Henry to have a fresh start in a new neighborhood. There were too many memories of his mother in your old place. You're a freelance journalist so you can work from anywhere."

Ray gave a solemn nod, as if seeing the logic in her words. He traced his fingers back-and-forth across his forehead. "You said there were some things we needed to talk about. If it's about Henry, I really appreciate you helping out, and I promise not to burden you with him too much longer. The doctor's coming by this afternoon. If everything checks out, they'll discharge me tomorrow. I can pick up Henry then." His eyes met Sonia's with a plaintive appeal. "I might need a ride home from the hospital. And a change of clothes—some sweats and a T-shirt."

Sonia flashed him a stilted smile. "Of course." She fished in her purse for the newspaper article she'd pilfered from his family room and smoothed it out on the bed in front of him. "I found this when I was picking up Henry's things at your house." Despite wanting to pepper him with questions, she forced herself to stay quiet—curious to see what his reaction would be. If he recognized the story, his expression might give him away.

Ray read silently for a few minutes and then gestured at the page. "Why are you giving me this? I don't remember this story." His brow creased. "Did you say you found it ... with Henry's things?" He suddenly sounded confused and tired. Sonia quashed a pang of guilt and pressed on. "No. It was in the family room, on the end table. You must have torn it out of the newspaper for some reason. Are you sure you don't remember anything about the story? Were you working on it, perhaps?"

Ray bit his lip and frowned. "It doesn't ring a bell." He folded the page back up and handed it to her." Maybe I tore it out to set my coffee cup on. I don't know." He sank back in his pillows with a weary sigh and closed his eyes.

Curbing her frustration, Sonia slipped the article into her purse. "Ray, do you remember telling me about your childhood? About your dad, and how abusive he was? You ran away from home when you were sixteen."

Ray's eyes shot open, bulging with the guarded look of a caged animal.

Sonia inhaled a shallow breath before continuing, "He made you sleep in the dog pen in the garage overnight."

A clip of pure terror flashed across Ray's face and then it was gone. He opened and closed his mouth a couple of times before stammering, "I remember ... something now ... fighting with a man."

"Anything else?" Sonia asked encouragingly. "Try to think."

Ray frowned. "I punched him, and he ... " His voice trailed off.

"It's okay, Ray. That's good. Keep going. Your memories are starting to come back."

"He fell ... backwards. There was ... blood ... everywhere." A sheen of sweat formed on his face. "I ... I think I killed him."

12

Sonia drove home from the hospital with Ray's words ringing in her ears. They had stared at each other for a long moment afterward, neither of them quite knowing where to go from there. Ray had admitted he couldn't be sure it was his father he'd been fighting with. In fact, he wasn't even sure if it was a real memory, or some fabrication his injured brain had dreamed up. Sonia reminded him that he'd told her his father succumbed to a heart attack shortly after he left home. But then he began to wonder if the fight had triggered the heart attack. Despite further prodding, Ray couldn't remember any additional details. "It's a foggy memory. I don't know when or where the fight happened. And I can't say for sure it was my father I was fighting with. It's just an impression I have of a man falling backwards, but each time the memory starts to resurface, his face blurs."

Sonia hadn't quite known what to make of it all. If Ray had killed his father, then Finn's instincts about him were right. It also meant that Celia had been covering for Ray all these years. And what about the large transfer of money she'd been making on a monthly basis? Was that to buy Tom's silence? Had he threatened to expose what his brother had done? In the end, Sonia had half-heartedly assured Ray that even if the fight had brought on his father's heart attack, he couldn't be held responsible for what was essentially a natural death. But the truth was, she was afraid of what Ray might be capable of, and more scared than ever for Henry's safety.

She pulled into her driveway and switched off the engine, leaning her head against the steering wheel to collect her thoughts before going into the house to face the inevitable barrage of questions from her mother. She'd intended to grill Ray and get some answers, but instead she'd returned from the hospital with more questions than ever. There must be some way to get to the bottom of it all. She couldn't in good conscience hand Henry back over to Ray until she knew the child was safe. If Ray was lying, he was frighteningly good at it—which made him a dangerous sociopath.

Glancing across at his house, she made a split-second decision to head back over there and take a closer look around. Buried somewhere in his belongings, there had to be a photograph of his wife—some record of her existence. The other question Sonia was desperate to resolve was what role Ray had played in his father's sudden death. Had there actually been a heart attack? The fragmented images could be the dregs of a guilty conscience whirling around in Ray's damaged brain. Celia had scores of old file boxes in the garage. Her husband's death certificate had to be in there somewhere.

Her mind made up, she climbed out of her car and tromped over the back lawn to Ray's house. After letting herself in, she sent her mother a quick text to let her know she was picking up some clothes for Ray. The last thing she needed was Evelyn calling the cops after spotting a light on in the house. Slipping her phone into the back pocket of her jeans, Sonia swept her gaze around the disused kitchen. It had taken on an ominous aura in Celia's absence. There were too many fossilized secrets in this house, too much unfinished business, and at the heart of it all was a little boy Sonia had made an impromptu promise to protect. Mustering her resolve, she headed out to the garage to begin her search for answers.

After retrieving a half-rotten wooden ladder she found buried under a pile of junk at the back of the garage, she balanced on the bottom rung and began weeding through the cardboard boxes and plastic tubs piled haphazardly on the sagging particle board shelves. Most of the boxes were filled with old household items, chipped ornaments, miscellaneous painting supplies, stacks of women's magazines, and similarly worthless items.

Fighting to keep her face free of the cobwebs dangling above her head, Sonia ascended the second rung and reached for another cardboard box falling apart at the seams. Grunting under the weight of her precarious load, she gingerly descended the ladder and pulled open the flaps. Beneath the crumpled newspaper on top, lay a silver picture frame. She flipped it over and examined the couple in the wedding photo. She recognized Celia immediately— slim and pretty, in a long-sleeved satin gown. Next to her stood a stocky, unsmiling man with a slick side part, dressed in a black suit. A small group of family members were positioned on either side of the couple.

Sonia rubbed the smudged glass with her sleeve. This had to be Ray's father, although it didn't look much like him. Ray definitely took after Celia's side of the family. She set the photo on a shelf and dug deeper in the box. Tossing aside several framed baby pictures, she stumbled upon a moldy file folder full of documents in plastic sleeves, including a marriage certificate, a death certificate, and two birth certificates. She perused the birth certificates first, surprised to discover that Ray was only eleven months older than his younger brother, Tom. Next, she pulled out the death certificate and confirmed that Rupert John Jenkins had died of congestive heart failure. There was no mention of any injuries or suspicious circumstances. Whatever memory Ray was wrestling with, apparently, he hadn't murdered his father, which provided Sonia with some small measure of relief.

She returned the box to the shelf and was about to reach for the one next to it when she heard her mother's voice drifting her way. "Sonia! Are you out there?"

Biting back her frustration, she scooted back down the ladder and leaned it against the wall. "Coming!" she called, pushing open the door into the kitchen while attempting to brush the dust from her clothes.

Evelyn ran a critical eye over her. "There you are. I was worried. I saw your car in the driveway, but I couldn't find you."

"I texted you," Sonia said with a wry grin.

"You did?" Evelyn patted her pockets in a flustered fashion. "I must have set my phone down."

"We should head back to the house," Sonia said. "I don't like leaving the kids alone, even if we are just next door."

Evelyn flapped a hand dismissively. "Mary's watching them. She stopped by with a lemon meringue pie. What are you doing here anyway?"

"I was ... looking for some clothes for Ray. They're discharging him tomorrow."

"He keeps his clothes in the garage?" Evelyn peered around dubiously.

"He thought he put a tub with some sweats in it out here," Sonia answered with a careless shrug. "I couldn't find them. He's probably confused."

"You weren't rifling through Celia's things, were you?" Evelyn asked, narrowing her eyes.

Sonia let out a defeated sigh. "I might have peeked in a couple of boxes. I was looking for a photo of Ray's wife—if she even exists. I have to make sure he's telling us the truth before he's discharged. If he's dangerous, he shouldn't have access to Henry."

Her mother puckered her lips. "Did you find Henry's birth certificate?"

"No. I can't find any paperwork for him, or any trace of Ray's wife. I did find a wedding photo of Celia and her husband though. He gives me the creeps, something about the cold way he's staring into the camera." A shudder ran across her shoulders. "Come on, let's get out of here."

The minute Sonia walked into the kitchen, she could tell something was amiss. The kids were coloring at the table, a trail of cookie crumbs across the pages. Jessica's eyes darted guiltily from adult to adult. Mary shot Evelyn a tense look before reaching for her stick and getting to her feet. "I should go. I need to let my dog out."

Wordlessly, Sonia followed her to the door and laid a hand on her arm. "Mary, did something happen? I saw the look you gave Mom."

Mary's shriveled lips trembled, her rheumy eyes filled with angst. "Not exactly. It's just that Henry—" She broke off and fixed an apologetic gaze on Sonia. "I don't want to stir up any trouble ... it was just so upsetting. Of course, he might have been making it up. He's only a kid, after all."

The knot in Sonia's stomach tightened. "Making what up? What did he tell you?"

Mary adjusted the strap of her varnished black purse. "Well, the kids wanted to draw, you see, so Jessica fetched her art supplies and she suggested they draw their families. Henry drew his mom, and everything was going great, but then I asked him if he was going to draw his dad too, and he shook his head." Mary hesitated and threw a nervous look over her shoulder. "Naturally, I asked him why. It's not that I was being nosy or anything, I just—"

"Of course not," Sonia soothed, desperate for her to get to the point.

"He said his dad was a bad man," Mary whispered loudly. "That's when Jessica asked him if he was bad because he choked his mom. At first, I thought I misheard her, and then I scolded her for saying such a thing—I could see Henry was fighting back tears." She pressed her lips together. "Jessica was upset with me, but I didn't realize it was something Henry had told her. At any rate, I managed to distract them with some cookies. The next thing I know Henry's drawing a picture of himself inside his house with tears running down his face. I asked him why he was crying, and he said, *because I was yocked in*." Mary arched her sparse brows. "I didn't know what the poor kid was talking about at first, but then Jessica caught on that he was saying, *locked in*. He told us he was locked in his room, *every day*."

Sonia frowned, her pulse thundering in her temples. "Did he say who locked him in?"

Mary gave a weighty nod. "Yes, his dad, but that's not all. He said his mother was locked in too."

13
———

The following morning, Sonia was still at a loss to know how much of what Henry had said to believe. She backed out of her garage, torn between driving to the hospital to pick up Ray, as promised, or going straight to the police station to report what his son had said. It seemed improbable that Ray could have kept his child and cancer-ridden wife locked in a room without someone finding out about it. His wife must have had family, friends, neighbors checking up on her—not to mention doctors, and appointments to keep.

Did Henry simply have an over-active imagination? Was he desperate for attention in the wake of the loss of his mother? Turning on her blinker, Sonia merged robotically with the traffic on the highway, her mind churning through the possibilities. There could be a more benign explanation. Ray might have locked Henry in his room to keep him safe while he ran an errand or something—the actions of a desperate parent. Maybe he'd dashed to the pharmacy for a prescription for his wife. Then again, if Ray thought he was capable of killing his father, then maybe he was capable of locking his child in a room as a form of punishment, or perhaps even to avoid having to care for him.

The traffic light up ahead turned red and Sonia slowed to a halt, tapping the palm of her hand on the steering wheel. The frustrating part was that Ray couldn't remember anything. When she'd broken the news to him that he had a son, he'd been genuinely shocked. But he'd also expressed concern for Henry's welfare—he hadn't sounded like someone who was likely to choke his wife in front of his young son, or lock them in a room, or deprive his kid of toys or treats. Was it possible he could have forgotten that he was a monster?

A horn blared behind her, jolting Sonia into action. She floored the gas through the intersection, and took a sharp left toward the hospital, sealing in the decision she'd been mulling over ever since she'd left the house. She would pick Ray up and bring him home. After that, she would decide what to do about him.

When she entered his hospital room, he was perched on the edge of the bed, clutching some paperwork.

"Did they discharge you already?" Sonia asked, handing him the clothes she'd brought from his house.

Ray nodded. "Doctor Robinson stopped by earlier with my test results. He said I'm good to go home with a responsible adult." He gave her a sheepish grin. "I told him you were very levelheaded. Although, I've no idea if there's any truth to that. You might be here to kidnap me."

Sonia gave a nervous laugh in response. How ironic that he felt he had as much reason to fear her as she did him.

He disappeared into the bathroom with his clothes and emerged a few minutes later dressed in sweats and a long-sleeved cotton shirt that Sonia had dug out of one of the moving boxes.

"I really appreciate you going out of your way like this," Ray said. "I don't want to become a burden, but the bummer is I haven't been cleared to drive yet, and the doctor wants to see me again in a couple of days."

Sonia managed to mask her irritation with a thin smile. "I'm sure I can get you to your appointment."

"That's kind of you," he said, stuffing the discharge paperwork into his pocket. "All right, let's get out of here."

Inside the elevator, the tension in the claustrophobic space seemed to pulse with a current of its own. Sonia kept her eyes forward, wondering, not for the first time, if she should be afraid of Ray. She tried not to think about how easy it would be for him to hit the emergency stop switch and strangle her. She could still feel Henry's hot little fingers digging into her neck. Goosebumps pricked her skin. She had to make a decision soon on whether to go to the police with the information she had. Did Ray sense she was keeping something from him, planning to rat him out while playing the friendly neighbor? More important, what was he keeping from her?

The doors finally dinged open revealing the hospital lobby. Exhaling a silent sigh of relief, Sonia led the way out to the parking lot and unlocked her car. Ray climbed into the passenger seat and reached for his seatbelt. That had to be a good sign. He hadn't forgotten the basics of life, at least. Hopefully, he still remembered how to use a computer, so he could order his groceries online. She had put a few staples in his refrigerator, but she didn't want to be obligated to keep him fed and stocked up until he was able to drive again. "Do you remember what your house looks like, yet?" she asked.

Ray furrowed his brow for a moment, before shaking his

head. "No. I can't even remember my own son's face. That's what worries me most."

"I'm sure you'll recognize him once you see him."

"I meant to ask you," Ray said, scratching the back of his head. "Does Henry go to school?"

Sonia grimaced, navigating her way through an intersection before answering. She'd hoped to avoid having this conversation until she'd decided whether to report Ray to the police. "He just started at the local preschool, Small Steps. I picked him up from there the day of your accident. The principal asked me to remind you that you haven't turned in all his paperwork. The registration process needs to be completed before he can go back to school."

Ray blinked, a befuddled look on his face. "Do you know what paperwork they're talking about?"

"They're missing his birth certificate and immunization record."

"That's odd. Maybe I haven't unpacked them yet," Ray said absentmindedly, before turning to look out the window.

Sonia darted a glance across at him. He didn't sound particularly concerned, or guilty. Either he'd forgotten that he didn't have a birth certificate for Henry, or he was an exceptionally smooth liar. A shiver of fear ran up her spine as Finn's words flitted back to mind.

Don't think for one minute that if anything happens to Jess I won't come after you.

Finn had called Ray a psycho, and Jessica thought he was creepy. What if they were right? What if they were more in tune to the danger Ray presented than she was? She didn't exactly have a good track record for knowing a villain when she saw one. The longer she delayed turning the information over to the police, the more risk she could be exposing her family to.

When they pulled back into her driveway, Sonia switched off the engine and turned to Ray. "Henry may not react the way you want him to at first. Remember, he lost his mother not that long ago, and then you suddenly disappeared out of his life. He's attached himself to my daughter, Jessica, and he may not want to go home with you right away."

Ray looked crestfallen. "We can't continue to be a burden on you and your family. He needs to come home with me tonight. We'll figure it out."

Sonia flashed him a sympathetic smile. "Let's just play it by ear." As far as she was concerned, Henry was welcome to stay for another night if it made things easier, but she wasn't about to offer Ray her guest room. She could just imagine Jessica telling her father that the strange man next door was now sleeping in the guest bedroom. The last thing she needed was CPS and a SWAT team swarming her house.

"Well, look who's back," Evelyn said, running an appraising eye over Ray as she untied her apron. "You look all tuckered out. How does a hot cup of tea sound?"

Ray gave an appreciative nod. "That would be great, thanks."

Sonia gestured to a chair. "Park yourself there. I'll go find the kids."

"They're outside playing on the tire swing," Evelyn called after her.

Sonia leaned against the back door frame and folded her arms across her chest, watching the children for several minutes. Her heart warmed at the rare sound of Henry's laughter pealing through the air. A few more days here, and he might start acting like a normal four-year-old. There was nothing she wanted more for him than to see the fear in his eyes gone.

You're safe here, I promise. I won't let anyone hurt you.

"Higher!" he shrieked as Jessica pushed him.

Reluctantly, Sonia straightened up, steeling herself to interrupt their play. She wasn't sure whether to let Henry know that his father was back, or simply to tell him it was time to come inside. All things considered, it was probably best to prepare him—it didn't feel right to blindside him.

"Watch this, Mom!" Jessica called out, pushing the tire swing with all her might. "Hold on, Henry!"

Sonia walked up to her and smoothed a hand over her ponytail. "I know you guys are having fun out here, but Henry's dad is back, and he wants to see him."

Jessica threw her a wary look before reaching for the rope and slowing the swing down.

"More!" Henry cried, kicking his feet excitedly.

"I'll push you some more later," Jessica said, in a motherly tone as she helped him off the swing. "First we have to go inside and see your dad."

"Why?" Henry asked, searching out his thumb.

Sonia took a shallow breath, trying to figure out how best to answer him. At least he wasn't completely freaking out at the news. Smiling, she reached for his hand, opting for a diversionary tactic. "Tell you what, let's go inside and get some of Grandma's cookies."

Ray's eyes lit up at the sight of Henry traipsing into the kitchen clutching Sonia's hand. He shot a hesitant look at her before addressing Henry, "Hey, buddy. Did you have fun on the tire swing?"

Henry nodded but made no attempt to approach him. Instead he took a half-step backward and peered around Sonia's legs.

"All right, cookie time," Sonia said briskly. She lifted Henry up and plopped him on a chair at the table next to his father before he had a chance to protest. Evelyn started fishing around in the cookie jar and arranged an assortment on a plate. The instant she set them on the table, Henry snatched up a chocolate chip cookie and began chomping on it. Sonia smirked, secretly pleased at how brazen he'd become when it came to the treats he'd been denied.

Ray wet his lips, his eyes riveted on his son. "I'm sorry I had to go away for a couple of days, Henry."

Henry stopped chewing, his cheek smeared with chocolate. "Can I have another sleepover?"

Ray bunched his brows together. "Maybe, in a day or two. But tonight, we need to sleep at our house."

Henry jutted out his bottom lip. "I want to sleep here." He pointed a finger at Jessica. "With her!"

Sonia winked reassuringly at Ray before turning to Henry. "How about Jessica and I walk you back over to your house?"

Henry considered this for a moment and then gave an underwhelming nod. Sonia smiled encouragingly at him. He might be hoping to try and convince them to let Jessica sleep at his house instead. But that was never going to happen.

After gathering up Henry's things, they all trooped across the back lawn to Ray's house, leaving Evelyn to tidy up the avalanche of crumbs beneath the table.

Jessica retrieved the key from the planter and proudly unlocked the door for everyone.

Ray trudged from the kitchen into the family room, shaking his head in bewilderment. "None of this looks familiar."

Sonia went over to the shelf beneath the television and

pulled out the photo album that Celia had put together of her sons. "Why don't you look through some family photos?" she suggested. "See if you recognize anyone."

Ray sank down in an armchair with the album and began turning the pages. "I'm guessing these are from my childhood." He frowned as he worked his way through the photos. "This must be my brother in all these pictures with me. What did you say his name was?"

"Tom," Sonia answered. "He's eleven months younger than you."

"Can I see?" Jessica cried, squeezing in between the arms of the chair and the couch for a better look.

"Me too," Henry echoed.

Ray angled the photo album to give them a better view as he continued flipping through the pages.

"Beach!" Henry said, pointing a finger at a photo of Ray and Tom digging in the sand with plastic shovels, their buckets half-buried next to them.

"That's right," Ray said, smiling at him. "Do you like going to the beach, Henry?"

He shrugged, never taking his eyes off the photo. The look of intense longing on his face made Sonia suspect he'd never played in the sand before.

Ray turned the last page and studied the photo of himself and his brother, Tom, for a long time. "He looks like me."

Jessica cocked her head to one side and curled up her lip. "Not really." She tilted the photo toward Henry. "What do you think?"

He pressed a tiny finger on Tom's face. "My dad."

_____

14

Later that evening, Ray heated up a plate of lasagne Sonia had left in the refrigerator for him and took it into the family room to eat in front of the television. They had all laughed awkwardly after Henry pointed at the picture of Tom and called him his dad. Thankfully, Sonia had acknowledged that Ray and his brother, Tom, really did look remarkably alike, and left it at that. Ray wasn't ready for any more probing questions—he needed time to think things through.

As Sonia had predicted, Henry didn't respond well when it came time for her and Jessica to leave. He'd burst into tears and clung to them, and Ray hadn't had the heart to force the poor kid to stay with him—or the energy to argue with him. In the end, he'd consented to Henry spending one more night with Jessica and coming home tomorrow instead.

He put a forkful of food in his mouth and chewed mindlessly. His head throbbed whenever he moved it too quickly. From time to time, patchwork images flashed to mind, but they always faded away in a blur before he could stitch a memory together. It was incredibly frustrating, but, at the same time, a hopeful sign that his brain would soon be firing on all cylinders again. At least he'd remembered how to use a microwave to heat his dinner—it wasn't as if he'd suffered any irreparable brain damage. He'd just have to put his trust in the doctors and hope his memory returned in full over the next few days. For now, he needed a distraction —thinking too much aggravated his headache. He picked up the TV remote and clicked through the channels: *I Shouldn't Be Alive*, *Win the Wilderness*, *Deadliest Catch*—eventually settling on an episode of Top Gear. After surviving a wreck that had totaled his truck, he wasn't in the mood for a survival-type show.

He hadn't had much of an appetite when he sat down, but Sonia's lasagne proved a refreshing change from hospital food, and he cleaned his plate. He wiped his mouth on a napkin and set the empty plate on the end table, his gaze falling on a folded-up page from a newspaper. Frowning, he reached for it. It was the article Sonia had brought to the hospital. He reread the story carefully—the original interview with Katie Lambert's father, and his desperate plea for her safe return, tugged at his heartstrings. Katie was only seventeen when she went missing. She was last seen waiting for an Uber after work. The police suspected she'd been abducted some time later that evening. Ray couldn't imagine the horror of losing a child, for any reason—let alone to some predator. No wonder Katie's father had committed suicide. The newspaper article indicated the poor man had already lost his wife to cancer—

Ray caught his breath, his heartbeat picking up pace as a memory blazed across his brain. Sonia had told him his wife had died of cancer too. He scrunched his eyes shut trying to remember what she looked like. Something—anything—

about her. Her name, for instance. Despite pushing through the pounding pain in his head, he couldn't drum up so much as the vaguest recollection of her face, her hair, or even the color of her eyes. Nor could he recall anything about her illness. Surely there would have been dozens of doctors' appointments, hospital visits, treatments. He must have accompanied her to some of them. He rubbed his brow in an effort to ease the tension. It must have been a traumatic time for Henry too—watching her slowly dying. At some point, it would have been impossible to hide the truth from him.

Ray blew out a heavy breath and reached for his plate to take it to the kitchen. He would do whatever it took to help his son move on from this. For starters, he needed to make a concerted effort to spend some quality time with him in the coming weeks. They felt like strangers forced together. No doubt, he'd been so wrapped up in taking care of his wife for the past few months that Henry had been sidelined, perhaps even shipped off to relatives. He frowned to himself. Were his wife's parents still alive? He tried to think of their names as he rinsed off his plate and silverware and stashed them in the dishwasher. With a bit of luck, he might have identified them as his in-laws in his contacts. If nothing else, his wife's phone number had to be in there. And then it hit him. The police had found his wallet, but his phone had been smashed beyond repair.

Gritting his teeth in frustration, he glanced around the kitchen for a laptop. He must have a computer in the house somewhere. He made his way down the hall, peering into each of the bedrooms in turn. His heart leapt when he spotted a MacBook on the nightstand in the main bedroom. A momentary flash of panic hit when he opened it and realized he couldn't remember his password. But the second he placed his fingers on the keyboard, they flew over the keys with a mind of their own. He pulled up his contacts and searched for the name, *Jenkins*. The only two listed were his own and his mother's. No contact information for his brother, and no one with the same last name who could possibly be his wife. Maybe she hadn't changed her name after they got married. He would have to dig up his marriage certificate—it had to be in one of the moving boxes, along with Henry's birth certificate. He scrolled back up to the first name in his contacts and began working his way through the list, checking the notes section for any additional identifying information. To his disappointment, he didn't recognize any of the names as those of his in-laws.

Disheartened, he closed the laptop and took stock of the moving boxes stacked in the room. Why had he not unpacked, yet? By all accounts, he'd been here for a couple of weeks already. With a resolute sigh, he got to his feet and approached the first box. Time to make a start on things while Henry wasn't around. After hanging up his shirts and pants in the closet, he cleaned out a few drawers in the dresser and put away his underwear and T-shirts. He flattened the cardboard boxes and stacked them in the hallway, before moving on to the guest bedroom. Judging by the night light near the bed, this was Henry's room. Ray ran a hand over his jaw, berating himself for not doing a better job of making the place more kid friendly. No wonder his son wanted to stay at Jessica's—his toys weren't even unpacked. Ray made a mental note to purchase some kid-friendly bedding as soon as possible—Henry's favorite superhero, perhaps. For several minutes, he stood staring out of the window, trying to remember what superheroes Henry liked, but he came up blank. No matter. He'd ask him about it tomorrow and then order something on Amazon. A couple of days from now, Henry's room would look a whole lot more appealing to a four-year-old boy. In the meantime, he could make a start on things by unpacking his son's belongings.

Opening up the flaps on one of the cardboard boxes at the foot of the bed, he was surprised to find it was packed full of books. He checked the remaining boxes, but found nothing of Henry's in any of them. They were mostly filled with work files. He straightened up and stretched out his back. Maybe he'd intended to make this room his office, but that still didn't explain where Henry's belongings were.

He reached for the Target bags on the floor and tossed them on the bed before rifling through the contents. It looked like he'd gone shopping for Henry recently. It struck him as odd that he hadn't bothered to empty the bags and put the items away. Despite his fatigue, he got to work folding the clothes and putting them in the lowest drawer in the dresser. Evidently, the contents of Henry's old room must still be in boxes somewhere. The most obvious place to look was the garage. He might have unloaded a bunch of boxes there and been too busy with work and getting Henry settled into school to get around to them.

After turning on the fluorescent strip light in the garage, he swept a glance around the musty space. The contents looked like they'd lain undisturbed for quite some time—no moving boxes in sight. His eyes traveled up and down the sagging shelving on the back wall, searching for anything that might have been a recent addition. Between the mice droppings and the thick layer of dust encrusted on every surface, he couldn't envision leaving his belongings out here —and definitely not his son's clothes and toys. The place was in desperate need of a thorough cleaning. He was about to head back inside when it occurred to him that his mother might have some things from his childhood stashed in the garage. Doctor Robinson had encouraged him to look through family photos and personal items in an effort to speed up his recovery. The photo album in the family room hadn't helped—but it couldn't do any harm to go through a few boxes of his mother's stuff.

He pulled out the ladder jammed between a lawnmower and a metal file cabinet on the back wall and leaned it against the shelving, surprised to see fingerprints in the dust. Maybe Sonia had borrowed the ladder recently for something or other. He climbed up a rung and lifted down a cardboard box that had burst a seam. Gingerly, he removed the crumpled newspaper protecting the contents and reached for a photo frame lying upside down on top. He flipped it over, his heart seizing so violently in his chest he thought he would pass out. He grabbed onto a shelf to prevent himself from crumpling to the floor. Beads of sweat needled his forehead. An all-too-familiar sensation of panic took hold, as a current of fiery fear moved steadily through his veins. He recognized that face staring back at him; the hard set of the granite eyes above the thick-lipped grimace. That same expression he always wore right before he turned, sliding his belt from his pants with serpent-like cunning.

Sick to his stomach, Ray tossed the frame back in the box and shoved it back into place before hurriedly returning the ladder to the spot he'd found it in. His legs trembled beneath him. He couldn't do this now, he was too weak, too confused. Broken images sparked in his brain, beckoning to memories he didn't want to face—shouts of anger, spittle flying, a flurry of fists. Blood—so much blood. He stumbled from the garage back into the family room, collapsing into the closest chair. For a long time, he sat slumped in it, staring across the room at nothing in particular, sweaty palms resting on the doilies draped over the arms. What had he done? The thought terrified him, but he had to know.

When his legs felt strong enough to support him, he retrieved the photo album of his childhood from the cubby beneath the television. He leafed through it again, stopping every now and then to study a photo, trying to coax some long-lost memory out from the rock it had scuttled under. He scrutinized the photo of himself and Tom on the last page—the picture of normality.

But the look of desperation in Tom's eyes told a different story.

15

___

The gears in Ray's mind went into overdrive as he tried to process the questions flying through it. Why did those disturbing images of a fight keep flashing to mind? He couldn't remember the abusive childhood he'd told Sonia about, but there was no mistaking the visceral reaction he'd had when he found that photo of his father and the hopeless look in Tom's eyes. Had he attacked his father in some misguided bid to protect his little brother? Was that why he'd run away from home? Each time he tried to lock on to a memory, his thoughts disintegrated like fraying string.

His gaze slid to the newspaper clipping on the end table. Sonia had wondered why he'd saved the article, but he didn't have an answer for that either. He didn't know the missing Booneville girl, or her family—or anyone else in this town, for that matter.

He eventually fell into a troubled sleep in the lumpy armchair, assailed by nightmares which left him gasping for air. His heartbeat raced to the point of explosion in his chest each time the images poked their way through to the surface of his mind—a volley of fists and blood, and always the hazy face of a man. Sometimes, he thought he could make out his father's cruel stare; at other times he found himself looking into Tom's terrified eyes. Confusion gripped his brain like a vice. Who had he been fighting? And what had they been fighting about? Was it possible he'd actually killed his father? Maybe it had been a terrible accident. He might have been trying to protect Tom. But that wasn't what was turning the blood in his veins to ice. Something bad had happened to instigate the fight—something very bad. He felt it in his bones.

After finally falling into a deep sleep in the early morning hours, Ray woke with a jolt shortly after 9:00 a.m. His head pounded mercilessly, and every joint ached from the awkward position he'd slept in, but he groaned and forced himself to his feet. He had promised to pick Henry up by ten, and he was determined not to show up late—he'd already asked too much of his neighbors.

Scrubbing his hands over his face to wake himself fully, he plodded down to the master bedroom and opened the closet to retrieve some clean clothes. His gaze fell on a shoebox overflowing with papers on the shelf above him. A quick glance inside revealed a sheaf of bank statements. Frowning, he set it aside to take up to the kitchen with him. Sonia had mentioned something about an unusual bank transfer he'd been trying to get to the bottom of.

His gaze drifted down to the black backpack shoved into the recesses of the closet. It didn't look remotely like anything that would belong to an elderly woman. Curious, he grabbed a strap and yanked it out. Inside, he found a large flannel shirt, jeans, and a pair of boots, along with a GPS and a small bag of toiletries. An overnight bag of sorts, perhaps? It must belong to him. But what had he packed it for? He slipped his fingers into the front pouch and pulled out a trail map.

Frowning, he spread it out on the bed and studied it. For some reason, he'd highlighted a loop into the Blue Ridge Mountains. Turning the map sideways, he took note of the coordinates printed neatly in the margin. It looked like his handwriting. There was no campground marked on the map at those coordinates, but there was a stream nearby—perhaps it was a favorite fishing spot he'd been planning on taking Henry to before the accident. But why didn't he have any camping supplies in his pack, other than a change of clothes, and nothing at all for Henry? It didn't make sense.

He slumped down on the edge of the bed, letting the map slide from his hand, a sliver of a memory, slippery as an eel, dancing in and out of his consciousness. Every time he tried to pin it down, it receded into the shadows. Head throbbing, he lay down on the bed and closed his eyes. Something about the coordinates was familiar to him, but he couldn't retrieve it from the scum-covered depths his memories had become bogged down in. Releasing a tired breath, he sat up, tucked the shoebox under his arm, and made his way to the kitchen. A strong cup of coffee was in order before he picked up Henry. He brewed a full pot in the relic of a coffeemaker he found on the counter and sat down at the table with the shoebox.

Frowning, he studied the stack of bank statements paper clipped together by year. It appeared he had been going through them and highlighting things, taking notes about things he needed to take care of, and accounts that had to be closed. He'd highlighted a monthly transfer of $4500 going back almost five years. Sipping his coffee, he contemplated the possibilities. Sonia had mentioned something about his mother sending money to his brother. It was a hefty sum of money for a grown man to be taking from his elderly mother—$54,000 a year. Granted, Celia had been comfortably off, but hardly wealthy. The transfers amounted to roughly two-thirds of her combined income from her social security, a small pension, and a modest rental property.

Ray drained his coffee and rinsed the mug out in the sink. He wasn't going to get to the bottom of things by staring at the statements. He would have to go into the bank and see if they could help him sort it out. Right now, he had a more pressing matter to attend to. For better or worse, it was time to pick up his son. Admittedly, he was overwhelmed at the thought of caring for a four-year-old by himself—and at a complete loss as to how to occupy him all day long. Hopefully, Henry would have his own ideas about what he liked to do for fun.

Ray pulled the screen door closed behind him and crossed the lawn to his neighbor's back door. Evelyn spotted him through the kitchen window as he raised his fist to knock. He could have sworn he saw her purse her lips in disapproval before she gave a small nod of acknowledgment and dried her hands on a tea towel.

"You're looking a little fresher this morning," she quipped, opening the door and ushering him inside. "Did you sleep?"

"A little," Ray said, not wanting to elaborate on the nightmares that had plagued him.

"Tea?" Evelyn asked, peering at him over her shoulder as she filled the kettle.

Ray shook his head. "No thanks, I just downed a huge mug of coffee. That should be enough to kickstart my system—hopefully, my memory too."

"Are you feeling better?" Evelyn asked, a gleam of curiosity in her eye.

"Pretty good. I've still got a nagging headache." He didn't add that it got worse every time he tried to dig up a memory. He got the impression Evelyn wasn't as concerned about his welfare as she was about releasing a four-year-old boy back into the care of a parent who'd forgotten he had a child to begin with. "How did Henry sleep last night?" Ray ventured.

"Like a baby," Evelyn answered, setting the kettle on the stove to boil. She cleared her throat before folding her arms in front of her. "He thinks the beds in Jessica's room are very comfortable. Apparently, he didn't have pillows in his old house." She quirked an eyebrow upward, as if awaiting an explanation.

Ray gave a nervous laugh. "I'm not sure where he got that idea from. Vivid imagination of a four-year-old, I suspect."

"Indeed," Evelyn said in a tart tone as she busied herself with her tea.

"Is Sonia here?" Ray asked, trying not to sound overly hopeful. It was apparent Evelyn had no intention of handing Henry over without giving him a grilling first. It was obvious, she still didn't trust him.

"She's in her office, trying to catch up on her work."

Ray swallowed hard, sensing the indictment in Evelyn's tone. "I can't tell you how much I appreciate you both going out of your way to help me. Maybe you can let Henry know I'm here, and we'll get out of your hair. I'm planning on doing something fun with him today."

Evelyn threw him a sharp glance over the rim of her mug. "What kinds of things does he enjoy doing?"

Ray hesitated, feeling the heat creeping up his neck. He had no idea what Henry liked to do—he couldn't remember. He opened his mouth to offer up some generic response, but he was spared when the door burst open and Jessica and Henry barged in.

"Can we have a snack, Grandma, please?" Jessica asked. " We're hungry."

"What? After that big pancake breakfast?" Evelyn's lips softened into a smile. "What would you like?"

"Goldfish, please," Jessica said.

Ray shifted in his seat, attempting to smile at his son. Henry had come to an abrupt stop at the sight of him, a crushed look in his eyes.

"It's time for us to go home now, Henry," Ray said, getting to his feet.

"Jess, why don't you put some crackers in a baggie for Henry to take with him?" Evelyn suggested.

"Okay." Jessica skipped across the kitchen and tugged open a drawer. She filled a Ziploc to overflowing and pressed it into Henry's hands.

"Please be sure and thank Sonia on my behalf," Ray added.

Evelyn gave a curt nod. "Henry's clothes are in the washer. I'll send them over later. Don't forget you need to look for the paperwork for his preschool."

"Yes, of course. Thanks for the reminder," Ray said. "I'll dig that out later today. Henry and I are going to do something fun together first." He smiled down at his son again as he reached for his hand but got only a blank stare in response. To his relief, Henry accompanied him out the back door without a fuss this time.

Back inside his house, a forlorn-looking Henry stood in the middle of the kitchen, clutching his bag of Goldfish crackers, as though waiting for further instructions.

Ray leaned back against the counter. "What do you want to do today, Henry?"

He shrugged, a detached look in his eyes.

Ray racked his brain, wondering what would appeal to a four-year-old. "Do you want to go to the park?"

Henry studied him warily, like a stray dog who'd been offered a piece of meat by the dogcatcher.

"We could throw the ball around for a bit," Ray suggested. No sooner had the words left his lips than he remembered he hadn't seen a ball anywhere in the house or garage. "Or you could play on the swings and the slide," he added hastily.

Ignoring him, Henry knelt down and began driving his truck back and forth over the floor, lost in his own world.

Ray scratched the stubble on his jaw. He'd never felt more at a loss than he did right now. Wasn't he supposed to know how to get through to his own son? Maybe he needed to be more direct and talk to him about his mother—acknowledge the pain he was in. "Henry, I know you miss your mom. And I get that you're feeling sad. But I want you to know I'm always going to be here for you."

Henry began making engine sounds, head bent low over his truck. Ray grimaced. There wasn't any point in pushing it if Henry wasn't ready to talk.

"Tell you what," Ray said, adopting a more chipper tone. "Dad's going to take a quick look for some paperwork for your school while you have a think about what you want to do today. Maybe you'd like to go get some ice cream or go to the movies. I'll be back in a few minutes, and then we'll decide."

Ray hurried down the hall to Henry's bedroom. He must have stashed a file of important documents somewhere in the house. He wouldn't have left anything as essential as Henry's birth certificate and immunization record behind, knowing he would need it for a new school. He took a quick look around the room for a file box, or anything that looked like it might contain paperwork, but came up short. A peek in the closet revealed nothing other than Celia's extra coats and the few items of Henry's clothing he'd retrieved from the Target bags. Frustrated, he backtracked down the hallway to his own room. Spotting his laptop bag stashed on the floor by the nightstand, he checked inside the pockets, but it contained nothing more than some drafts of miscellaneous articles he'd been working on. Maybe he'd intended to make another run back to his old house to fetch the rest of their things before the accident happened—that could have been why he'd packed an overnight bag.

He blew out a heavy breath and walked over to the closet, yanking out the backpack he'd come across earlier. He rummaged around in the outer pocket again to make sure it contained nothing other than the map, and then dumped the clothes out on the bed. Peering inside the bag, he spotted an inner pocket he'd missed earlier. He unzipped it and slid his fingers inside. Frowning, he pulled something out. Blood drained from his head as he stared, slack-jawed, at the photo of the blonde teenager on the driver's license.

Katie Lambert.

16

A cold sweat broke out on Ray's forehead. The driver's license slipped from his fingers and he shrank back from it, trembling all over. Katie Lambert was the name of the missing girl in the article he'd torn out of the newspaper—the very one Sonia Masterton had asked him about. How was this possible? His throat was suddenly dry as sandpaper. His head felt like it was about to explode. Was this some kind of horrible coincidence? His brain was screaming at him for a logical explanation as to why the missing girl's license was in a backpack in his closet. Was she a relative of his? Maybe the police had returned it to him. His hand shook as he picked it up off the floor, desperately searching the face for any resemblance to his own.

His eyes traveled to the backpack lying on the bed next to him—the backpack that contained a change of clothes and a map of the Blue Ridge Mountains with a highlighted trail. Slowly, it dawned on him that there could be an entirely different explanation. One that left him reeling, but that had to be considered. What if he was involved in the missing girl's disappearance?

Bile crept up his throat, his eyes locked on the fresh-faced teenager staring accusingly up at him. This little piece of plastic in his hand was as incriminating as a lock of her hair. A killer's souvenir. He'd watched enough crime shows to know that murderers often kept something belonging to their victims as a trophy of sorts. He slumped to the ground and dropped his face into his hands, rocking back-and-forth on his knees as he moaned softly. What had he done? Had he abducted Katie Lambert? Buried her and marked a trail to her grave?

A sound behind him startled him. He spun around to see Henry watching him intently. Pulling out his thumb he asked, "Is you sad?"

Sucking in a jagged breath, Ray took a moment to compose himself. He couldn't remember Henry directing a question at him since he got home from the hospital, or taking any interest in him at all, for that matter. Yet, Henry always seemed to be looking at him as if he knew something Ray didn't. If he could keep him talking, he might get some much-needed answers. Maybe if Ray displayed some vulnerability, Henry would reciprocate.

"Yes, I am," he answered. "I'm sad, and frightened, and confused. Sometimes dads get that way, you know."

Henry blinked solemnly at him. "I'm sad too."

Ray scooted over the carpet and lifted Henry into his lap. His first inclination was to reassure his son that he would always be there for him, but the words stuck in his throat. If he had something to do with Katie Lambert's disappearance, then he was a criminal. For all he knew, he could be on the run. Thanks to the concussion, he had no way of knowing what the truth was. He swallowed the barbed knot in his throat. If he was arrested, Henry would face a life without either of his parents. He fought to calm his thumping heartbeat. "What are you sad about, buddy?"

Henry squirmed in his lap, avoiding looking directly at him.

"It's okay," Ray said, softening his tone. "You can tell me anything. You're not in trouble."

"*Never ... tell ... them*," Henry whispered into his fist, almost as if he was reminding himself. With a valiant wriggle, he escaped from Ray's grasp and darted out of the room.

"Wait!" Ray called after him, scrambling to his feet. He caught up with Henry in the hallway and swooped him into his arms in a playful fashion. Whatever was troubling his son, he couldn't force it out of him. First, he needed to build some trust—beginning with keeping his promise to have some fun together. He would figure out what to do about Katie Lambert's driver's license later. "How about you and I grab some water bottles and head to the park? It's about time we got out of here."

After Googling the closest park, Ray reached for Henry's hand and set off down the road. Henry insisted on bringing his toy truck, and Ray gave up on trying to dissuade him. The last thing he wanted was to instigate another tearful outburst. To his relief, Henry seemed content to hold his hand as they strolled to the park. Several times, Ray tried to engage him in conversation, commenting on the various dogs they passed, talking about the different things they could do at the park, even suggesting they go for ice cream afterward—but Henry trotted along at his side in silence, his little face only lighting up when the playground came into view and he saw the other kids laughing and chasing each other around.

"What do you want to do first, Henry?" Ray asked,

surveying the scene as they approached the play equipment for younger children. "That slide sure looks like fun."

Henry stood on the sidelines observing the other children for several minutes, then took a tentative step toward them.

"Want me to hold your truck for you?" Ray offered. "That way you have your hands free to climb."

Henry shook his head, tucking his toy truck protectively under his arm, before trotting over to the play equipment.

Ray folded his arms across his chest and watched him make his way laboriously up the steps to a slatted rope bridge connected to a bright red plastic slide. Henry's one-handed progress soon began to frustrate the other children, drawing attention to himself. Ray glanced around, catching the curious glances of a couple of the mothers watching from the benches dotted around the park. He smiled uneasily back at them. The last thing Henry needed was an ardent mom brigade descending on him to hurry him up. He watched as Henry crossed the bridge and went down the slide, a smile breaking out on his face. A little girl with pigtails and glasses laughed and grabbed his hand, and the two of them ran back around to the steps to climb up again. Ray blew out a relieved breath. It looked like Henry had made a new friend.

It wasn't long before the pair abandoned the slide and moved on to the sandbox, digging with what Ray assumed were the little girl's plastic shovels. Her mother, or nanny, sat off to one side on a bench, rocking a baby in her arms. She was carrying on a conversation with the kids, and Henry appeared to be conversing with her, but Ray couldn't make out what they were saying. He was deliberately standing close enough to keep an eye on Henry, but far enough away so as not to intimidate him into silence. He didn't want a stranger at the park picking up on their awkward father-son dynamic.

After a few minutes, the kids grew bored with the sand and ran back over to the slide. Ray waved and smiled encouragingly at Henry, but he merely stared at him in passing. Ray couldn't help feeling deflated that his son warmed more easily to anyone other than him. He watched as the little girl skipped over to the woman to take a drink from the water bottle she was holding out to her. After taking a quick sip, the girl began talking animatedly, pointing at Henry. The woman pulled out her phone, apparently distracted.

All of a sudden, she peered pointedly around her daughter in Ray's direction, phone still pressed to her ear. Ray smiled back at her, groaning inwardly. Now he would have to go over there and meet and greet. It would appear rude if he didn't introduce himself when she'd looked directly at him. He waited until she'd put her phone away, then stuffed his hands in his pockets and walked over to the bench where she was sitting. "Our kids seem to have hit it off," he said, slapping on a smile. "I'm Ray Jenkins, Henry's dad."

"Ann Whitmore," the woman responded. "That's my daughter, Ivy, playing with Henry. And this is Jack." She adjusted the baby in her lap, her eyes shifting uneasily around. "I haven't seen you here before."

"We just moved here a couple of weeks ago," Ray said, wondering if he should mention that his wife had passed away recently. He quickly nixed the idea, anticipating the follow-up questions which would be impossible to answer. " Henry started at Small Steps preschool."

"I know," Ann said abruptly. "Ivy goes there too."

"Ah, so that explains the instant connection." Ray shuffled awkwardly from one foot to the other. He couldn't put his finger on what it was that was off-putting about Ann's manner—it felt as though she'd assessed him and found him wanting as a father, almost as if she knew the guilty secret he was hiding in his backpack. He shook himself free of the paranoid thought. His head was beginning to throb again. He really should go home after this. He needed to figure out what to do. More to the point, what he'd done.

"Ivy talks about Henry all the time," Ann went on. "He has ... quite the imagination."

Ray threw her an uncertain look, detecting a hostile undertone to the throwaway comment. "Don't all four-year-olds?" he said, tagging on a forced laugh. "He probably gets it from me. I'm a writer. We creatives are known for our propensity to embellish the world around us."

Ann fidgeted on the bench as though growing increasingly uncomfortable with the conversation. Maybe it was time for her baby's nap, and she was too polite to tell him.

"Well, it was nice to meet you, Ann," Ray said. "Henry and I should get going."

He turned to leave when she blurted out, "Do you write fiction or non-fiction?"

"I'm a freelance journalist, so mainly articles and opinion pieces," Ray answered, surprised at her sudden interest in reviving their flagging conversation.

Ann gave a tight smile, peering furtively around him.

He glanced over his shoulder in the direction she was looking in time to see a squad car pull into the parking lot. His heart began to beat a little faster. *Nothing to be concerned about,* he reassured himself. Cops regularly patrolled parks as a matter of course. It wasn't as if they knew he had Katie Lambert's license at his house.

He turned back to Ann. "Enjoy the rest of—"

"Wait! What, uh ... what magazines are you published in?" she stammered. "I'd like to read some of your work."

Ray frowned. Put on the spot, he couldn't recall the name of a single publication he'd written for. He waved a hand dismissively to cover his embarrassment, "Oh, nothing that would earn a Pulitzer."

"Are you Ann Whitmore," a deep voice from behind him asked.

Ray spun around to see two police officers walking toward them.

"Yes," Ann answered, a strained expression on her face as she jiggled Jack on her lap. She gestured to Ray. "This is the man I called about."

17

"That's the kid over there," Ann said, pointing to Henry who was gawping at the police officers. "He says that man's not his father."

Ray's jaw dropped, shock ricocheting through him. "What are you talking about? Of course I'm his father!"

"That's not what he told me," Ann retorted, staring defiantly back at him. Her faltering tone had been replaced by an air of assertiveness—emboldened, no doubt, by the presence of the police officers.

One of the officers took up a perimeter position, resting a hand casually on her gun. A male officer stepped toward Ray, his aviator shades glinting in the sun. "Do you have any ID on you, sir?"

Ray fired a wounded look at Ann before reaching into his back pocket and pulling out his wallet. He could scarcely believe how duplicitous she'd been, pretending to connect over their kids' preschool, even expressing an interest in his work—all the while waiting on law enforcement to show up and interrogate him. "I live a couple of blocks from here," he said, handing his driver's license to the officer. "That's my old address. My son and I moved here a few weeks ago."

The officer glanced at his driver's license and then walked over and knelt next to Henry. "Hey buddy! Is this your dad?"

For a long moment, Henry stared back at the officer, his bottom lip protruding. Then, he darted over to Ray and ducked behind his legs.

Ray put an arm around him, resting his hand protectively on his shoulder. "He lost his mother recently—my wife. And as if that wasn't enough, I was just released from hospital yesterday. I wrecked my truck and sustained a head injury. As you can imagine, my son's somewhat traumatized. Whatever he said, I can assure you it was only to get attention." Ray tilted his head toward Ann, still seated on the bench. "He saw his friend's mother interacting with her daughter and he wanted her to notice him too. He misses his mom dreadfully."

The officer handed him back his license. "I'm sorry for your loss, sir. I'm sure you can appreciate that we're obligated to look into any calls about suspicious child-adult relationships. Can you verify any of what you've told me?"

Ray wet his lips, immediately regretting bringing up the subject of his dead wife. "I can show you the police report of the accident. It's at the house. My neighbor will be able to verify everything. She looked after Henry while I was in the hospital."

The officer jotted down a few notes and then turned to Ann. "Thank you for your vigilance, ma'am. It would appear that everything's in order."

Far from appeased, Ann narrowed her eyes. "Henry's been saying strange things to my daughter, Ivy, at preschool too."

"What kinds of things?" the officer asked.

"He told her he was locked in his house without any food."

Ray flattened his lips, barely able to curb his frustration as he glared at Ann. "Like I told you, he has an overly vivid imagination, and he's been through a lot lately. I guess I was hoping for some sympathy when I shared that with you, not a criminal investigation."

"All right, sir," the officer cut in. "Let's take a quick drive to your place of residence and talk to your neighbor just to put Mrs. Whitmore's mind at ease."

Ann held a defiant gaze as Ray ushered Henry toward the squad car. There was nothing else to do but to go along with the officer's request. Anything else would look suspicious. And the last thing he needed right now was for the officer to obtain a warrant to search his house and discover Katie Lambert's driver's license.

When they pulled up outside Sonia's house, Ray took a quick calming breath. He'd been trying to rehearse what to say during the short trip, but the minute Sonia opened the front door, the officer took charge. "Sorry to bother you, ma'am. We wanted to verify that this gentleman here is your neighbor. His son told a woman at the park that he wasn't his dad, and we got a call to follow up. Can you confirm his identity?"

A look of alarm flashed across Sonia's face. She glanced at Ray, before turning her attention back to the officer. "Yes, his name's Ray Jenkins. He moved here with his son, Henry, a couple of weeks ago. His mother lived in the house before him. We were neighbors for close to ten years."

The officer jotted something down in his notebook before continuing. "I understand Mr. Jenkins was involved in an accident recently?"

"That's right," Sonia confirmed. "I looked after Henry for a couple of days while he was in the hospital."

The officer slipped his notebook back into his shirt pocket and tipped his hat to her. "Thank you for clearing that up, ma'am." He turned to Ray. "Sorry for the inconvenience, sir. We appreciate your cooperation. I'm sure you can understand that we're obligated to follow up on these types of calls from concerned citizens."

Ray gave a distracted nod, his heart clattering in his chest like a rollercoaster. "If that's all, I'd like to get back to spending the rest of the day with my son. This is the first chance we've had to be together since my accident."

"Absolutely. You have a good day," the officer said, before turning on his heel and retreating to the curb where the female officer was waiting in the squad car.

"Do you want to come in?" Sonia asked, one hand on the door as if to indicate she'd rather he didn't.

Before Ray could respond, Henry shot past him and darted down the hall in search of Jessica.

Ray gave a resigned shrug. "I guess I'm coming in now, if only to retrieve my son."

"So, what exactly happened at the park?" Sonia asked, leading the way to the kitchen. She sat down at the table and pushed aside a pile of carpet samples.

Ray pulled out the chair opposite her. "Thanks for smoothing things over out there." He let out a dejected sigh. "This woman at the park, Ann Whitmore, called the cops on me because Henry told her I wasn't his father."

Sonia forwarded him a sympathetic look. "Actually, he told Jessica the same thing." She hesitated, lowering her voice, "Ray, is it possible Henry's adopted?"

He frowned, then shook his head slowly. "I don't ... think so. Not that I can remember. Apparently, Ann's daughter is in Henry's preschool class, and he's been saying unsettling things there too—that he was deprived of food and locked in his room." He rubbed a hand over the back of his neck. "It sounds bad, I know, but it's not uncommon for a young child who's lost a parent to make stuff up for attention."

"Or embellish something that happened. Kids often do that," Sonia said, picking at a strand of wool on one of the carpet samples. "Did you or your wife ever discipline Henry by sending him to his room without dinner?"

Ray flinched. "I can't imagine doing that. He's only four-years-old. But of course, I can't remember, can I?"

"You need to be patient with yourself. Have you remembered anything else since we last spoke?"

Ray knit his brows together in concentration. "Bits and pieces. It's too fragmented to make any sense of it. It's almost as frustrating as fishing. You know how you can see a fish just below the surface of the water, but you can't get it to bite. That's how I feel when I'm trying to remember something. I keep getting flashes of a fight scene. I'm not sure who I was fighting with—probably my father. My brother might have been there too." He paused for a moment. "I think I punched someone. I keep seeing a man fall backward, but his face is blurred. There was blood everywhere. I don't know ... I really hope I didn't kill my father." His voice broke and he cleared his throat to cover his embarrassment.

"You didn't. Celia told us her husband died of a heart attack," Sonia assured him. "Granted the fight scene's not the happiest of memories, but at least it shows that your brain's beginning to heal. Did you try looking through the photos again?"

"Yeah, it didn't help." He hesitated, wondering if he should enlist Sonia to help him with an idea he'd been toying with ever since he'd discovered the license in his backpack. He wouldn't be able to tell her the truth—that he suspected he was somehow involved in Katie Lambert's disappearance—but maybe he could pass his request off as a benign appeal for help. After all, Sonia struck him as the type who liked to lend a helping hand. She'd given him the benefit of the doubt, so far, unlike her mother who signaled her disapproval of him at every opportunity.

"I found something this morning that might help jog my memory," Ray went on. "It was a map of the Blue Ridge Mountains with a highlighted trail. I must have been intending to hike it before the accident. Or maybe it's a fishing spot I've been to before—there's a stream nearby. At any rate, I was thinking it might help to go back up there and see if it jogged my memory. You know how they always say nature heals." He paused, then twisted his lips into an apologetic grin. "The thing is, I can't drive myself. I would rent a car, but the doctor hasn't cleared me to drive yet and—"

"I'd be happy to take you if you think it will help," Sonia interrupted. "My mom can watch Henry for a few hours. She's getting around much better these days."

Ray raised a skeptical brow. "I doubt she'll go for it—the part about you driving me, I mean. She's made it clear she doesn't trust me."

Sonia shrugged. "I won't tell her. I'll say I'm going to a job site, and you have to go to the hospital for a follow-up appointment. Why don't you call an Uber to pick you up at your place so she's not suspicious? I'll meet you in town."

"Well, if you're sure," Ray responded.

"It's not a problem. I can even hike the trail with you, in case you get disoriented or something. How far is it from here?"

Ray squeezed his jaw. "It's about an hour's drive." He

didn't add that he estimated it would take another hour to hike to the end of the highlighted trail after that—a hike he would be making alone. If the coordinates led to Katie Lambert's grave, he couldn't risk Sonia finding out.

They glanced up at the sound of the front door opening.

"That's probably my mother," Sonia said.

Evelyn shuffled into the kitchen, frowning almost imperceptibly when she spotted Ray. She slipped off her coat before joining them at the table. "I'm surprised to see you here, Ray. I thought you had plans to do something with Henry today."

Ray exchanged an uncomfortable look with Sonia. He'd rather not relay what had happened at the park, but Evelyn would find out soon enough. He was under no illusions that anything that happened in the neighborhood escaped her attention.

"I took Henry to the park," he said. "We bumped into a little girl from his preschool. Everything was going great until Henry told her mother I wasn't his dad. She called the cops on me." He scrubbed a hand over his face. "I explained the whole situation to them, that Henry's mother passed away recently, and that he was just trying to get attention. The cops were decent about it, but they drove me home so they could verify my story with Sonia."

Evelyn pinned a hawk-like gaze on him. "But she can't really verify anything, can she? The only story she can verify is the one you told us."

"Mom!" Sonia protested. "Give him a break. He's had a rough morning and he's still recovering from the accident."

"Is he?" Evelyn pursed her lips. "It's pretty convenient that his memory was wiped out. There are plenty of questions I'd like answered myself."

Ray stood abruptly, the chair leg screeching on the travertine floor. "I should go."

"Why don't you let Henry stay and play for a bit so you can get some rest," Sonia suggested. "The kids will enjoy hanging out together."

Ray glanced at his watch. "I think I will go lie down for an hour. My head's pounding."

"I'll bring Henry back over later," Sonia said, seeing him to the door.

Back in his mother's house, Ray sank down on the couch, reeling from everything that had happened. The incident at the park had been extremely stressful. His heart had been juddering against his ribs the whole way home at the thought of the police discovering Katie Lambert's driver's license. Not to mention the fact that he still hadn't found Henry's birth certificate. What if the police had asked to see it? It would have looked incredibly suspicious if he hadn't been able to produce it, especially in light of what Henry was telling people. He had to locate that birth certificate ASAP. He would have to make a trip back to his old house right after he checked out those coordinates. He shifted onto his side and adjusted the cushion behind his head. Gradually, his eyelids grew heavy, and he abandoned himself to the heavy feeling seeping through his bones.

He woke with a start at the sound of the doorbell. *Henry!* Had it been an hour already? He pulled himself up on the couch and rubbed his eyes, muted images flitting through his mind like ghosts. He'd been dreaming of the fight again. Raised voices, exchanged blows, the stench of fear and blood—always the elusive face.

Suddenly, a new memory from his dreams sprang to mind. Rough-sawn timber, a whiff of woodsmoke. A gasp escaped his lips when it dawned on him. The trail he'd highlighted wasn't a hike he'd been intending to take. He'd taken it before.

It led to a cabin in the woods.

18

Ray stumbled to his feet and hurried to answer the door, his mind a blur of activity—streaming images he couldn't process quickly enough to comprehend. Pressing his fingertips to his temples, he willed himself fully awake before wrenching open the door. "Hey, sorry to keep you waiting, Sonia." He grinned at Henry and made an awkward attempt to ruffle his hair.

"Are ... you all right?" Sonia asked, blinking at him questioningly.

"Yes, I'm fine, thanks. I conked out on the couch." He made a point of smothering a yawn. "Just need a few minutes to regroup."

"Do you want me to keep Henry a little longer?" Sonia offered.

"No, not at all." Ray let out an embarrassed laugh. "I'll put some coffee on. That should do the trick."

Sonia gave a dubious nod as she released Henry's hand. She got down on one knee and looked him in the eye. "Be sure and tell your daddy to bring you over for some cookies tomorrow."

Ray closed the door behind her and exhaled a rough breath. His brain felt like it was on fire, the wiring reconnecting, flashing bits and pieces of important information at him—too swiftly to assemble into a meaningful sequence. But he had to figure it out. He needed to know everything that was stored in the recesses of his mind. Even the dark, disturbing things. More than anything, he desperately needed to know what he'd done. He could scarcely bring himself to entertain the possibility that he had something to do with Katie Lambert's disappearance. But how else could he explain how he'd come to be in possession of her driver's license? He had to get to the bottom of it—and quickly. He would start by writing down everything that came to mind, no matter how disjointed. He could figure out how to put the pieces together afterward.

His gaze drifted down to Henry. First, he needed to find something to occupy his son with. Stationing him in front of the television wasn't the most desirable option, but it was a surefire way to hold his attention. "Come on, Henry. I'm going to turn on the TV. You can watch some cartoons while dad finishes up his work."

Henry trotted obediently into the family room and positioned himself on his knees in front of the television, his toy truck peeking out of the pocket of his jeans. Ray opened the heavy, velvet drapes to let in the light he had blocked out earlier to nap. After settling on a suitable channel, he pulled the door partly closed behind him and left a mesmerized Henry to watch his shows. Back in the kitchen, he fumbled with the coffee pot, barely able to focus as fragmented memories drifted by like wispy clouds in his brain, vanishing the minute he tried to catch them. He grabbed a pen and a pad of paper and sat down at the kitchen table to jot down some notes.

As he began to write, it felt like a dam in his brain suddenly burst. The memories came fast and furious, tumbling over themselves to be heard. Ray's forehead grew slick with sweat as a picture began to build. He glugged down a second mug of coffee, his fingers shaking so violently he could hardly read his own writing.

When he was done, he set down his pen and skimmed over the words he'd put on the page. A shiver shot down his spine. He'd been writing about his dream last night. He'd described the hand-built log cabin in intricate detail: the saddle notched interlocking beams framing the roughly twelve by sixteen-foot space, a gable roof built from spruce and covered in sod and moss, the eight-point deer antlers nailed above the rough-hewn steps, the painstakingly crafted front door, and the bench beneath the south-facing window. A smell of damp bark and smoke greeted him as he stepped inside, his eyes sweeping over the unpretentious furnishings. Next to the stone fireplace, staring into the crackling flames, stood the cabin's sole inhabitant—*his younger brother, Tom!*

Ray leapt to his feet and plowed his fingers through his tousled hair. His body tingled all over as the certainty of it sank in. *Tom was alive.*

In a trance, he walked over to the coffee pot and poured the dregs into his mug with shaking fingers. He grimaced as he swallowed a bitter mouthful, before dumping the rest in the sink and returning to the page of notes he'd left on the kitchen table. He rubbed his aching forehead as he tried to absorb the enormity of it. After years of searching for his brother—even going so far as to hire a private investigator—he had given up all hope that he was alive. To think that all this time Tom had been living only a short distance from their mother. Evelyn had mentioned that Tom used to call

Celia regularly. His mother must have known all along where he was.

Ray folded his arms on the table in front of him. He had probably found the coordinates to the cabin among her belongings after she died. And, at some point in the past few weeks, he had hiked up to Tom's cabin. He could see it clearly in his mind now—inhale the scent of it even when he closed his eyes. He glanced over at the counter, furrowing his brow when he spotted the pile of paper clipped bank statements he'd been going through. Why had their mother been sending Tom such a large sum of money each month? What could he possibly have been using it for? He certainly wasn't spending it on his cabin—everything in it had looked handmade or recycled.

Ray scrunched his eyes shut in a desperate bid to remember what had gone down at Tom's place. All at once, the fight scene flashed to mind again. And this time, he distinctly saw the face of the man he'd punched to the ground. His fingers curled into fists as the truth hit home. It wasn't his father he'd been fighting with at all—it was Tom. But what had the fight been about? Had he confronted his brother about the money he'd been taking from their mother?

Ray stood and began pacing the floor. Another memory sprang to mind, stopping him in his tracks. This time he was in his truck, heading to the cabin, the black backpack on the seat next to him. He had driven up the mountain as far as he could and parked in the closest campground to the trail. As he'd hiked up to the cabin, the dense trees had slowly begun to close in around him, shutting out the light and sounds of the outside world—sealing in the scent of pine and the chittering of squirrels. Just when he'd begun to fear he was hopelessly lost, he'd bumped into a hunter. The stranger had been wary of him, and Ray had been equally cautious, noting the rifle casually slung over his shoulder and the large hunting knife strapped to his person. But, after explaining that he was Tom's brother, the hunter's demeanor changed—in fact, he'd gone out of his way to direct him to Tom's place.

Ray flinched out of his reverie when the door creaked open.

Henry pottered into the kitchen. "I'm hungry."

Brushing a hand over his jaw, Ray hurriedly tried to disentangle his brain from the muddled memories it was sifting through and focus on the more mundane task of feeding his son. "All right, let's see what we've got here." He opened the refrigerator and assessed his options. "How about a cheese stick?" Without waiting for an answer, he peeled off the plastic and held the string cheese out to Henry, who stared at it in bafflement before accepting it. He clutched it like a toothbrush and asked, "What is you doing?"

Ray gave a nonchalant shrug. "Nothing, buddy. Just … thinking."

"Why is you not working?"

"Why *are* you not working?" Ray said, with a wink. "I am working in a way. It's work that I do in here." He tapped a finger on his head for emphasis.

"Okay," Henry said, before taking a bite of his cheese stick and exiting the room.

Ray held his breath for a long moment and then tiptoed after him, peering into the family room to make sure Henry was safely back in position in front of the television. He padded quietly down the hallway to his bedroom and pulled the backpack out of the closet once more. He urgently needed to return to the cabin and find his brother.

Whatever they had been arguing about, it couldn't be more important than reestablishing their relationship now that they'd found each other again. It had likely been about the money—not that Ray cared about their mother's money. Maybe Tom had some kind of addiction problem. Whatever it was, it could be resolved with the right kind of support. And Ray intended to give it to him. He loved his brother fiercely. They had been through so much together. Tears spilled freely down his cheeks. He felt a twang of guilt that he didn't feel the same level of connection to his own son. Then again, the brother he'd thought was dead was alive. Under the circumstances, his whacked-out emotions were understandable.

His heart lurched against his ribs when he suddenly remembered the driver's license. Slipping shaking fingers into the inner pocket of his pack, he pulled it back out and stared into the innocent eyes gazing up at him. A cold sweat broke out on the back of his neck as another thought struck.

Was Katie Lambert the reason he'd fought with Tom?

19

Sonia threw herself down in an armchair opposite her mother. "Any chance you can watch Henry for a few hours tomorrow? I have to go out to a job site, and I'll be gone most of the day. I've organized a ride home from school for Jessica."

Evelyn narrowed her brows. "Why? Where's Ray going?"

"He has to go to the hospital for a follow-up appointment. And he needs to sort some things out at the bank afterward. He'll be tied up most of the day."

"I take it he hasn't located Henry's birth certificate yet," Evelyn said in a prim tone.

Sonia hesitated. When she'd questioned Ray about the documentation the preschool needed, he'd told her his files were still at his old place. Sonia suspected he was lying, but she'd let it slide. His memory was still a mess—his whole life was a mess at the moment. He'd probably forgotten where he'd put the birth certificate and was too embarrassed to admit it. "He left it at his old place," Sonia said breezily. "Once he gets the all-clear from the doctor to drive again, he's going to pick up the rest of his stuff. So, can you watch Henry tomorrow?"

Evelyn let out a dissatisfied humph. "I suppose I could bake some cookies with him."

"You're the best," Sonia said, getting to her feet and hugging her mother. "Don't feel you have to do anything special with him. It's fine if he watches cartoons while you knit. It's only for one day."

Evelyn sighed, a wistful look in her eyes. "It's the least I can do for Celia after all the kindness she showed Jessica. I sure do miss her."

SHORTLY BEFORE EIGHT the following morning, Sonia was huddled in her car outside The Busy Bean coffee shop, hands wrapped around a paper cup of steaming French Roast, listening to the drumming of the rain on the roof. She could barely see past the wipers swishing back-and-forth across her windscreen. It was hardly an ideal day to hike up into the mountains. She'd done her best to dissuade Ray from attempting the hike until the weather cleared—she couldn't imagine it being a healing experience in this downpour—but he was insistent they stick to the plan.

Sonia had thought long and hard about going to the police to report the things Henry had told her, but something held her back. Maybe it was the fact that Ray genuinely seemed to care about Henry. It just didn't seem plausible that he had done some of the things Henry said he had. But what really settled the matter in her mind was when Henry pointed at the photo of Tom and called him, *dad*. Tom and Ray did look remarkably alike, and it had made her think that perhaps Henry had only ever seen Ray in photos before. If Ray and his wife had been divorced,

Henry might have been living with his mother up until her death—which meant the man Henry referred to as his dad —the man who had choked his mother, deprived him of food, and locked him in his room—could have been his mother's boyfriend. Sonia had decided she would give it a day or two for Ray's memory to fully recover and then ask him outright. If she was wrong, she could still go to the police with her concerns after that.

She glanced up at a sharp rap on the passenger window. Ray opened the door, tossed a black bag into the back and slid into the seat next to her, shaking his hair like a drowned dog. The drooping bags under his eyes only added to his weather-beaten look. He didn't appear to be sleeping well.

"Sorry to keep you waiting," he said. "It took longer than I expected to get an Uber."

"Are you sure you still want to do this? It's dumping pretty hard," Sonia said. "I'm happy to take you another day when the weather's better."

"It's supposed to clear up a little later," Ray replied. " Besides, I came prepared with my boots and waterproof rain gear. I really want to do this today."

"Your call," Sonia said with a shrug as she put the car in gear and pulled out of her parking spot. She set the wipers to maximum speed, but it made no difference to the visibility. Hopefully, Ray's prediction about the weather was right. She didn't like driving in heavy rain. Nevertheless, she'd volunteered to help him and she was determined to see this through. She was as eager as Ray was for answers. "Any new memories since?" she asked, reaching for her coffee.

Ray frowned, staring straight ahead as though wrestling with how to answer. "I think that trail I highlighted on the map leads to a cabin—my brother's cabin, to be precise."

Sonia's jaw dropped. "What? Tom's ... alive? Are you sure?"

Ray interlaced his hands and rested them in front of him. "As sure as I can be. I remember hiking up to his cabin. I can see every detail in my mind. I'm pretty sure that's where the fight happened. I told you I knocked someone out, right?"

Sonia gave a perturbed nod. "You said you thought you did."

"I was half-afraid I'd killed my father—believe me, I thought about it enough growing up," Ray went on. "But it's Tom's face my fist slams into every time the images come to mind now."

"But you thought Tom was dead," Sonia said. "How did you find him?"

"I must have found the coordinates to his cabin when I was going through our mother's stuff. Evidently, I drove out there and confronted him about ... something." Ray turned and stared out the side window into the battleship-gray morning that stretched out in every direction like a seething ocean.

"Are you sure it's wise going back up there if you two were throwing punches?" Sonia asked.

Ray smoothed a hand over his jaw. "I don't have a choice. Our mother's wishes were that the estate be divided equally between the two of us. I need to talk to him to figure out how we're going to handle the money."

"Do you think that's what you were arguing about?" Sonia asked.

Ray's expression darkened. "That would be my guess. I probably hit him up about the money he was siphoning from our mother's account. I keep thinking the only thing he could have been using it for was drugs or alcohol. Maybe

I even accused him of being an addict and wanted him to give me power of attorney. He might have thought I was trying to screw him out of his rightful share. Who knows what was said? I just need to get back up there and sort things out with him."

"I hope you're not making a mistake. You could do this through lawyers, you know," Sonia said. "It doesn't sound like Tom wants anything to do with you."

Ray shifted uneasily in his seat. "I have to try and reach out to him again. We were close as kids. Tom's all I've got left."

Sonia narrowed her eyes at him. "What about your son?"

"Well, yes, of course I have ... Henry," Ray said hastily. "I meant, you know ... Tom's all I have left from my past. He and I went through a lot together."

"What if he won't listen to reason? He might pull out a gun or something."

Ray gave a sad shake of his head. "Tom and I were best buddies once. We can work this out."

Sonia slid him a discreet glance, hearing a wobble in his voice. "So, tell me more about the cabin," she said brightly.

Ray squeezed his forehead between his thumb and fore-finger. "I can see it clearly in my mind. It's a small log cabin, built by hand—Tom's a good craftsman. Completely off grid. No running water, no sewer, no power, no modern amenities whatsoever. We always talked about doing stuff like that as kids, but I was never as handy or outdoorsy as he was." He paused before continuing, "I can't remember much about the trail to the cabin. I recall getting hopelessly lost, going in circles at one point. Thankfully, I bumped into a hunter who took me the rest of the way to Tom's place. I think he might have lived up there somewhere too. Big guy, all kitted out with a rifle and a wicked-looking knife."

They fell silent for a while, listening to the rain pounding on the roof. Before long, they found themselves turning onto the gravel road that led to the Deep Creek Campground marked on the map. It turned out to be little more than a root-ridden dirt parking lot replete with an outhouse, a couple of fire pits and a bear-proof trashcan. Sonia switched off the engine and turned to Ray. "Looks like the rain is easing up a bit. Do you want me to come with you?"

"No, I need to be alone so I can think. You don't have to wait here, either," Ray replied. "Why don't you drive back to the main road and find a café or something where you can hole up and stay warm?" He pulled out his phone and frowned at it. "No service. Let's just plan on meeting back here in four hours. It will take me about an hour to hike up to the cabin and an hour to hike back so that still gives me two hours to talk some sense into Tom."

Sonia gestured to her portfolio lying on the back seat. "I brought my work with me. I don't mind hanging out here." She quirked a grin. "Trust me, I rarely get this kind of solitude to work in."

Ray reached into the back and tugged his pack out by the strap. His eyes raked over her face. "It's pretty isolated here. Don't talk to strangers."

Sonia swallowed hard as she watched him climb out of the car and disappear into the rain.

But you're a stranger.

20

Out of sight of Sonia's car, Ray pulled out his handheld GPS and turned it on. He hadn't wanted her looking over his shoulder to see where he was going—he couldn't take the chance that she might decide to follow him. Just because she'd agreed to drive him out here didn't mean she trusted him. He suspected Evelyn was filling her head with suspicions about him at every opportunity. Not that he could fault Evelyn for wanting to protect her daughter. After all, Henry had been saying some very disturbing things that he needed to get to the bottom of. First, he had to deal with Tom.

As soon as the bars on the device turned green, confirming he'd picked up a satellite signal, he punched in the coordinates for the cabin. Seconds later, the GPS located his position, and he saved it as a waypoint for his return trip down the mountain. He had no intention of getting lost up here a second time. He grimaced when he pictured the impending encounter with his brother. Hopefully this visit would go better than the last one.

Bracing himself against the rain, he set out along the

programmed route. Progress was frustratingly slow, the earth churning beneath his boots as the elevation grew more challenging. As he hiked, he went over in his mind what he was going to say to Tom. More than anything, he wanted a relationship with his brother. But was that even realistic if what he feared most was true? He had told Sonia he was afraid Tom might be a drug addict or an alcoholic, but that wouldn't stop Ray from trying to help him. On the other hand, if he had had something to do with Katie Lambert's disappearance, all bets were off. Ray's initial thought on seeing her driver's license in his backpack was that he had been involved. But the other possibility was equally disturbing—that the brother he'd believed was dead all these years was alive, and a monster. If Ray had found the license at Tom's cabin and questioned him about it, that would have been reason enough for them to have fought.

Then again, he could be jumping to the worst conclusion unnecessarily. Tom might have stumbled across the license when he was out hunting. It wasn't outside the realm of possibility. Katie Lambert's abductor might have been searching for a remote location to dump her body. But, if that was the case, why hadn't Tom turned the license over to the police? Was it possible his brother didn't know about the missing girl—living the secluded life that he did? Maybe he thought a hiker had dropped it. Or maybe he had his own reasons for wanting to avoid law enforcement. Ray frowned to himself as he pondered the possibilities. Wherever the truth lay, he had to face it. He had to know if he or his brother had done the unthinkable.

Halfway to the cabin, he searched out a fallen tree to rest on. He pulled out his Hydro Flask and took a long draught of water. He was still bruised from the accident, and already feeling the effort of the climb. Thankfully, he'd allowed plenty of time, knowing he might struggle in his weakened state. He only hoped Tom would be reasonable once he got there—he certainly wasn't in any condition to fight him again. His thirst temporarily quenched, he stashed his canteen in his pack and got to his feet, determined to finish what he'd started.

The second half of the climb proved more challenging, but his efforts were rewarded when the rustic cabin he remembered finally came into sight. He approached slowly, not wanting to startle his brother and risk facing down the barrel of a shotgun.

"Tom, are you in there?" he called out in a loud voice. "It's me, Ray."

He walked up to the front door and banged his fist on it.

"Tom, it's your brother, Ray. We need to talk."

He waited for a minute or two, then tented his fingers over his eyes and squinted through the dirty window to the right of the door. There was no sign of his brother inside, and the fire was unlit. Surely, he wouldn't be out in this dismal weather. Ray tried the door, surprised to discover it was unlocked—but then crime was hardly a consideration this far off the beaten path. Other than the occasional stranded hiker, it was unlikely Tom ran into too many strangers.

Ray threw back his hood and stepped inside, peering warily around the dark space. He doubted Tom was wandering around in the woods. It was too wet to go hunting, but it was possible he might have gone into town. If he'd discovered that his monthly payment hadn't gone through, he might even be trying to call their mother. Ray frowned to himself, trying to recall if he'd cancelled the phone service at the house, yet. He remembered making a list of tasks to take care of, but some of the details leading up to the accident were still lost in the lingering fog in his mind.

He shrugged off his backpack and tossed it on the floor. Damp and shivering, he sank down in a rocking chair and stretched out his legs to catch his wind. He could afford to hang around for an hour or so. With a bit of luck, Tom would come strolling through the door at any minute. If nothing else, he could rest and dry out a bit before hiking back down to the car. He was tempted to light a fire, but Tom mightn't take kindly to that level of intrusion, given the hostile terms they'd parted on.

Ray cast a curious glance around the interior of the cabin. He could sit here killing time, or he could do a little digging in Tom's absence. Intrusive or not, this was the best opportunity he might have to search the cabin and see if there was anything in it linking his brother to Katie Lambert's disappearance. If Tom was involved, he wasn't likely to cop to it if Ray confronted him.

Beginning with the rustic loft bed, Ray patted all along the logs and stuck his fingers in every cobwebby chink— going so far as to squeeze the seams of the bedding to make sure nothing had been stitched into it. After retreating down the ladder, he searched inside the storage bench, and rummaged through the pockets of a fur coat and a leather hunting pack hanging on a rack by the door. In the kitchen area, he opened all the tin canisters on the carved shelf above the table to check the contents; coffee, tobacco, flour, and dried beans—nothing untoward. Next, he felt for loose stones in the fireplace, and ran his hand over the mantle, dislodging a small can of Grizzly chewing tobacco in the process. He cracked it open and took a whiff, pulling back in disgust. Tom's teeth must be yellow and rotten after years of gnawing on this stuff. Ray wrinkled his brow, trying to remember if his brother had any teeth left at all. But he could only picture his gnarled beard and the smoldering anger in his eyes as they'd exchanged blows.

He was about to return to his seat when he heard footsteps approaching the cabin. His chest tightened. He threw a panicked glance around the small space. Too late to hurry back outside and act as if he'd been waiting patiently for Tom's return. Bracing himself for a confrontation, he took up a nonchalant position next to the fireplace and waited anxiously for the door to open. Minutes ticked by and Ray wet his lips nervously, wondering what Tom was doing. He could hear him shuffling around. Did he realize someone was inside his house?

Ray rubbed his jaw, weighing his options. He needed to make his presence known. If he waited any longer, it would look like he'd been trying to hide. He quieted his breathing and slipped out of the cabin, only to find himself looking into the brooding eyes of an imposing stranger. He took a step backward, momentarily caught off guard. The bushy-bearded, mountain man staring back at him looked vaguely familiar.

"Who ... who are you?" Ray stuttered.

The man's brows shot up. "You're having me on, right?"

"I mean, I feel like I should know you—" Ray broke off and gave an apologetic shrug. "I'm sorry. I ... just got out of hospital. I suffered a concussion. It affected my memory."

The man leaned a hand against the side of the cabin, a curious gleam in his eyes. "You really don't recognize me?"

"No, I'm sorry. Should I?"

"I'm Buck." He stepped closer, the hard edge leaving his voice. "You're Ray Jenkins, Tom's older brother. I bumped into you a couple of weeks back."

Ray rubbed his forehead as it suddenly dawned on him who he was talking to. "Of course! You led me to the cabin."

Buck dipped his head in acknowledgement, eying Ray as if he was waiting on him to say something else.

Ray cleared his throat and gestured sheepishly at the cabin door. "I don't suppose you know where Tom is. I need to talk to him, but I only have an hour or two before I have to head back down the mountain."

Buck smoothed out his bushy mustache, his eyes firmly latched on Ray's. "We'd best go inside and talk."

"I ... don't know if that's a good idea," Ray said, scratching the back of his head. "Tom mightn't be too happy to find us making ourselves at home in his cabin."

"Trust me, Tom won't say nothing about it one way or the other," Buck replied.

Trying to mask his reluctance, Ray walked back inside. He took a seat on the storage bench and motioned to Buck to take the rocking chair. Ignoring him, Buck slung his pack onto the floor and walked over to the fireplace. He stared down at the ashes for what seemed like forever before turning to Ray. "What do you remember about your last visit here?"

Ray shifted uncomfortably in his seat. He wasn't sure how much he wanted to share with Buck about what had gone down, although, it was possible Tom had confided in him—Ray had no idea if the two men were close friends or merely casual acquaintances. At any rate, he had no desire to air his dirty laundry with a stranger if it could be avoided. "Not much, to be honest. Like I said, I'm recovering from a concussion. I had an accident a few days ago—totaled my truck and ended up in the hospital."

Buck folded his arms in front of his chest, and tucked his

fingers into his armpits, giving Ray the impression he was about to be reprimanded.

"Are you telling me you don't remember the fight?" Buck asked, in a scathing tone.

"Well, I wouldn't call it a fight, exactly." Ray pulled his brows together, a flush creeping up his neck. "We did get into a bit of a heated argument. Our mother passed away recently, and we were trying to sort out her affairs."

"You punched Tom square in the jaw," Buck said, his voice dripping scorn. "Any way you skin it, that's a fight in these parts."

Ray gave a resigned shrug. "Okay, so we fought. But, I only remember bits and pieces. I can't even remember what we were fighting about. You probably know more than me. It sounds like Tom's already told you the whole story."

Buck moved his jaw slowly side-to-side. "He didn't have to. I saw it for myself."

Ray frowned, racking his brain for any memory of Buck being there with them. "I don't remember that. If you were there, why didn't you try and stop us?"

"It was all over by the time I walked in. Tom was out cold on the floor."

Ray twisted his lips in an apologetic grimace. "I've no idea why I lost my cool like that. I really regret punching him. That's why I'm here. I need to make amends. Tom's all I've got left—well, other than my son."

Buck threw him a sharp look, a glint of morbid fascination in his eyes. "Where is your son?"

Ray blinked, surprised by the question. "He's with my neighbor."

Buck turned abruptly and walked over to the rocking chair. He sank down in it with a distracted air, staring off into a corner of the cabin.

"Do you happen to know where Tom is?" Ray prodded. "If he went into town, there's not much point in me waiting around—"

"He didn't," Buck cut in.

"Okay," Ray said, trying to curb his frustration at the man's increasingly clipped tone. "Do you know when he'll be back?"

Buck scowled. "He's not coming back, Ray. You killed him."

21

Ray sat still as a statue on the storage bench staring across at Buck's face which was suddenly swimming in and out of focus against the log walls of the cabin. He tried to speak, but his throat felt like it was on fire. His mind raced through a maze of confusion, as he grasped in vain to make sense of Buck's words. He must be hallucinating—that was the only explanation. Had he passed out after the strenuous hike up here? Or was he dreaming about the cabin again? Was Buck even real? He scrunched his eyes shut and blinked them open, sucking in a jagged breath at the sight of the living, breathing, bearded man opposite him.

Buck leaned forward in his chair. "You okay?" he asked gruffly.

"No," Ray choked out. "Of course I'm not okay. Why did you say that ... about my brother?"

Buck skewered him with a look that was not to be trifled with. "It's true, Ray. You slugged him and he fell backward and cracked his head on that very bench you're sitting on. It happened right as I was walking in the door." He got to his feet and trudged over to where Ray was seated.

Ray shrank back as Buck's shadow fell over him, half-afraid the man was about to take a swing at him. Instead, he pointed to a dark stain on the other end of the bench. "That's his blood you're looking at right there."

Ray stared in horror at the rust-colored patch on the wood. *No!* His heart felt like it was seizing up in his chest as he struggled to breathe. It couldn't be true. Tom couldn't be dead. He'd only just found him after all these years. Whatever they had been fighting about, they could have worked it out. Even if Tom had something to do with Katie Lambert's disappearance, Ray would have been there for him. Got him the best lawyers, cooperated as a witness in his defense, made sure the mitigating circumstances of their abusive childhood were taken into consideration.

He buried his head in his hands, choking back sobs. He wasn't sure what he was crying for anymore. A tangled ball of emotion that went all the way back to his childhood. His life had started out a mess and now it had come full circle. If what Buck was saying was true, he was a murderer. He had confessed to Sonia the nagging fear that he might have killed his father. Never in a million years had he suspected the deep, darker truth—that he'd killed the brother he loved. He shook his head slowly, trying to clear his thoughts. Something didn't make sense. If Buck had witnessed the murder, why had he let him walk away a free man? He straightened up and wiped his eyes with the backs of his hands, studying Buck's deadpan expression. "Why didn't you turn me in?"

"It's complicated. I handled it."

Ray furrowed his brow. "All you had to do was go into

town and make an anonymous call to the police. They would have picked me up within the hour."

Buck grunted. "Folks on this mountain have their own way of dealing with things. We don't like cops sniffing around. Next thing you know they're asking about gun permits and dog licenses, and every other dumb thing they can harass us with."

Ray fixed his gaze on the blood stain on the bench, contemplating Buck's reasoning. He was right. If he'd made an anonymous call, the cabin would instantly have become a crime scene, cadaver dogs combing the mountain, every recluse in a shack questioned as a potential witness. So how exactly had Buck *handled* it, as he'd put it?

"Where ... where's Tom's body?" Ray rasped. The words seem to echo around the space, the log walls closing in on him like prison bars. Like it or not, this was his prison now. He'd spilled his brother's blood here. A part of them both would live on here forever.

Buck blew out a heavy breath. "It's been taken care of."

"What does that mean?" Ray demanded, his voice rising.

"I buried him."

"Where?" Ray cried out, leaping to his feet. "Take me there, *now*! I want to see where you buried my brother."

"Not gonna happen," Buck said, with an adamant shake of his head. "We can't be wearing a path to his grave and risk someone discovering it. We talked about this. No grave marker, no visits. You agreed to stay away."

"What are you talking about?" Ray yelled. "I would never have agreed to anything like that. Tom was my brother. You have no idea what we lived through and what he meant to me."

Tom told me plenty about what went on." Buck's eyes

simmered with a hint of molten anger. "He was pretty screwed up, you know."

Ray swallowed the prickly knot mushrooming in his throat, all at once aware he was sweating profusely beneath his damp jacket. He fought to keep his composure. "What do you mean?"

A wary distance entered Buck's eyes. "Never mind. I shouldn't have said anything."

Ray could feel a wave of panic mounting inside. What was Buck alluding to? "You can't just throw something like that out there and then leave me hanging," he said, trying in vain to keep the tremor of desperation out of his voice. "What do you mean, he was screwed up?"

"It doesn't matter anymore. He's dead and buried now, and maybe it's a good thing."

Before he even realized what he was doing, Ray leaped to his feet and grabbed Buck by the throat. "Don't you dare talk about Tom like he was a piece of garbage! His life was worth something to me!"

Buck shoved him backward with a single thrust of his brawny arm. "Get your hands off me! You're just as messed up in the head as your brother!" he growled. "What are you trying to do, kill me too?"

Ray gasped, shrinking back in horror, dizzy and disoriented. He stared down at his hands, half-expecting them to be covered in blood. "I ... I'm sorry. I don't know what came over me. When you said that about Tom being screwed up, I ... I flipped."

"I'm not telling you anything you don't already know," Buck huffed. "You're the one who found it on him."

The hairs on the back of Ray's neck prickled. "Found what?"

Buck scratched the side of his cheek, his gaze flitting

briefly to the door and back. "Look, Ray, I feel bad about you losing your memory and all, but we swore we'd never talk about it again."

Ray thought for a moment. He desperately needed a compelling reason to overcome Buck's reluctance to keep talking. "I don't remember any of what you're telling me, but I believe you. The problem is, if I don't know what I'm not supposed to talk about, I might accidentally say something. My brain's still a scrambled mess from the accident." He lowered his voice. "Buck, please. I'm begging you. I need answers, and you're the only one who can help me. My brother was as good as dead to me for twenty years—until I found out he was alive. I came here today to patch things up after our fight, and now you're telling me I killed him. Can you imagine how I feel? I'm gutted. I don't remember him dying, and I don't remember you burying him. You've got to tell me everything. It's important. What did I find on him?"

Buck turned and paced across the floor for several minutes before abruptly resuming his seat. He gestured for Ray to sit back down on the bench. "I'm only going to tell you this once and then it's over and done with—for good this time."

"Yes, of course," Ray said, with a vigorous nod.

Buck cleared his throat, his brow trenched. "That day on the mountain when I ran into you, I'd lost my hunting dog, Drake. I'd been out looking for him for hours, whistling for him, backtracking my route. He found his way home later on that day, and I came by to tell Tom—he'd been helping me look for him." He broke off and rubbed his hands over his knees, as though preparing himself for what he was about to divulge. "When I got to the cabin, I heard hollering and shouting so I hung back for a few minutes—didn't wanna get in the middle of anything. Anyway, it got worse.

Sounded like you guys were smashing the place up. I didn't know who you were. I thought I'd better show my face and make sure Tom was all right." His voice trailed off and he stared morosely at the floor.

"Did you ... see me punch him?" Ray asked.

Buck gave a reluctant nod. "Right when I pushed open the door, he fell backward and hit his head. Your fist was raised. It was pretty obvious what had happened. I ran over to Tom and shook him, yelled his name a bunch of times, but he didn't respond."

Ray pressed his clenched fingers to his lips. "Are you sure he was dead?"

"He had no pulse," Buck mumbled in response. "There was nothing I could do."

"Did you at least try to save him?" Ray hissed through gritted teeth. "Don't you know all that CPR stuff, living out here on your own?"

Buck glared at him coldly. "I'm not a doctor. I can set a bone or tend to a wound. I can't bring a man back from the dead."

"I'm sorry," Ray said, raising his hands in a placating gesture. "It's hard to hear, that's all."

"You're the one insisted on talking about it," Buck shot back.

"I know. So, what happened once you—we—realized Tom was dead?" Ray asked, only too aware his voice was shaking uncontrollably. He still couldn't believe it. It was inconceivable that he had killed his own brother and let a stranger bury him. He'd covered up a crime—his own brother's murder. This wasn't who he was. Or was it? He frowned, rubbing his temples. He didn't know who he was anymore.

"I knew we had to bury the body right here in the woods

—keep the cops out of it," Buck answered. "You didn't want to go along with the idea, at first. You thought someone would report him missing. But no one's going to miss a mountain man. You live out here, you die out here. Your stuff gets passed around, and someone else takes over your cabin. Cycle of life." He hesitated before continuing. "I told you to check Tom's pockets before I put him in the ground." He gave a self-conscious shrug. "No sense burying a good knife or a pipe. That's when you found it—the driver's license." He trained his eyes on Ray. "I never saw a grown man turn white so quickly. You were shaking worse than you are now. I asked you what was wrong, and you handed me the license without saying a word. It didn't mean anything to me. I figured some camper must have lost her pack and Tom found it. Then you told me it was a Booneville girl who'd gone missing years ago."

"Katie Lambert," Ray said, his stomach twisting as the hard truth sank in. He should be relieved it wasn't him behind her disappearance. But all he felt was empty inside. It was equally gut wrenching to think that his own brother had abducted a young girl, murdered her, and buried her in these woods—he figured she had to be dead, or she'd have turned up by now.

Buck gave a grunt of acknowledgment. "Lambert, yeah, that's the one. Once you found her license, you got on board with me getting rid of Tom's body. You didn't want to spend the rest of your life in prison for ridding the world of a monster."

Ray let out a despairing sigh. "So you buried him right away?"

"Before his body was cold," Buck said. "I agreed to keep my mouth shut, so long as you took the boy with you."

22

For a short while after Ray left, Sonia sat in the campground parking lot with the car engine running and the heater on. She stared out at the drenched forest, questioning whether she had done the right thing by bringing Ray here. She'd wanted to help him get the answers they both needed. But, after learning that he believed his brother was alive, she realized she might have taken on more than she'd bargained for. What if they got into another fight and Ray got hurt? He wasn't in great shape after his accident. Or what if he became disoriented on the way up to the cabin? It would be on her head if anything happened to him. His doctor had stressed the importance of someone keeping an eye on him for several days. A strenuous hike in inclement weather was hardly what he had in mind. He hadn't even cleared Ray to drive, for good reason. He was supposed to be at home resting, allowing his body and mind to heal in a warm, safe environment. And she was supposed to be the levelheaded neighbor tasked with overseeing his recovery.

Sonia nibbled nervously on her nails. Her mother would

be livid if she knew what she'd done. She didn't feel much empathy for Ray—even after his accident. She didn't trust him. The fact that he'd neglected his mother all these years had sealed her opinion of him before they'd even been introduced. Sonia couldn't blame her. Evelyn's suspicions weren't entirely unfounded. But Sonia had always trusted her instincts about people. When Ray opened up to her about his childhood, she'd heard the pain in his voice, recognized his wounded spirit. She felt sure his intentions toward Henry were good.

Whatever the reason for the distance between him and his son, Ray needed help getting to the bottom of it. Hopefully, this trip to the cabin would be a good place to start. Ray seemed eager to mend the broken bridges in his relationship with his brother. Maybe meeting up with him again would be healing for them both in more ways than one, if they could keep their tempers in check this time.

Sonia glanced at her watch. Time to quit procrastinating and get something done while she was here. Several design deadlines were looming, and she could use the uninterrupted time to knock out a few sketches. She slid across into the passenger seat, so she'd have more room to work, and reached into the back for her portfolio. After unscrewing the flask of hot tea she'd brought along, she poured herself a cup, and then leaned over to turn off the engine. Running the car for four straight hours wasn't an option. Besides, it wasn't as cold as she'd expected it to be—between the hot tea and her North Face jacket, she reckoned she'd stay toasty.

Opening up her portfolio, she studied the design schematic she'd prepared for her new clients who had recently moved to the area from New York. It was an exciting project at the higher end of her usual budget allocation, which gave her a lot of room to play around with the ideas they had gathered on Pinterest. Now, it was her turn to translate their motley collection of pins into a perfectly coordinated vision for a functional and stylish house. They favored the industrial loft look which would be an interesting challenge to pull off in their new four-thousand-square-foot single-family home. She would begin by sketching room layouts for the three different options they had requested.

She hummed happily to herself as she worked, enjoying the inspirational backdrop of nature and the gentle tap of the rain on the roof. The creative process was particularly liberating without access to Wi-Fi or Photoshop. She sketched swiftly, the ideas flowing steadily, already envisioning blowing her clients' minds with her imaginative presentation. It wasn't just about the design itself—knowing *how* to present her ideas was half the battle, and Sonia had a knack for helping her clients catch her vision for their space in a way they could relate to.

Reaching into the back seat for her case of colored pencils, she caught sight of something peeking out from underneath the passenger seat. Frowning, she reached around and retrieved it with the tips of her fingers. A driver's license. Had it fallen out of Ray's bag when he tossed it into the back? Flipping it over, she frowned at the photo. Was this Ray's wife? She looked so young. She read the name, repeating it under her breath, disbelieving what she was seeing. *Katie Lambert.* Of course! She recognized that face now. An icy chill crept slowly up her spine. The air in the car had suddenly turned deathly cold.

She clapped a hand to her mouth, her eyes riveted on the headshot of the young woman. What was Ray doing with Katie Lambert's driver's license? A strangled scream escaped her lips as the horror of it descended on her. *The newspaper article!* He'd claimed he didn't know anything about the story. Was he lying? Had he abducted Katie? Was the whole memory loss thing a sham? And then another sickening thought struck. She had driven him out here. Could she be tried as an accessory to the crime? She shook her head free of the thought. She needed to pull herself together and think rationally.

Shaking, she dropped the license into the cup holder in the console, trying to make sense of it. It must have fallen out of Ray's backpack—there was no other way it could possibly have ended up in her car. She shoved her stack of drawings haphazardly into her portfolio and tossed it into the back before scrambling across to the driver's seat. She had to get out of here. She needed to go straight to the police. This was no longer about Henry. Ray must have had something to do with Katie Lambert's disappearance. At the very least, he knew something about it. Maybe that was why he was here. He might be keeping her holed up in a shack on the mountain. His brother could be in on it with him. Sonia let out a despairing groan. Katie might have gone without food and water while Ray was in the hospital. What if she'd died of thirst? No wonder he'd been so insistent on coming up here in the pouring rain.

Fumbling with the key in the ignition, she yanked it to the right, inhaling a sharp breath at the clicking sound that resulted. *No!* This couldn't be happening. Desperation mounted inside her. She turned the key again, hoping for a miracle, but to no avail. Her scalp prickled with fear. She must have left it in the accessory position when she'd switched the engine off. A sick feeling surged up her throat as the enormity of her predicament sank in. Ray was due back any time. He'd already been gone over three hours.

She had to get out of here before he returned. She darted a fearful glance around at her unfamiliar surroundings, relieved to see no sign of him. After zipping up her coat, she threw up her hood and reached for her purse. As soon as she got a cell signal, she would call 911. They might have to comb every inch of the woods to find Ray, but they would catch him in the end. He had no way off this mountain now that the battery in her car was dead.

Her thoughts tumbled over one another as she clambered out of her car and into the rain. Trembling with a mixture of cold and fear, she locked the door and dropped the keys in her coat pocket. With a final searching look around, she took off down the rough road leading out of the campground parking lot. The forest that had earlier been her source of inspiration and calm had morphed into a potential death trap. At any minute, Ray might appear from behind a tree. One look at her, and he would know she'd discovered his secret. And then what? Would he try to abduct her too, or strangle her on the spot?

Her mother had been right all along not to trust him. He was unhinged. There was no telling what he had in mind. Perhaps he'd lured her here because he suspected she knew too much already. He might be planning to return to the car with a gun and force her to accompany him to his brother's cabin—if it even belonged to his brother. What if he'd killed Tom, and their father? She had no idea what he was capable of. Maybe his disjointed memories were more accurate than he realized. She moaned as she quickened her pace, thrashing through the damp undergrowth. He might actually be a serial killer. She knew she wasn't thinking straight, but then monsters didn't think straight either. They did the unthinkable, especially to those naive enough to lend a stranger a helping hand.

She'd only been underway five minutes or less, when she heard the distinctive sound of a twig snapping like a firecracker behind her. She froze, turning her head slowly to scan her surroundings. Her heart was pulsing so hard in her chest it felt like it might burst. Scarcely daring to breathe, she crept as quietly as possible off the dirt road and slipped behind the trunk of a tree. Minutes ticked by, but she heard nothing more to indicate she was being followed, only the sound of her ragged breathing. Maybe it had been an animal moving through the brush. She peered cautiously out from behind the rough, corrugated bark of the tree, before continuing down the mountain. This time she elected to weave her way among the trees that lined the dirt road rather than remain exposed. Her purse strap kept slipping off her shoulders and she berated herself for not bringing something more practical. But then, she hadn't been planning on fleeing down the mountain. Her Vans weren't the best option for hiking in either, but at least she wasn't wearing heels.

Just when the tension in her shoulders had begun to dissipate, she picked up on a rustling sound a short distance behind her. The hairs on the back of her neck tingled. Someone, or something, was definitely following her. Adrenalin surged through her as she struggled with a split second-decision—hide again, or run? She turned and ran.

Branches clawed at her face in passing as she thundered blindly through the forest. Her purse slipped from her shoulder again, and she frantically threw the strap over her head and continued running, unhampered apart from the canvas shoes slipping on her heels. She barely felt the pain of the blisters forming as she squelched her way through a watery bed of mud and leaves, her one goal to reach the main road and flag down help.

She could no longer hear if anyone was following her. But she couldn't risk slowing down enough to look over her shoulder. Her only hope was that she was in better physical shape than Ray. Maybe the memory loss was a ruse, but he hadn't been faking the bruises she'd seen in the hospital. Her hair slowly worked its way loose from the makeshift ponytail she'd put it in to work on her sketches, but she didn't dare stop to adjust it. Pumping her arms, she propelled herself to go faster, hair plastered across her face.

In the next instant, her shoe caught in a tree root and she tumbled forward, throwing her arms out in a desperate bid to break her fall. She landed on her hip in the dirt with a thud and let out a strangled yelp. Panting, she jerked her head around in terror, but there was no one in sight. She rubbed her hip, trying to calm her rapid breathing. Somehow, she had to get up and keep going. Wincing, she got to her feet and hobbled back for her shoe. As she bent over to pick it up, she froze at the sound of footsteps.

"Sonia! Are you all right?" a voice cried out.

She didn't dare move a muscle. She couldn't have moved anyway. Shock had turned her to stone.

23

TWO MONTHS PRIOR

A myriad of emotions swirled around in Ray's head as he exited the law offices of Smith & Buchanan, the firm in Booneville handling his mother's modest estate. He'd driven down from Richmond the previous day and stayed in a hotel overnight, hoping to wrap everything up in one day. The minute he climbed back into his truck, he tore open the envelope the lawyer had given him and slid out the keys to his mother's house. A familiar heaviness gripped his chest as memories he'd buried deep inside ripped through his consciousness like tree roots breaking through the dirt. Some small part of him was sorry to learn his mother was dead, but he was mostly numb. If he was grieving for anyone, it was for himself and the happy childhood he had missed out on. If he had been a drinker, he would have opted for a stiff drink right about then. But it wasn't an appealing option for the child of an alcoholic. Even the smell of hard liquor, the very fabric of his childhood, was enough to turn his stomach to this day.

In some ways, the physical beatings and deprivation had been easier to take than the mental and verbal abuse his father had hurled at him and Tom—an unremitting barrage of cruel taunts, and hurtful words that he could still hear echoing through the chambers of his mind during sleepless nights. A nightmare of a life that Celia had been adept at covering up in public. But behind closed doors, it was a different story. Often, their father would start drinking early in the evening and stay up all night watching television, growing increasingly aggressive and unpredictable as the hours wore on. Half the time, Ray and Tom were too terrified to go downstairs to eat their dinner, and too traumatized to fall asleep, praying their father would pass out before he could stumble upstairs to unleash his anger on them for some perceived offense or another. The only respite they ever really had was when he occasionally disappeared for days on end. Ray had no idea where he went, but he was pretty sure he wasn't working, as Celia claimed.

It had taken years of therapy for Ray to work through the scars from his childhood: the flashbacks, the anxiety, the depression. It had handicapped him in life relationally. In the jobs he'd held when he was younger, he was known as a loner. But his colleagues had no idea how hard it was to put your faith in people when those closest to you let you down time and time again.

On many occasions growing up, Celia had promised him and Tom that she would leave their father, but she'd always chickened out in the end. A part of him hated her for her cowardice, even though he knew how scared she'd been. He would never put a child through anything like what they had suffered. Maybe that was why he shied away from serious relationships. It wasn't as if he hadn't had his chances. He could have been married by now, but he always panicked and ended the relationship when it came time to commit. It was too terrifying a prospect to pledge yourself to someone for the rest of your life when you were convinced it would only be a matter of time before they hurt you.

He tossed the envelope from the lawyer's office on the passenger seat and put the truck in gear. He was dreading making the trip to the house his mother had been living in. But, like it or not, it had been left to him to handle her affairs. Her will had stipulated that everything was to be divided equally between him and Tom. Unsurprisingly, Smith & Buchanan had been unable to get in touch with Tom. After Ray explained that his brother had vanished without a trace when he was sixteen, the lawyer suggested filing a petition with the court requesting he be *presumed dead.* Ray wasn't sure how he felt about that. It seemed too final—too cutthroat.

For years, he'd clung to the hope that his brother was alive. He'd spent a fair amount of time and money trying to find him—even going so far as to put a highly rated private investigator on the job. She'd been thorough in pursuing all possible avenues but concluded that Tom was either deceased and law enforcement had been unable to determine his legal identity, or he was living off-grid somewhere and had no wish to be found.

Ray and Tom had talked about the idea a lot when they were younger—romanticizing the notion of living off the land and being accountable to no one. But Ray doubted Tom had actually gone through with it. As hard as it was to accept, the more likely scenario was that his brother had succumbed to a life on the streets. The cards were stacked against him with addiction running in the family.

Forty-five minutes later, Ray pulled into the driveway of a tired-looking craftsman-style bungalow. He sat in the truck staring at the building for several minutes before he became aware of an older woman sitting on her porch peering curiously across at him. He snatched the envelope off the seat and climbed out, ducking his head to avoid having to acknowledge her as he made his way to the door. The less contact he had with his mother's neighbors, the better.

His plan was to look around inside and assess the situation. With a bit of luck, the house would only require a fresh coat of paint to get it ready for sale, and he could unload it quickly. He didn't relish the idea of spending weeks on end sprucing it up and carrying out repairs. Nor was he interested in listing the contents on Craigslist or hosting a garage sale. Depending on the condition the furniture was in, he would either donate it or toss it. The quicker he got out of there, the sooner he could get on with his life.

Stepping inside, he wrinkled his nose at the musty smell pervading the space. Every appointment bore witness to the age of the departed inhabitant. The kitchen was straight from the seventies—laminate cabinets and countertops, an avocado green dishwasher, and a harvest yellow tile backsplash. The wood cabinets were topped with wicker baskets overflowing with plastic ivy and faded fake flowers. Ray curled his lip in distaste. The color palette alone was enough to induce a migraine.

With a mounting sense of dread, he made his way into the family room, groaning aloud at the hideous statement-stone fireplace wall that greeted him. Every square inch of space in the room was cluttered with lamps, ottomans, footstools, and nesting tables overflowing with ornaments and knickknacks. The arms and backs of the couch and chairs were bedecked with yellowing lace doilies. The entire room smacked of a love affair with the color brown, culminating in a particularly distasteful carpet that resembled dead leaves on a forest floor.

Resigning himself to tackling a bigger job than he'd anticipated, Ray searched out Celia's bedroom next. He grimaced as he took in the space: the obligatory shag carpet, a gaudy, floral window treatment that matched the comforter on the queen-sized bed, an uncomfortable-looking tufted chair upholstered in Wedgewood blue, and a lopsided oak dresser with grooves for handle pulls. There was no getting around it. The whole house would have to be renovated, beginning with renting a skip to handle all the junk he'd encountered so far.

He slid apart the mirrored closet doors, almost gagging from the overpowering stench of mothballs that hit him. He didn't relish the idea of going through his mother's clothes. Maybe he could bag them up and donate them as is. By the looks of things, he would have more than enough to handle without sifting through an elderly woman's wardrobe and trying to figure out what was worth saving.

Eying the shoeboxes on the shelf above the clothing rack, he reached for the nearest one and peeked inside. It was jammed full of papers—letters and the like. Probably trash, but he would have to go through them all to make sure. He sat down on the edge of the bed and began rifling through the contents. Three shoeboxes later, he stumbled on a pile of bank statements. As he leafed disinterestedly through them, the sum of $4500 caught his eye. Scrutinizing the statements more closely, he was surprised to see that $4500 had been transferred out of Celia's account every month for the past five years. Where on earth was the money going? It was almost two-thirds of her monthly income. She owned a modest rental property, but, apart from that, her only income was a small pension and her social security check.

Ray returned the shoeboxes to the closet and took the

pile of statements down to the kitchen. He would call the bank and see if they could help him get to the bottom of it. First, he needed some coffee. He rummaged through the array of brightly colored ceramic canisters on the countertop until he found what he was looking for.

As he waited for the coffee to brew in the archaic machine, he ran his eye over a calendar hanging above the phone documenting his mother's last known movements: a trip to the hairdresser, a doctor's appointment, a grocery list; bread, milk, tuna, oranges. He pulled out the alphabetical address book beneath the phone and thumbed through it. The breath caught in his throat when he came to the letter "J."

Tom Jenkins, 35.7647° N, 82.2653° W

24

For several days, Ray went back-and-forth about what the coordinates meant, debating what to do about them. Was Tom alive—living off-grid someplace? Had he given Celia the coordinates? That would mean his mother and younger brother had been in contact with one another. It could also explain the $4500 Celia was transferring into an unidentified account each month. But why would Tom need the money? And why had no one told Ray his brother was alive?

A wave of remorse coursed through him as the harsh truth hit home. He was the one who had cut off all contact. Even if his mother had wanted to tell him, she had no way of getting in touch with him—he'd made sure of that. He'd kept tabs on her through the years from a distance, but he'd never suspected that all this time Tom was alive. His heart shuddered when he pictured his brother's small, pale face, taut with fear, as they'd huddled together in their bedroom listening to the sound of their father going on another rampage, dreading the moment they would hear his footsteps thumping up the stairs.

He couldn't put it off any longer. If Tom was alive, he had
to know. He opened up the map he'd bought of the Blue
Ridge mountains and jotted down the coordinates in the
margin, then marked an approximate course with a yellow
highlighter. After stashing a change of clothes in his backpack, he grabbed his GPS, some snacks and water, and
headed out to his truck, already second-guessing his decision. He couldn't be sure what he would find when he
arrived. Maybe it was wishful thinking on his part believing
Tom was alive. What if the GPS led him to a mound of rocks
and a makeshift cross? Perhaps their mother had spread
Tom's ashes in the mountains and recorded the coordinates
so she could visit his grave.

An hour later, he turned off the main highway, and
traversed along a dirt road for a mile or so up into the
mountains, before parking his truck in the Deep Creek
Campground. There was no official trail to the coordinates,
which would make for slow going navigating his way
through the shadowy, hulking forest. Despite all his talk of
living like a prepper in the back country, he had ended up
working in the city all his life. Without Tom, the off-grid
dream had lost its appeal. Even with the GPS, he would
have to be careful not to lose his bearings—he wasn't good
at directions. As best he could estimate, it would take him at
least an hour to reach the coordinates, possibly longer. After
adjusting his pack, he set off, a cautious swirl of excitement
building inside him as he pictured reuniting with Tom after
all these years.

He was making good progress until he attempted to
cross a stream and lost his footing on a moss-covered rock.
As he fought a losing battle to keep his balance, the GPS
slipped from his grasp and fell into the water with a sickening crack. He scrambled out onto the opposite bank, fran-

tically trying to dry it off, willing the dead screen back to life. Despite his valiant efforts, it was apparent the device was shot. He had no choice now but to rely on his map to make it the rest of the way. He tried to stay calm and approach the setback in a logical manner, although his brain was screaming at him that he was an idiot for allowing this to happen. He wasn't cut out for the backcountry. He hadn't even brought a gun with him—just some snacks and enough water for a short hike. He'd been counting on making it to Tom's cabin and spending the night, if things went well. Or making it back down the mountain before dark if it turned out to be a wild goose chase. The last thing he wanted to do was spend a night alone and lost with the risk of hypothermia or a deadly encounter with a wild animal.

After consulting the map, he set off once more in what he hoped was a northwesterly direction. It wasn't long before he came upon another stream and realized something wasn't right. According to the map, he shouldn't have to cross any more water to reach the coordinates. Was this the same stream he'd crossed earlier? He glanced at his watch. Only a little after noon. No need to panic, yet. He still had plenty of time to make it safely to Tom's cabin, or back down the mountain, before nightfall.

Pulling out his map, he sat down at the base of a tree and munched on a granola bar while he got his bearings. After re-orienting himself, he adjusted his route and set off once more. Unused to the physical exertion, his joints were already protesting the steep incline. The hush of the forest had become unbearable, almost as if it were holding its breath and watching him—waiting for him to make a mistake. He only hoped he was hiking in the right direction this time. Without his GPS, he could be going in circles. The wisest course of action would probably be to turn around and try and find his way back to the campground.

The sound of pinecones crunching underfoot startled him. Spinning around, he found himself face-to-face with a bearded man dressed head-to-toe in a mixture of camo and fur, a gun slung over his shoulder, and a menacing knife glinting at his waist. Ray swallowed down his apprehension at the imposing figure, only partially relieved to find himself no longer alone. He gave a tentative nod by way of greeting. "Glad I ran into you. I think I'm lost."

The man cocked his head to one side, sizing him up, his eyes resting briefly on his canvas backpack. "You're a long way past the last campsite. Where are you headed?"

"My brother has a cabin up here. Our mother passed away and I'm trying to get in contact with him."

The man drew his shaggy brows together in a skeptical manner. "What's his name?"

"Tom Jenkins." Ray gave a self-conscious shrug. " Although, to be honest, I don't know if he's going by that name anymore. I'm Ray, by the way."

A flicker of shock, mingled with some other emotion Ray couldn't pinpoint, crossed the man's face. "Tom Jenkins is your brother?"

Ray gave a hesitant smile. "Yes, my younger brother."

The man moved his jaw side-to-side, weighing Ray up with heightened interest. "I'm Buck. Didn't mean to sneak up on you like that. I lost my hunting dog. I've been looking for him all morning, but I'm on my way back to my place— figured he might have found his way home by now. I can take you by your brother's cabin on the way."

"Wow, thanks. I really appreciate that," Ray said. "I dropped my GPS and cracked the screen. I've been trying to figure out where I'm at from my map, but I can't make much sense of it."

"My condolences on your mother's passing," Buck said, gesturing to Ray to follow him.

"To be honest we weren't … close," Ray said falling in behind Buck as he waded deeper into the undergrowth. "We hadn't spoken in years."

"How about Tom?" Buck asked.

Ray puckered his brow. "I think he kept in touch with our mother. I didn't realize it until I was going through her things and found the coordinates for his cabin. He and I were pretty tight when we were kids, but we lost touch when we were teenagers."

"Brace yourself. He might not be too happy to see you," Buck warned. "He's a strange one. Keeps to himself."

"Tell me about it," Ray replied. "I hired a private investigator years ago to try and find him but he even stumped her."

"That's kind of the point of living here," Buck retorted with a grunt.

They fell silent for the rest of the way until Buck came to a halt and pointed up ahead. "That's Tom's cabin straight through that clump of trees." He tipped his fingers to his forehead. "Good luck. And watch your back."

His forbidding tone sent an icy shiver down Ray's spine. Did Buck know something about Tom that he wasn't telling him? Was he dangerous? Had he become a raging alcoholic like their father? Whatever the case, Ray intended to take the warning to heart. He hadn't even considered the possibility that he might be endangering himself by dropping in on Tom unannounced. He almost wished now that he'd packed a weapon. It had been twenty years since he'd set eyes on his brother, and he knew nothing about the man he'd become.

He waited until Buck disappeared into the wooded mountainside and then took a few deep breaths. He couldn't back out now. He needed to muster his courage and go knock on the cabin door. The fact that his brother was alive was enough to propel him forward. Surely the bond they had once shared would guarantee a heartfelt reunion, despite the divergent paths their lives had taken. It was unlikely after all these years that Ray would be able to talk Tom into returning to civilization. But with the money he stood to inherit from his mother, that option was open to him.

Ray approached the cabin cautiously, his heartbeat ratcheting up several notches with each step. He wasn't sure how he was going to react when he actually set eyes on Tom. The well of suppressed emotion inside him ran deep. He blinked to clear his vision as he padded quietly toward the front door. Evidently, Tom didn't have a dog to alert him to the presence of strangers. He stepped up onto the porch and peered through the small window to the right of the door. His eyes widened, the breath leaving his lungs at the sight that greeted him. Despite the unkempt hair and bristly beard, there was no mistaking the man hurriedly shoving items into a leather hunting pack laid out on the table. *Tom!*

Abandoning all caution, Ray depressed the wooden door handle, and swung the door open.

Time rolled to a standstill as their eyes met—each drinking the other in.

"Ray?" Tom blurted out at last. His voice was rough and resonant, nothing like the thin, trembling voice of the broken child Ray remembered.

He took a step forward to embrace him, but Tom drew

back. He threw a skittish glance at the pack in his hand, his expression hardening. "You shouldn't have come here."

Ray winced at the caustic tone—so like their father's—that cut to the core. He gave an embarrassed laugh in a vain attempt to hide how hurt he was. "What kind of a welcome is that after twenty years?"

Tom sniffed and ran the back of his hand under his nose. "What do you want, Ray?"

"I came to tell you that our mother passed away. I found the coordinates to this place when I was going through her stuff." He paused and swallowed the lump scratching at his throat. "I thought you were dead all these years, Tom. Did she know you were alive?"

He grunted, avoiding Ray's penetrating gaze. "I sent her the coordinates when I built the place. Figured someone should have them."

Ray gestured to the hunting pack on the table. "You didn't know she was dead, did you? Is that where you're going, to visit her?"

A dark look settled on Tom's face. "I haven't set eyes on her since the day I left. You of all people should know better than to think I would want a relationship with her."

"But you were quite happy to take her money," Ray shot back.

"I don't care about her money—you can have it!" Tom darted an uneasy glance at the door. "You should go. I can't do this right now."

"Why not? When should we do it?" Ray protested. "I spent the best part of two hours hiking up this mountain, not to mention getting lost, just to see you. He unhitched his backpack and dropped it on the floor. I thought I could spend the night. We need to talk—get reacquainted."

Tom wet his lips in a nervous fashion. "You can't stay here. It's too dangerous."

"What are you talking about? You live here. You're not making any sense," Ray replied. "Look, I don't know what's going on with you, Tom. I don't know what you need the money for. Maybe you're hitting the bottle like our father, But, whatever it is, I'm here for you now. I want to help."

Tom closed the flap on his leather pack and pulled the drawstring tight. "You can't help me, Ray. I don't need rescuing anymore. I need you to leave, now."

"What? You can't be serious! I only just got here. Are you really going to throw me out?"

Tom reached for the rifle on the wall behind him and fixed a cold gaze on Ray. "I will if I have to."

Ray held up his hands in front of him. "Okay! Easy, Tom. Look, I realize I sprung this visit on you. But we need to talk —not just about the estate, about everything that's gone on in our lives since I saw you last. How about I leave you my number and you can call me from town when you're ready? I'll come and pick you up." He rummaged around in his pack for one of the pens he always carried with him in case he ran across a story. He tore off a corner of the map and scribbled down his number. "Don't wait too long," he said, setting it on the table. "It's been far too long already."

He swung his backpack onto his shoulders and turned to go, hesitating at a rustling sound above him. Glancing up at the loft bed, he let out a sharp gasp.

A small boy with terror-filled eyes was peering down at him.

25

Ray blinked up at the loft bed in disbelief. "Am I ... seeing things or is that a child up there?"

Tom flapped an arm angrily at the boy. "I thought I warned you not to show your face!"

Quick as a fish darting into a reef, the boy vanished beneath a blanket.

Aghast, Ray turned to his brother. "Tom! What's that kid doing here?"

Tom sniffed hard, his eyes shifting all around the room. "He's my son. Not that it's any of your business."

"You ... you have a son?" Ray shook his head, incredulous. "I can't believe this. First, I find out you're alive, now I learn I have a nephew. How ... I mean, who's—"

"His mother left us," Tom said abruptly. "It's nothing I want to talk about, so don't ask."

"Can you at least tell me your son's name?" Ray asked, fighting to keep his tone calm.

Tom scowled and reached for a coat hanging by the door. "His name's Henry."

"Henry Jenkins," Ray muttered, trying to collect his

thoughts. He couldn't wrap his head around the idea that Tom was a father. Was that the reason Celia had been sending him money each month? It made sense that she would be concerned about her grandchild's welfare, especially knowing where he was living. But something didn't add up. Looking around the humble surroundings, it was apparent Tom wasn't spending the money on taking care of the kid.

Beyond that, the more pressing question on Ray's mind was whether Tom was a fit father for a young child. It was alarming to think the boy was up here in the mountains without his mother, or access to healthcare, or education, or any friends his own age. Tom didn't even have a dog for him to play with. Ray gritted his teeth. He needed to make his brother see sense. But he had to tread carefully. Judging by the way Tom had snapped at the boy, he was basing his parenting style on habits he'd learned in his own childhood —none of which were healthy. "Did our mother know about Henry?" Ray asked.

Tom looked surprised by the question. "Course not."

"How old is Henry?"

After a beat of silence, Tom answered, "He's ... four."

Ray's heart sank a little further. He had a sneaking suspicion "four" was Tom's best estimate. Talk about being a negligent father. Was he not keeping track of his own son's age? History repeating itself. Their father had never known when their birthdays were—nor had he cared.

"Tom," Ray said, doing his best to keep his voice level, " You can't raise a small boy out in the mountains alone like this. It's not good for him. He should be in school. He needs to have friends. What if he gets sick or something?"

Tom's eyes glinted with anger. "Don't stick your nose into

my business. I know what's best for him. I'm taking care of
him."

"Really?" Ray motioned to Tom's leather hunting pack. "
Looks like you were getting ready to head out alone when I
arrived. Henry was in bed. Do you leave him here by himself
when you go hunting? Is that what you call taking care of him?"

Tom jutted his chin out. "I'm bringing him with me."

Ray frowned. "Didn't look like it—the way he was hiding
under the blanket like that. Regardless, he's only four years
old, way too young to take hunting. It's dangerous to have a
small child around guns."

"You have no idea of the kind of danger he's in." Tom
threw him a dark look as he yelled up to the loft area, "
Henry! Get down here, now! We're leaving."

"Tom!" Ray gasped. "Quit threatening him like that! He
didn't do anything."

"Hurry up!" Tom barked up the ladder.

Stewing in a mixture of anger and helplessness, Ray
watched as the little boy's face reappeared from under the
blanket. He stared solemnly at Ray but made no attempt to
climb down.

Tom muttered something unintelligible under his
breath, then stood on the bottom rung and grabbed the boy
around the waist. Henry wriggled in his arms, whimpering.

"Knock it off!" Tom snapped as he set Henry down on
the floor. "We have to go. And you can't make a sound."

Trying to mask his shock, Ray took stock of the boy's
neglected appearance. His dark curls were filthy and
matted, his face so engrained with dirt that his eyes looked
like marshmallows set in mud. He was wearing pants that
were way too big for him, held up at the waist by a piece of
string. Judging by the dried stains on the front, he was

having difficulty undoing the string quickly enough to relieve himself.

Ray rubbed a shaking hand over his jaw. This was child abuse. If the authorities knew the conditions Henry was living in, they would remove him immediately. He had to do something. Kneeling in front of the boy, he smiled gently at him. "Hi there, Henry. My name's Ray. Nice to meet you."

Henry jammed his thumb into his mouth, his eyes flitting anxiously between Ray and Tom.

"Where are his toys?" Ray fumed. "Doesn't he have a teddy or something? He looks half scared to death."

Tom frowned as he reached for his hunting pack. "You best get out of here now. Me and the boy have stuff to do."

"The boy?" Ray echoed. "Is that how you refer to your son when he's standing right here in front of you. Can't you at least use his name? Don't you remember what it felt like when dad yelled at us, *get over here, boy*?"

"I never had a dad," Tom growled, elbowing past him. He gripped Henry by the shoulder and stared defiantly at Ray. "Whether you like it or not, Henry's none of your business."

"He is my business, Tom. This is my nephew we're talking about. I've never seen a more neglected child in all my life. You ought to be ashamed of yourself. How can you call yourself a father? You're depriving him of everything a kid needs to grow up happy and secure."

"You don't understand," Tom hissed. "I'm doing the best I can."

"Well, your best isn't good enough," Ray fired back. "He's not being properly taken care of, not by a long shot. This isn't right."

Tom reached for his gun. "I'm not gonna warn you again. Get off my property!"

"Are you crazy?" Ray asked. "Put the gun down! You're scaring Henry." He bent down and picked the boy up in his arms, trying not to gag at the stench of him. He smelled as if he'd been steeped in four years of filth and never been bathed. "Is your daddy scaring you, buddy?"

Henry started sobbing so quietly it was almost as if he'd been trained not to make a sound even in the depths of despair. Ray's heart ached for him. He knew how that felt. "It's okay," he soothed, rubbing Henry's back in small circles.

"I ... m-m-miss Mommy!" he sobbed.

Ray pinned a steely gaze on Tom. "Where is his mother?" he demanded. "Have you tried to reach out to her at all?"

Tom raised his rifle and pointed it at Ray. "It's time for you to leave. Put the boy down."

"Okay, okay," Ray said in a placating tone. His heart thudded against his ribs. He needed time to think this through. He couldn't leave the child here, but he couldn't push Tom to the breaking point either and risk Henry taking a stray bullet. He set him down in a rocking chair—the only seating in the shack, apart from a storage bench—and reached for his backpack, sick to his stomach. Did Tom make the kid sit on the floor to eat? Or was he forced to stay up in the loft bed? Ray couldn't decide which was worse, eating on the floor like a dog, or being a virtual prisoner in your own bed. A chill passed over him. Tom wasn't right in the head. He couldn't in good conscience leave Henry here with him one more day.

Tom slowly lowered the rifle and laid it on the table. He folded his arms in front of him, a sullen look on his face as he waited for Ray to exit the cabin.

"I'm leaving, but I'm taking Henry with me," Ray

announced. "He needs medical attention. What you're doing to him is criminal."

"Don't you dare threaten me," Tom snarled, reaching for his hunting pack. "If you're so concerned about his welfare, maybe you should think about the fact that Henry's been through enough already losing his mother. How do you think he's going to feel if you rip him away from me too?"

"You're not a fit father, Tom," Ray said. "Open your eyes and take a good look at your son. He looks like a refugee. You're every bit as bad as our father was—you're full of pent-up rage. Are you hitting the bottle too? Henry's terrified of you. I saw it in his eyes the minute he peered down from the loft. After everything we went through as kids, I can't believe you would bully and abuse an innocent child."

"You've no idea what you're talking about," Tom spat back, dropping his pack at his feet. "You don't even know me anymore."

"You're right, Tom. I don't know you. And I don't like what I see now that I'm here."

Fists flying, Tom lunged for him, spittle flying from his mouth. Instinctively, Ray threw a defensive punch, catching him square on the chin. Tom stumbled, clearly dazed, before toppling backward over his hunting pack.

The last thing Ray heard before Tom hit the floor was the crack of his head as he slammed against the storage bench.

26

R ay stood frozen in place, eyes planted on his brother sprawled motionless on the cabin floor. His shoulders sagged in relief when Tom moaned softly and stirred. Ray stole a glance at Henry, his little body trembling in the chair, before making a split-second decision. Any minute now, Tom would be back on his feet, more enraged than ever. He couldn't leave Henry here with him. It wasn't safe. Neglect was one thing, but Henry's cowering demeanor suggested Tom was also physically abusive—he'd lunged at Ray, after all. At the very least, he was unstable, and unwilling to listen to reason. This was no environment for a small child.

Before he could change his mind, Ray hurriedly threw on his pack, picked Henry up in his arms and fled. With a bit of luck, Tom would be too dazed to follow them—at least until they had got enough of a head start to make it safely out of his reach. Ray had no idea how to get back to the Deep Creek Campground where he'd left his truck, but if he could just get down the mountain, he could figure out his bearings after that.

He set off at a jog in the direction he thought he'd come from but was soon forced to slow to a walk. The brush was too thick and the terrain too treacherous to risk a spill with Henry in his arms. He considered abandoning his pack and putting Henry on his back, but the child was clinging to him like a limpet, and he feared peeling him off his chest might only traumatize him further. Instead, he focused all his efforts on putting as much distance as possible between themselves and the cabin.

Fifteen minutes in, Ray was feeling the strain of his load. After checking over his shoulder to make sure they weren't being followed, he searched for a hollow to rest in. Sinking down on a lichen-covered log, he pulled out his Hydro Flask and offered Henry a swig of water. The child stood there staring at him with a bewildered look on his face, a tell-tale tremble revving up in his bottom lip.

"It's okay, buddy," Ray soothed. "I know you're scared, but everything's going to be all right."

He dug a granola bar out of his pack and held it out to Henry. After a moment's hesitation, he grabbed it and clutched it in his fist like a lollipop.

Ray frowned as he screwed the cap back on his flask. Was Henry waiting on permission to eat or something? "Go ahead," he said, smiling encouragingly at him. "You can eat it."

A confused expression flitted across Henry's face as he looked more closely at the granola bar in his fist.

It suddenly dawned on Ray that he might need help opening it. "Here, let me get that for you." He reached out his hand, but Henry let out a piercing wail and jerked the bar away.

"Shhhh!" Ray said, casting a nervous glance around them. He rooted around in his pack for another granola bar and tore it open, then handed it to Henry. He watched in shock as the child gobbled it down in seconds, then held out the other one for Ray to open. Watching him scarf it down just as quickly as the first one, Ray was sobered by the thought that Henry might have been deprived of food. He was thin, but Ray hadn't noticed just how malnourished he was until now—his oversized pants hiding the dire reality of the situation. Anger bubbled up inside him. How could Tom of all people do this to a child? Hadn't they suffered enough themselves to know better?

As soon as Henry had satisfied his hunger, Ray persuaded him to drink a little water before setting off again. His hopes began to surge that they were heading in the right direction when they came to a stream and he recognized the spot he'd dropped his GPS at earlier. Henry appeared to be fascinated by the water, peering down at it from Ray's arms, and craning his neck to look back at it after they crossed over. It struck Ray as odd. Surely, he must have seen streams before. It seemed to fit Ray's theory that Tom left the boy alone in the cabin when he went out—a prisoner in his loft bed. His stomach knotted at the disturbing thought.

At long last, the Deep Creek Campground parking lot came into view. Ray almost collapsed with relief when he spotted his truck parked where he'd left it. He jogged toward it and unlocked the doors, exhaustion hitting him as the adrenalin oozed from his veins. Henry began to protest the minute he set him in the back seat and attempted to strap him in.

"All right," Ray said, too weary to argue with him. "You can sit next to me up front. But you can't sit in my lap. I have to drive." He buckled Henry in as best he could, resorting to slipping the top half of the seatbelt behind him to avoid it cutting uncomfortably across his throat. When he turned the key in the ignition, Henry tensed, his eyes widening.

"Nothing to be scared of," Ray promised, winking at him. "This will be fun."

He pulled out of the parking lot and began the bumpy ride along the dirt track back down to the main road. As he drove, he thought about his next move. He should probably go straight to the authorities, but he questioned if that was the wisest course of action. Naturally, they would dispatch cops to the cabin to question Tom. There was no telling how he would react. He might pull a gun on them too. And what if he told them he wanted to file assault charges against Ray? They could both end up in jail. Then who would be there for Henry? With his mother out of the picture, he'd be dumped into the system, with no guarantee he wouldn't go from one form of abuse to the next.

By the time they reached the outskirts of Booneville, Ray had formulated a plan. Pick up some clothes for Henry, book a motel room, and get him cleaned up. They could spend the night in anonymity while he thought things through. He wouldn't make any rash decisions about reporting Tom to the authorities. His head was still spinning from everything that had happened. If it weren't for the ragged child seated next to him, he'd be tempted to think it had all been a crazy nightmare.

He didn't dare take Henry to his mother's place in case any of the neighbors spotted him, and he couldn't go back to the hotel he'd stayed in last night—there was no way he could sneak him through the lobby in his current condition. He drove slowly down Main Street, eying the stores on either side: Harmon Feed & Supply, The Busy Bean coffee shop, Second Chance thrift store, a Chevron station, a post office, Smith & Buchanan law offices, Delaney Engineering,

The Buffalo Gal restaurant, Delia's Gift Shop, Main Street Mini Mart. Maybe they didn't have a children's clothing store. It was either the thrift store or try and wash what Henry was wearing. He clenched his fingers around the steering wheel. He couldn't take Henry into the thrift store in the state he was in, and he couldn't leave him in the truck either. Someone might catch a glimpse of him and alert the police. One look would be enough to tell an alert citizen that something was terribly wrong.

Ray drove to the far end of town where he'd spotted a small motel on his way in the day before. Judging by the dingy exterior, the staff weren't likely to be too judgmental about the cleanliness of their clientele. Still, he would leave Henry in the truck while he checked in—better safe than sorry. He pulled up outside the office and switched off the engine. As an afterthought, he removed the keys from the ignition. "Henry, I need to run inside for a couple of minutes. I want you to wait here. Don't open the truck door, and don't look out the window at anybody. In fact, you can hide on the floor if you want." He felt bad for suggesting it, but he suspected Henry was used to squirreling out of sight on Tom's command. He unplugged Henry's seatbelt and squeezed his shoulder. "Be a good boy, I'll be right back."

It wasn't as if he really trusted Henry not to press his face to the glass and stare out at any passersby, but he could keep an eye on him easily enough from the office through the oversized glass window. To his surprise, the minute he stepped inside the motel, Henry slid to the truck floor. Ray twisted his lips. Evidently, the child wasn't willing to risk the consequences of disobeying an order. Ray dreaded to think what those consequences might have been.

After procuring the room key, he drove to the other end of the motel where he'd requested a room next to the laundry facilities. He grabbed his backpack and, after a quick glance around to make sure no one was ogling them, ushered Henry inside their room. It was standard cheap motel fare, a dark forgiving carpet to disguise every bodily fluid on the spectrum, a heavily patterned bedspread to serve the same function, a pair of mismatched rickety night-stands, an archaic-looking television, an ugly, and extremely loud, wall heater, and a chipped and scarred desk with a lamp that looked like it had been knocked over one too many times.

Ray turned on the television and found a cartoon channel. Henry immediately sank down on the floor and leaned against the end of the bed staring up at the screen with his mouth hanging open. It was obvious he'd never seen a television before. Ray took the opportunity to gently undress him, horrified to see the remnants of bruises on his back. He was tempted to ask Henry about them, but hesitant to upset him—it could wait until morning. By then, he would have made his decision on what to do.

"Stay here," Ray said to him. "I'll be right back."

He hurried next door to the laundry room and tossed Henry's clothes, sneakers and all, into the washing machine, trying not to gag at the offensive odor, like the breath of death itself, that emanated from them. As he set the machine to run, his stomach rumbled, reminding him that he hadn't eaten anything, other than a granola bar, since breakfast. As soon as he got Henry looking halfway presentable, he would head back out and pick up something to eat. They couldn't sit inside a restaurant until he got Henry some decent clothes that fit properly. Maybe they should make a run to the thrift store.

His mind was going in circles, wondering if he'd done the right thing. After all, he had no legal claim on Henry.

He'd abducted a child—broken the law. Granted, it was his own nephew, but this was the first time he'd set eyes on him. No judge would look favorably on what he'd done, no matter how good his intentions had been. Not to mention the fact that he'd assaulted the child's father. The more he thought about it, the more he realized he'd inserted himself into a bad situation and made it worse.

By the time he finally coaxed Henry away from the television and into the bath, the water had turned cold. But that was the least of Ray's concerns. He felt sick to his stomach as he took a closer look at the tell-tale bruises on Henry's tiny torso, confirming what he'd feared most. Tom had been physically abusing his son. His own childhood had turned him into a monster. Bile oozed its way up Ray's throat. It would have been easier to learn that his brother had overdosed in a gutter somewhere. Tears tracked down his cheeks as he rubbed a washcloth gently over Henry's back. To his relief, the child seemed to enjoy the sensation, and quickly took to the water, splashing, and playing with the bubbles the cheap bath gel made.

In the end, it took even more persuasion to get Henry out of the bath than it had to get him in. After entertaining himself happily for half an hour, he'd completely soaked the floor, evoking a strong aroma of mold. Judging by the telltale spots in the corners of the ceiling, a half-hearted attempt had been made to paint it over. It didn't make the prospect of overnighting here any more appealing, and Ray was tempted to abandon his plan and drive back to his own home in Richmond. But until he had come to a firm decision on what to do about Henry, he needed to stay in Booneville.

After dressing him, Ray took Henry by the hand and led him back out to the truck. The clothes he had pulled from the dryer still looked somewhat stained, but they smelled significantly better. They would have to do for now. He drove back through town, debating whether to pick something up at the mini mart or go into a restaurant and order takeout. The latter sounded considerably more appealing—they both needed some real food.

"Okay, listen up," he said to Henry as he pulled up outside The Buffalo Gal. "We're going to go inside and pick up something to eat and take it back to our motel room. I want you to be a good boy and hold my hand. If anyone talks to you, pretend I'm your dad. It's really important, Henry. Do you understand me?"

He gave a solemn nod, his tiny face instantly filling with fear. He knew what Ray was telling him to say was wrong. But he was too young to realize that Ray had his best interests at heart—that the real injustice had been perpetrated on him by his father. Ray's heart ached when he remembered how Henry had sobbed for his mother. He patted him on the head, smiling down at him to mask the emotions tearing him apart on the inside.

In that moment, he made Henry a silent promise to do whatever it took to find his mother.

27

Between worrying about Henry waking up, and wrestling with what he'd done, Ray barely slept. As soon as it was light out, he slipped quietly out of bed and made himself a cup of cheap coffee on the cracked plastic coffeemaker above the microwave, then headed into the bathroom to get ready. Standing under the low-pressure shower, he reluctantly concluded that he had no choice but to go back to his brother's cabin and try and reason with him. At a minimum, he needed to let him know his son was safe. The second pressing matter was that of Henry's mother. He had to find a way to persuade Tom to tell him who she was. It was possible she really had abandoned them, and didn't want anything more to do with Henry, but Ray needed to hear it from her own mouth.

Henry still hadn't stirred by the time Ray was showered and dressed. He leaned over the creaky bed and rested a hand gently on Henry's shoulder. "Hey, buddy, it's time to get up." Despite shaking him several times, he had to resort to lifting him into a sitting position before Henry finally opened his eyes. He blinked uncomprehendingly around his strange surroundings and fixed a sleepy gaze on Ray.

"Are you hungry?" Ray asked, attempting to pull Henry's shirt over his head. He had no idea if the average four-year-old could dress himself, but he doubted Henry knew how to. Judging by the state his clothes were in, he'd been sleeping in them for an awfully long time.

Henry yawned and pointed to Ray's backpack.

Ray chuckled. "You want a granola bar for breakfast? I reckon we can do better than that. Let's get you dressed and get out of here."

FORTIFIED by the egg-and-bacon sandwiches they gobbled down in the truck, they set off for the cabin once more. An hour later, they were winding their way up the dirt road to the Deep Creek Campground where Ray had parked the previous day. He'd purchased a new GPS at the gas station and already plugged in the coordinates. He was determined to do whatever it took to make his brother see sense—even if it meant groveling.

The only hitch in his plan was what to do with Henry. He couldn't risk taking him back up to the cabin in case Tom turned violent. His only option was to leave him in the truck. It wasn't an ideal solution by a long stretch, but he had picked up some crayons and coloring books at the mini mart to keep him occupied. He was counting on the fact that Henry was used to being left alone for hours on end and complying unquestioningly with whatever he was told to do. When they pulled into the parking lot, Ray could see the anxiety settling in Henry's expression as it dawned on him where they were.

"Everything's going to be all right, Henry. I need to go

back up to your cabin for a couple of hours, but you can stay here in my truck. You'll be perfectly safe. I brought you some snacks and coloring books." He pulled the supplies out of a plastic bag and handed them to Henry. As an afterthought, he leaned over and demonstrated what Henry was supposed to do with the crayons.

"Don't eat them. Just color the pictures."

He watched as Henry selected a crayon from the box and began swiping it back and forth over a picture of farm-yard animals. As he'd suspected, Henry's fascination suggested he'd never held a crayon in his hand before.

Ray ruffled his hair to get his attention. "If you hear another truck or car, I want you to hide on the floor in the back under this blanket, just like you did at your cabin, okay?"

Henry tore his gaze away from the coloring books and glanced at the blanket Ray was pointing at. He gave a distracted nod before turning back to the coloring book in his lap.

"It's important that you stay here. You can take a nap under the blanket, if you want. Just don't get out of the truck, for any reason." Ray hesitated and then handed Henry an empty water bottle. "Use this if you need to pee. I don't want you opening the door."

After double checking the route on the GPS screen, he waved goodbye to Henry and set off at a brisk pace.

A little less than an hour later, he found himself back at his brother's cabin—this time with no unnecessary detours. The GPS had done its job, and the urgency of getting back to Henry had spurred him on.

"Tom, it's me, Ray." He banged his fist on the door, shuf-fling his feet impatiently as he waited for Tom to answer. He yelled out again, then pushed the door open and peered inside. The first thing he noticed was that the fire hadn't been lit overnight. The second thing that struck him like a thunderbolt was that Tom was still lying in the same spot he'd left him in.

The hair on the back of Ray's neck prickled. Even from where he was standing, he could tell something was horribly wrong. "Tom?" he called out, his voice trailing off as he made his way across the floor. He fell on his knees next to his brother, gasping at the ashen hue to his features. Tom's eyes were closed, but not in the restful pose of sleep. His head was pillowed in a pool of congealed blood. Ray stretched out a trembling hand and touched his forehead, confirming what he knew in his heart.

Tom was dead!

Sinking back on his haunches, Ray dragged his fingers through his hair and let out a guttural scream. His heart was galloping in his chest, his brain racing to catch up with the hard fact staring him in the face—he had killed his brother! Not only that, but he had abducted his child afterward. There was no possibility of talking his way out of this in any court of law. No one would believe his version of events. And even if they did, he would still be found guilty of manslaughter. There was only one place he was going to end up when he got down off this mountain, and that was behind bars. He pressed his fingertips to his temples, desperately trying to untangle his thoughts, almost jumping out of his skin at a sudden knock on the door.

"Tom, you in here?" a familiar voice called out.

Ray scrambled to his feet and spun around as the door swung open. "Buck! I ... " He broke off, struck dumb by the flinty expression on the man's face. He watched with mounting dread as Buck strode over to him, his rifle slung over one shoulder. Lips set in a grim line, he eyed Tom's body stretched out on the floor. After a long moment of silence, he turned to Ray. "You did this."

It was more of a statement than a question, but his tone demanded an explanation.

"It ... was an accident. We were arguing, and ... Tom took a swing at me, so I punched him." Ray swallowed the thickening knot in his throat before continuing, "He tripped and fell backward, and he ... he hit his head on the bench. It knocked the wind out of him, but I thought he was all right. He groaned and went to sit up. I was afraid he might go for his gun—he'd threatened me with it earlier—so I took off ... with Henry."

Buck narrowed his eyes at him.

"You ... knew he had a son, right?" Ray said.

Buck rubbed a hand over his jaw. "Yeah." He frowned. "Where's the kid at?"

Ray wet his lips, trying to buy himself some time to think. He couldn't bring himself to admit to leaving Henry in the truck. He could be prosecuted for leaving a four-year-old alone. Not that it was any worse than the trouble he was already in. "He's ... with a friend."

Ray shifted uncomfortably as Buck's unswerving gaze bored into him. "Look, I didn't come here intending to kill Tom, or even fight with him, for that matter. We got into an argument over Henry. He's been badly neglected. I told Tom it was child abuse to keep him out here without access to education or healthcare. I threatened to report him to the authorities. That's when he lost it and tried to clock me. I reacted instinctively. You have to believe me; this was a horrible accident."

Buck shifted his weight to his back leg, staring down at Tom's body with a pensive look. He tugged on his beard thoughtfully. "I don't doubt things went down like you said. I know what a hothead Tom could be."

Ray let out a heavy sigh. "Thank you. I know it's a huge ask, but if you could just tell the police what you told me—about Tom being a hothead—it might help my case."

Buck mumbled something incoherent and began pacing back-and-forth across the floor. "I'm not going to tell them anything."

"What? Aren't you going to turn me in?"

Buck threw him a cutting glance. "Mountain folks handle their own affairs."

"So what do I do now?" Ray asked, his voice tapering off into a quiver.

"The only thing you can do," Buck replied, a stoic expression on his face. "Bury the body, and keep your mouth shut."

Ray gawked at him. "But someone's bound to report him missing."

Buck grunted in disdain. "You disappear in these parts, folks reckon you either got taken out by a bear, or you disappeared because you wanted to."

Ray silently digested Buck's words. What he said might hold true in this isolated neck of the woods, but, in the real world, it was a crime to dispose of a body improperly, especially someone you had murdered.

Buck reached for a coil of rope hanging on a hook by the door, then walked over to the storage bench and pulled out a blanket. "Best get to it. No sense delaying what needs to be done."

Ray gulped, his legs trembling beneath him at the thought of putting Tom's body in the ground. Could he really do this? If it weren't for Buck, he would head straight back to his truck and turn himself in at the nearest police station. "Why are you helping me?" He choked out.

Buck tossed the blanket and rope next to Tom's body and pressed his lips tightly together. "I'm going to help you under one condition. You take Tom's kid and you raise that boy as your own. He's your blood—he's your responsibility now."

Ray stared at Buck, jaw askew, as the weight of his words sank in. Was he serious? How would he ever be able to look Henry in the eyes and lie to him about what had happened to his father? Besides, he wasn't ready to be a father himself —he might never be ready. Even after years of therapy, he'd never been able to form a deep bond with anyone, much less a child. But he could hardly refuse Buck's demand given the circumstances he found himself in.

"Do we have a deal?" Buck asked.

Ray gave what he hoped was a convincing nod. "Yes, of course. I'm indebted to you for doing this."

Buck waved off his thanks. "Quit rambling. Go outside and fetch a shovel. You'll find one leaning up against the back wall of the cabin.

By the time Ray returned, Buck had already dragged Tom's body onto the blanket. "You might want to search his pockets before I wrap him up," he said, gruffly. "No sense wasting a good knife or a pipe."

Ray swallowed back his trepidation as he approached Tom's body. He still couldn't come to terms with the fact that he'd killed his brother. His chest ached at the thought of how differently this could have played out. They might have been able to establish a real relationship going forward. He would have had a nephew to take fishing—to buy presents for at Christmas. Instead, with one punch, he'd become a criminal, and a father, and now the rest of his life was about to become one big lie.

He knelt at Tom's side and dug around in the outer pockets of his hunting jacket, retrieving a fishing lure and an Irish tin whistle. He stared at the whistle, suddenly overwhelmed by sadness that he'd never heard his brother play it. A part of him wanted to keep it, but it was too dangerous. It was evidence of what he'd done.

After replacing it, he reluctantly slid a hand along the inside pocket of Tom's jacket. His fingers closed over a small piece of plastic. He pulled out a driver's license and stared at it curiously. His heart began to race. Could this be Henry's mother? She looked so young. What was she doing with someone like Tom? He read the name, *Katie Lambert*, repeating it under his breath. It sounded vaguely familiar. His mind raced through the catalog of articles he'd written over the years, searching for a story buried in the recesses of his brain.

And then a headline hit him.

Seventeen-year-old Booneville girl believed to be abducted.

"What ... what are you doing here?" Sonia choked out. "I don't understand—" She broke off, blinking up through the rain at Finn in disbelief. Was she seeing things, disoriented after her fall? It made no sense.

"I'm home on leave," he muttered in a low, urgent tone, crouching down next to her. "I've been keeping an eye on you and Jessica. I put a tracker on your car. But never mind that now. We've got to get out of here before Ray returns. He's dangerous, Sonia. There's a lot you don't know about him. I had a buddy in the army look into him after Jessica told me some disturbing things about him. Trust me, you have no idea who you're dealing with."

Sonia clutched his arm. "Finn, I think he abducted her ... Katie Lambert ... that girl who went missing from Booneville five years ago. I found her driver's license in my car. It fell out of Ray's backpack."

Finn set his jaw in grim determination. "I told you he was a psycho, but you wouldn't listen to me! What if he'd taken Jessica? Do you have it—the license?"

Sonia shook her head. "It's in my car, at the Deep Creek Campground. I ran the battery down. Where are you parked?"

"Down by the main road," Finn replied. "I couldn't risk Ray realizing he was being followed. But we need to go back and get that license first. It's the only evidence we have against him to take to the police. We need to get that creep locked up before he does anything else." He smacked a fist into his palm. "I won't stand for him living next door to my daughter one more day."

Sonia bit her bottom lip to keep it from trembling. "What ... what if he comes back to the car while we're there?"

Finn opened his jacket to reveal a gun strapped to his chest, and then held out a hand to help her to her feet. "I was trained for this. Has it really been so long that you've forgotten?"

Feeling somewhat self-conscious, Sonia placed her hand in his. As his calloused fingers closed around hers, it struck her that she hadn't touched him in seven years—scarcely set eyes on him, for that matter. She winced as she stood and forced her blistered heel into her shoe. "I hurt my hip when I fell."

"Lean on me if you need to," Finn offered, slipping his arm under hers for support. "Which way?"

"Follow the road," Sonia answered. "Although, we should probably try and stay out of view, just in case Ray's discovered I'm not in the car."

They set off for the campground, hugging the edge of the dirt road, allowing themselves the option of diving for cover behind a screen of trees, if need be. Sonia was far from thrilled at the prospect of going back to retrieve the license, but she couldn't argue with Finn's reasoning—it was a crucial piece of evidence. His military training and years of special ops experience gave her some measure of comfort. If it came down to it, he wouldn't hesitate to take Ray out, and he wouldn't be easily ambushed either.

"Jessica didn't say anything about you coming home on leave," Sonia said between breaths.

Finn gave a disgruntled shrug. "I didn't tell her. I figured you wouldn't want me stopping by, and I didn't want to disappoint her."

Sonia bit back the assortment of sarcastic responses that came to mind. He hadn't cared one iota about disappointing her up until now—that's pretty much all he'd done her entire life. The odd phone call here and there hardly equated to being a father. But this wasn't the time to get into a spitting contest with Finn. For once, he had come through for her. And for that she was grateful.

They could talk about him coming by to visit Jessica once they'd retrieved the license and Ray was safely behind bars. Despite Finn's lengthy record of broken promises, Sonia wasn't about to deprive her daughter of the chance to see her father when he was home on leave—no matter how little he deserved it. It would mean the world to Jess—she was still too young to understand what a flakey father he really was.

When the Deep Creek Campground came into view, Finn motioned for Sonia to stay out of sight behind a nearby cluster of trees. "Give me the keys and I'll grab the license."

Sonia pressed the key fob into his palm. "It's in the console."

"Be right back," Finn muttered. "Stay out of sight."

Breath on pause, Sonia watched as he moved stealthily toward the car and slowly cracked the door open. Moments later, he returned and hunkered down next to her. He examined the driver's license and then shook his head sadly. "She looks so young."

"She used to work at The Busy Bean," Sonia said. "She was always so friendly and helpful to everyone."

Finn quirked a wry grin. "Kind of like you, huh? Except this time you picked the wrong person to help. Ray Jenkins is a dangerous man. He's messed up in the head."

"I realize that now," Sonia said. "He told me about his abusive childhood, but I had no idea it had left him so screwed up." She threw a fearful glance over her shoulder. "We should get out of here before he shows back up."

Finn gave a hesitant nod, clenching and unclenching his fist, but made no attempt to move.

"What's wrong?" Sonia asked, picking up on his agitation.

He locked a worried gaze on her. "What if ... she's still alive—that girl, I mean? What if Ray went back up there to finish her off and get rid of the evidence?"

Quivering in fear, Sonia let the picture sit in her mind for a moment. The sounds of the forest grew faint as the thumping of her heart increased. Everything in her railed against spending one more minute here. But her compassionate nature wouldn't allow her off the hook so easily. Finn was right. If Ray was keeping Katie Lambert prisoner somewhere on this mountain, they had to make every effort to find her. Much as she hated to admit it, Finn was well equipped to handle a situation like this. She'd asked him once if he ever got scared on missions. He'd shrugged and told her courage was being scared and doing it anyway. Now was as good a time as any to prove that to herself.

"I have the coordinates to his brother's cabin," she squeaked out. She fished her phone from her purse and pulled up the photo she'd snapped of the map.

Finn frowned. "Where did you get this?"

She hesitated, loathe to admit she'd been snooping around in Ray's closet. "I saw the map on his kitchen counter. I knew he was hiding something, so I took a picture of the coordinates. I meant to look them up later."

Finn grunted as he punched them into his GPS. "I wish you'd stayed away from him to begin with, but, as it turns out, you might have done Katie Lambert's grandparents a favor. Let's go."

Sonia's heart bobbed in her throat as they hiked up through the damp forest in the direction of Tom's cabin. She flinched at every rustle of branches, every startled squirrel that scurried up a tree, every critter that scampered across the mulched leaves on the forest floor. She was still trying to wrap her head around the fact that Finn, of all people, had come to her rescue. Why couldn't he have been there all those times when she'd needed him in the past?

A part of her was furious at him for putting a tracker on her car. Surely that was illegal. But another part of her was grateful that he'd had the gumption to insert himself into the situation, alerted by the red flags she had ignored. Jessica would be ecstatic to see him, and for once she had something to be proud of her father for. But Sonia wasn't going to lead Finn on. If he thought a single, heroic act would be enough to right all past wrongs, he was sorely mistaken. She had no intention of letting him back into her life.

The throbbing in her hip grew worse as they climbed higher, the pain crowding out the questions about Ray she was toying with in her mind. She had lost all track of time when Finn suddenly motioned to her to be quiet.

"What is it?" she whispered, her empty stomach churning up acid.

"I can see a cabin up ahead."

"Any sign of movement?"

Finn didn't answer. Instead, he pulled out a small pair of binoculars and stared silently through them for several minutes.

Sonia couldn't help thinking about the many covert missions he'd been on over the years and how often she'd accused him of putting the military before his family. Maybe she'd been too hard on him for the sacrifices he'd made. It was what he loved to do, after all. And now, he was using his training to protect his family and rid them of the threat next-door. For the first time, she allowed herself to envision how the situation might play out. If Ray came at them with a weapon, Finn would have little choice but to shoot him. And she would have to serve as a witness for the defense. The last time they had gone to court, she had fought him with everything she had, but this time she would have his back.

Finn lowered the binoculars. "I'm going to circle round and approach the cabin from the back. Stay right behind me and try not to make a sound."

Sonia's throat felt torched with fear as they crept quietly through the trees around to the rear of the cabin. Suddenly, Finn came to an abrupt halt and held up a hand.

"What is it? Do you see him?" Sonia whispered.

Finn knelt and gestured to something on the ground in front of him. Sonia leaned over his shoulder, her eyes widening when she caught a glimpse of what he was pointing at.

"Tripwire," he said in a grim tone. "It must trigger some kind of primitive alarm system."

Sonia sucked in a sharp breath. "I can't believe you spotted it!"

He threw her a bemused look. "Bet you're glad I do this kind of thing for a living now, huh? I've been scanning our environment every step of the way. The stakes are a lot higher when it's IED's you're trying to avoid."

"Finn," Sonia stammered. "I know I made it hard for you to choose between the military and your family. Even though things didn't work out between us, I want you to know I appreciate what you do every day for our country."

A flicker of sadness crossed his face before he turned away. "Make sure you don't touch the wire when you step over it."

Gingerly, they made their way up to the cabin. Finn peered through a filthy window. "He's not in the main living area. Looks like there's another smaller room. Wait here."

Sonia darted several nervous glances into the trees while Finn crept around the perimeter of the cabin. She let out a relieved sigh when he reappeared a few minutes later.

"Ray's not here," he said. "We should go inside and search the place anyway. Maybe we'll find something to prove Katie Lambert was here."

Sonia pressed her lips together, reluctant to delay their return any longer. "What if he's watching us from the cover of the trees—waiting on us to go inside? What if it's a trap? He set up a tripwire, after all."

"He's not here. I would know if he'd been following us," Finn said. He padded quietly over to the front door and nudged it slowly inward, sweeping the room with the barrel of his gun. "It's clear," he confirmed, motioning for Sonia to follow him.

She stepped inside, blinking around the shadowy interior. The cabin was surprisingly orderly, a pair of boots lined up neatly by the fireplace, kitchen utensils dangling from hooks in perfect symmetry, a blanket meticulously folded and hanging over the back of a chair. The minimalistic interior was a far cry from Celia's cluttered house where he was currently living. She held her breath as Finn tiptoed across the floor and cracked open the door to the smaller room. " He's not in here." He lowered his weapon. "No sign of the girl either."

"Maybe he took her somewhere," Sonia said. She couldn't bring herself to voice her worst fear—that he'd taken her into the woods to dispose of her.

"I'll take a look around outside and see if I can find any recent footprints," Finn said.

"Be careful," Sonia warned him, wrapping her arms around herself as he disappeared out the door.

She glanced around the cabin with an air of apprehension. Despite Finn's reassurance that Ray wasn't here, she could feel an ominous presence. Maybe there was some kind of hiding spot in the cabin that Finn had overlooked. Frowning, she picked up one of the boots by the fireplace and examined it more closely. They were too big to be Ray's. He wasn't a large man, a good six inches shorter than Finn. Her mind went back to the day Ray had told her about finding his way to his brother's cabin, and the burly stranger who had helped him, a mountain man called Buck. Was it possible they were at the wrong cabin?

The minute Finn reappeared, she blurted out her suspicions. "Finn, take a look at these boots, they're size thirteen. I'm fairly sure Ray's feet are smaller than that. I think we're at the wrong cabin. This might be his neighbor's place. He told me about this mountain man who gave him directions. He called himself—"

"Buck," Finn said, his lips curling into a smile. "I know who he is."

29

"How do you ... " Sonia's voice trailed off at the strange look in Finn's eyes. A swirling mass of confusion invaded her head, muddying her thoughts. "I ... don't understand. How do you know Buck?"

Finn threw back his head and laughed, a caustic laugh that dragged a sack of memories back to the surface she'd sooner forget. The ridicule, the intimidation, the threats like low-lying clouds constantly hanging over her head.

"Sonia, Sonia, Sonia. Ever the trusting, helpful, kind-hearted woman to everyone around her." His cold eyes raked her face. "Except me. You didn't extend the same kindness to me when you shoved those divorce papers under my nose, did you?"

"Stop it, Finn! This isn't about us. Ray's still out there somewhere, and he might have Katie with him. Maybe Buck can help us track him down. How do you know him anyway? Is he military?"

Finn laughed again in an overly casual manner that didn't jive with the danger they were in. "He was—up until his dishonorable discharge six years ago when he lost his benefits and moved up into the mountains."

Sonia frowned. "I don't remember you mentioning anyone called Buck being discharged from the army."

Finn folded his arms in front of his chest, studying her like she was a petulant child. "Sonia, my love. I am Buck."

"What ... what are you talking about?" Sonia stumbled backward, her legs wobbling beneath her.

Finn gestured around him with a jerk of his chin "How do you like the place?" His lips curled into a cunning smile. "I fixed it up with you in mind."

Sonia retreated another couple of steps, her thoughts colliding with her senses in an explosion of terror. "But you ... you were on a mission last month. That's why you couldn't call Jessica on her birthday."

Finn let out an amused snort. "I was on a mission of sorts. I was hunting."

"You mean ... you haven't been overseas all this time?" Sonia asked in a breathless whisper.

Finn chuckled, clearly enjoying watching her struggle to catch up to the reality of the situation. But what exactly was that reality? And what did he mean by saying that he'd fixed up the cabin with her in mind? She needed to keep him talking—try and figure out what was going on in his head. "I still don't understand, Finn. How did you keep up the child support payments without your benefits?"

He pulled a chair out from the table and motioned for her to sit down. She sank down in it gratefully, unable to stop the shivering that had taken over her entire body. Finn leaned back against the table, his cruel eyes skewering her. " I told you I'd always provide for our daughter. I found a way."

"How?" Sonia demanded. "You're obviously not working

if you're living up here. Did you steal the money or something?"

He gave a reproving shake of his head. "You never did have any faith in me, did you? Of course I didn't steal it. I didn't have to. Our delightful neighbor, Celia, was only too happy to help when I shared our plight with her. I fed her a sob story about how the assault charges that led to my discharge were bogus, and how much Jessica was going to suffer if I wasn't able to provide for her."

He leaned closer, his breath hot on her cold skin. "I also told her you would use it as an opportunity to cut me out of my daughter's life entirely if I got behind on the child support payments, and how desperately I wanted to patch up our family. Celia offered to give me the money. She was very fond of Jessica. I think she took pity on me because she knew what it was like to have an estranged child she never got to see. I used to call her every month—she liked that. I told her to say it was Tom if anyone ever asked."

Sonia stared at him, appalled, her brain grappling to take it all in. "You were taking money from Celia Jenkins to support our child?"

"See, that's precisely the reaction I expected you to have." Finn cocked an amused grin. "I warned Celia not to mention it to you because you wouldn't accept the help. I told her my brave military wife would be too proud."

Sonia shook her head in disbelief. "How could you? Were you the one who stole her purse that time too?"

Finn smirked. "Stupid cow left it sitting out in plain view on the kitchen table with the door unlocked. What did she think was going to happen?"

Sonia glared at him. "The child support was only $1100. What did you do with the rest of the money?"

A sly grin spread over Finn's face. "I knew old Celia

wouldn't last forever. I've been building a nice little nest egg so I can take care of you and Jessica. You see, when Celia showed me the coordinates to her son's cabin and asked me to find him, I realized it would be the perfect spot to move my family to. I befriended Tom and took over this abandoned cabin. I cleaned it all up and patched the roof, and even added on a room so I could build a bunker beneath it." He paused and gestured to the door that led into the smaller room. "I'll show you around your new digs in a minute. "Anyway, I told Celia I couldn't find Tom— that he'd moved on and hadn't told anyone where he was going. I knew he would have a good chunk of money coming to him once Celia passed, so I planned on getting his signature giving me power of attorney over his inheritance."

"Where ... is Tom?" Sonia stammered, dreading the answer.

Finn gave a mockingly sad shake of his head. "Ray killed him. Couldn't stand to share the inheritance with him. I heard them fighting over it. A shame, really. I liked the guy."

Sonia's breath came in short, sharp bursts as she tried to digest the information quickly enough to keep up. Conveniently, Tom was dead. She had no doubt Finn had somehow orchestrated that, despite what he was telling her. But where was Ray, and how did he play into this? Maybe he'd found out that the transfers had been going into Finn's account all along and he'd come here to confront him.

Her blood ran cold when it occurred to her that Finn had had plenty of time to prepare for their arrival. He might even have watched Ray get out of her car and followed him up to his brother's cabin. Had he killed him too in a bid to get his hands on the rest of Celia's money? Her heart sank when she thought of Henry and what it would do to him if anything happened to his father. "Where's Ray?" she asked, in a jittery whisper.

A cunning smile spread across Finn's face. "He's on a mission to save poor little Katie Lambert before it's too late. He knows who the bad guy is who took her."

A cold chill crept slowly over Sonia. So if Ray hadn't abducted her, was Finn behind that too? "You know where Katie is, don't you?"

"How perceptive of you, my love. I'm afraid Ray's going to be extremely disappointed when his gallant rescue mission comes to a screeching halt."

Sonia lunged at Finn, dragging her nails across his face and drawing blood. "Is Katie dead? Were you and Tom in on this together? Did you kill him to stop him from talking? Did Ray find the driver's license in Tom's cabin?"

"Whoa! So many questions," Finn said in a mocking tone as he shoved her back down in the chair. "Save them, for now. I'm going to track Ray down and let him know you're safe." He let out an amused chuckle. "Then I'll offer him a generator to charge your car battery. Of course, he'll have to come back to the cabin to pick it up."

"Finn, I'm begging you, please. Leave Ray out of this. He has a young son and—"

"Henry, right? Four-years-old, dark curls, big round eyes, sucks his thumb?"

Sonia's stomach dropped. "How .... how do you know all this?"

"I knew his mother." Finn twisted one corner of his lips into a cruel smile, watching her reaction—as if waiting for something to click. And then it hit her like a thunderbolt. No wonder Henry had looked vaguely familiar. *He had Katie Lambert's eyes.* But that wasn't the only resemblance she'd picked up on.

Her gaze traveled slowly over Finn's thick, dark wavy hair as she finally connected the dots.

Finn was Henry's father.

30

Reeling from everything Buck had told him, Ray stumbled back down the slick mountainside in the direction of the Deep Creek Campground parking lot where he'd left Sonia. *Henry was Tom's son*. It all made perfect sense now. It explained why he and Henry had always felt like strangers to one another, and why, after his accident, he hadn't even remembered he had a son. No wonder Henry acted so traumatized around him, so bereft of words—he barely knew him. He'd been confused by a man who looked like his father, pretending to be him.

The only question left in Ray's mind was who Henry's mother was. But, deep down, he was pretty sure he already knew the answer to that. The driver's license he'd found in Tom's pocket was a cry for justice from beyond the grave. If he was right that Katie Lambert was Henry's mother, then Tom was even more of a sadistic monster than he'd thought him to be. He'd abducted a young girl and imprisoned her for his own evil purposes, either in his cabin or in some shack nearby—a girl who might still be alive. Henry talked about her as though he remembered her. He'd mentioned playing ball with her in his room. Just like he remembered being locked up and deprived of food, and all the other terrible things Tom had done to him.

Sickened to the core, Ray quickened his pace through the thick drizzle, relieved when the campground parking lot finally came into view. As soon as he got back to the main road, he would call 911. He would keep Henry out of it—for now. He jogged over to Sonia's car, groaning in frustration when he saw she wasn't there. He desperately needed to get off this mountain to process everything whirling around in his head. More than anything, he needed to figure out how he was going to move forward shackled by what he had done, and the lies he had bound himself to. He cast an uneasy glance at his surroundings, confirming that Sonia was nowhere in sight.

"Sonia!" he called out, walking over to the outhouse. "Are you in here?" He nudged the swing door gingerly inward, recoiling from the stench and the flies buzzing around. Maybe she'd got bored and decided to stretch her legs and take a walk. After all, he'd been gone for several hours. Returning to the car, he tried the door, surprised to find it unlocked. Perhaps she'd left him a note. He slid into the passenger seat and rummaged around. The keys were lying in the console so she couldn't have gone too far. There was nothing else for it but to hunker down and wait for her to return.

His head throbbed every time he thought about Tom lying beneath the dirt on the mountain somewhere, without so much as a headstone to mark his grave. Buck had helped jog his memory of that awful day. He remembered bits and pieces—fetching the shovel, agreeing to bury Tom in an unmarked grave. Accident or not, it was too horrific to dwell on what had happened, and too painful to think about what might have been if they could only have kept their anger in check.

Searching for a distraction, Ray reached into the backseat for Sonia's black portfolio and flipped through it curiously. Her eye for detail was extraordinary. He couldn't help but admire her artistic skills, as well as her generous nature. She'd sacrificed an entire day to drive him out here, purportedly to allow him to heal in nature. A stab of guilt assailed him. He'd lied to her and used her, and now he would be forced to keep lying to her. There was nothing she hated more. She deserved better.

He drummed his fingers on the dashboard wondering what time she had to be back in Booneville to pick up Jessica. Maybe if he started the engine, it would alert her to the fact that he'd returned. He stuck the key in the ignition and twisted it, his stomach sinking at the unmistakable metallic clicking sound that followed. Somehow, she'd let the battery run down.

Maybe she'd decided to walk down to the main road to get help. Or maybe she'd gone looking for him. Ray slapped a frustrated palm on the dash before climbing back out of the car. What was she thinking heading out alone in this rain? Why couldn't she just have waited until he got back— hopefully, she hadn't gone too far.

He set off at a brisk pace down the dirt track, counting on the fact that she would most likely head to the main road first to call for roadside assistance. Every few minutes, he stopped and called out her name, listening for even the faintest response. He had to consider the possibility that she might have slipped in the mud and twisted an ankle or something. Fifteen minutes later, sweating and hurting, he hadn't found any trace of her. If he reached the main road, and there was still no sign of her, he'd be forced to trek all the way back up to Tom's cabin in case she'd headed up the mountain to look for him.

Leaning on his thighs, he took a few deep breaths, exhausted from the exertion. As he lifted his head, a familiar figure came trudging into view. Relief surged through him. "Buck!" he blurted out. "You couldn't have timed that better! I need your help. My friend who drove me here has gone missing. Her car battery's dead. I think she might have set out to look for me."

Buck chuckled. "That she did. I found her wandering on the mountain, half-drowned and disoriented. I took her to my place and told her to sit tight in front of the fire while I tracked you down. Her heels were all blistered up from those stupid canvas shoes she was wearing."

Ray blew out a heavy breath. "That's a relief to hear she's safe. Now I just need to figure out how I'm going to jump-start her car. I guess I'll keep hiking down to the main road and hitch a ride into town. It could be a few hours before I'm back."

"No need," Buck said. "I have jumper cables and a generator you can borrow."

"Really? Wow, that would be a huge help." Ray cleared his throat. "Listen, Buck, obviously I can't say anything in front of Sonia, but I didn't thank you properly earlier for what you did. To be honest, I'm totally torn up about it. With the concussion and everything, I'd forgotten a lot of what happened. But I realize I owe you a huge debt of gratitude."

Buck gripped Ray by the shoulder. "We did what we had to do for the kid's sake. Enough said."

"Thanks, man," Ray replied. "By the way, your cheek's bleeding."

Buck brushed a hairy hand nonchalantly over it. "Yeah, I

took a shortcut through some heavy brush. Wasn't paying attention. I was in too much of a hurry to find you. Speaking of which, we should make tracks so we can get you guys back on the road before dark."

They hiked at a steady pace, stopping once or twice for Ray to catch his breath. He was hurting all over but determined not to complain. The sooner he got the car started, and got back to the main road, the sooner he could call 911. He hadn't told Buck what he was planning to do. Buck was convinced Tom had long since killed Katie and buried her, and he'd made it clear he didn't want police crawling all over the mountain. But Katie's grandparents deserved answers—the right to give their granddaughter a proper burial, if nothing else.

"Nice place you have here," Ray said politely when Buck's log home came into view. It was more spacious than Tom's, but utilitarian-looking—lacking the craftsmanship that Tom had painstakingly worked into every detail of his cabin.

"Well, you know what they say, it's not much, but it's home," Buck chuckled, ushering him inside.

"Where's Sonia?" Ray asked, glancing around.

"She's sleeping in the other room. I told her to make herself at home while I was gone. She was exhausted and her heels were bleeding pretty badly." He led the way across the cabin to the adjoining room, opened the door, and stepped aside for Ray to enter.

Shock tightened around Ray's chest like cords of rope at the scene that awaited him. Sonia was sitting on the floor in the far corner of the room, gagged and zip tied, her feet fastened to an iron ring in the floor next to a wooden trapdoor. He spun around, only to find himself staring down the barrel of a gun.

"Walk slowly over there and sit down next to her," Buck growled. "Sonia will tie your hands for you. If you don't cooperate, I'll shoot her."

Ray opened his mouth to protest, but the look in Buck's eyes stopped him in his tracks. He inched his hands into the air. "All right. Take it easy. Do you want to tell me what's going on here?"

Buck's lips curled into a malevolent grin as he waved the gun impatiently in front of him. "We'll get to the fun part."

Ray grimaced, assessing his limited options. Faced with a deadly weapon, he had little choice but to comply with Buck's orders and try to reason with him afterward. He walked over to Sonia and sat down next to her on the dirt floor, eying the zip tie in her trembling fingers. "It's okay, do what he says," he whispered, holding out his hands to her. Hampered by the zip tie around her own wrists, it took her several attempts before she succeeded.

When she was done, Buck tightened their wrist restraints, and then fastened Ray's feet to the ring in the floor. Satisfied that their bonds were secure, he removed Sonia's gag, then sat down on a wooden stool and eyed them both with an air of satisfaction.

"I don't understand, Buck," Ray said. "Is this about money? Are you going to try and blackmail me now for covering up what I did?"

"His name's not Buck," Sonia said, her eyes filling with tears. "It's Finn—he's Jessica's father ... and Henry's."

31

Ray blinked uncomprehendingly at Sonia, wrestling with which shocking revelation to respond to first. "What are you talking about? Henry's Tom's son—he's my nephew."

"No." Sonia shook her head. "Finn lied to you about that. He's Henry's real father."

"But ... you told me Finn was stationed overseas."

Sonia's face crumpled. "I thought he was. He lied. He's been lying about everything. He's not even with the army anymore."

Ray turned his head slowly in Finn's direction, his stomach twisting as he grappled with the enormity of what was becoming clearer by the minute. "Tom didn't abduct Katie Lambert—it was you! You planted that driver's license on my brother's body, didn't you? Sent me outside to get that shovel so you could set me up. You saw the perfect opportunity to cover up your crime along with mine."

Finn sneered at him. "Yeah, about that, Einstein. Tom wasn't dead after your puny right hook, just dazed. It took a few good whacks with the butt of my rifle to finish him off. He was a tough old bird."

A chill passed over the back of Ray's neck. Of course! All that blood. It had never made sense that Tom bled that much after hitting his head on the bench. His death had been no accident. It had been a cold-blooded and heartless murder—perpetrated on a helpless man.

"Why?" Ray whispered. "What did Tom ever do to you?"

"It's not about what he did; it's about what he knew," Finn said, lifting his gaze to stare out the window. "Turns out Katie was a lot more resourceful than I gave her credit for." He gestured to the trapdoor in the floor. "I kept her and the boy in the bunker when I wasn't around. When I was home, I sometimes let them stay up here so they could move about. I was chopping wood at the back of the cabin one day, and she managed to pick the lock on the door with a nail and escape with Henry. Took me a couple of hours to track her down, but I found her, eventually, hiding in a hollowed-out tree like a scared rabbit." He fell silent, anger sparking in his steely eyes. "She wouldn't tell me where she'd hidden Henry. Tom must have found him shortly before you showed up at his cabin—probably heard him whimpering or something. Henry wasn't much of a talker, but he knew his mother's name. It wouldn't have taken Tom long to put two and two together. I couldn't let him live."

"And Katie?" Sonia asked, fixing an accusing gaze on Finn. "Where is she?"

Finn grinned, and began crooning in a mocking fashion. "If you go down to the woods today, you're sure of a big surprise." He laughed and slapped his thigh. "The forest's full of wild surprises, my love: bear, wild boar, coyotes, cougars. Take your pick."

"You're the only animal here!" Sonia spat at him. "You killed her, didn't you?"

Finn laughed again before turning back to Ray. "I wasn't looking for a dog that day when I bumped into you—I was looking for Katie. She fought me like a banshee when I found her, screaming and hollering. I had to get rid of her. I passed Tom's cabin on my way back and overheard you telling him Celia was dead. And then you two started getting into it over Tom neglecting his son. I hung around and watched you take off with Henry. When I saw Tom trying to get up off the floor, I knew it was my chance to unload Henry on you."

"How could you murder two innocent people in cold blood like that?" Sonia screamed at him. "Are we next, Finn? Is that your grand finale?"

He smoothed a hand over his beard. "It doesn't have to be. I have a proposal for Ray if he decides to cooperate."

Ray scowled at him. "That depends on what you have in mind."

"You agree to sign Celia's estate over to me, and I'll let you live. Of course, I'll have to keep you in the bunker until the money hits my account, but, once it does, I'll put in an anonymous call to the police and let them know where to find you."

"And if I agree, what about Sonia?" Ray asked.

Finn narrowed his eyes. "You got something going with my wife, or what? Why do you care what happens to her? She goes where I go."

"I'm not your wife anymore!" Sonia hissed through gritted teeth.

"Either she stays here with me, or there's no deal," Ray said.

Finn smirked. "That's heroic. She can stay here, for now,

so long as you keep up your end of the bargain. Otherwise, you'll both be digging graves by the light of the moon."

"You've done nothing but lie to me ever since I met you," Ray said. "Why should I believe you now?"

Finn gave a nonchalant shrug. "Your choice." He ran a finger along the gun in his hands. "So, do you want to die today, or do you want to sign the paperwork I left at Tom's cabin?"

Ray threw Sonia a searching look. Her pale face was streaked with tears and dirt, her hair damp and tangled, and her eyes filled with the fear of prey that had walked into a trap and knew it was a fatal blunder. This was all his fault. He had dragged her into this mess by asking her to drive him to the cabin. Somehow, he needed to get her out of here. The first step was to buy some time. "All right, I'll sign it."

Finn grunted his approval and got to his feet. He paused at the door and flashed them a broad grin. "Tell you what, I'll even throw in Henry for good measure. Then you can all be one big happy family."

Ray clenched his teeth until the sound of Finn's maniacal laughter gradually faded.

"I'm so sorry—" he began.

Sonia cut him off. "No, I'm the one who should be sorry. I can't believe my family has been living off your mother for the past five years—stealing from her."

"You didn't know," Ray said. "That was all on Finn."

Sonia shook her head. "I should have been paying more attention to what was going on. I remember thinking at one point it was odd that I wasn't getting military-related correspondence anymore. But to be honest, I was just so glad to have Finn out of our lives that I didn't question it. I didn't even notice that the child support had started coming from

a new account. I never told your mother Finn was abusive—
I didn't want Jessica to find out. If only I'd said something,
he would never have been able to dupe her like he did."

"None of this is your fault," Ray assured her. "I really am
sorry I dragged you into this mess, and I'm sorry for lying to
you about my wife dying of cancer. I made that up to shut
down any questions about Henry's mother. It's all coming
back to me bit by bit."

Sonia suppressed a sob. "Finn was so angry when I filed
for divorce. He always told me he would win in the end. If
he kills me, he'll get custody of Jessica."

"Henry too," Ray added grimly. "But we're not going to
let that happen. We need to figure out a way to escape
before he gets back. He has no intention of letting us live
once he gets his hands on the money. You heard him. He'll
march us into the forest and make us dig our own graves.
We have no chance of escaping with a gun trained on us.
This is our best shot."

Sonia threw a helpless look around. "How exactly are we
supposed to get out of here?"

"I'm not sure," Ray admitted. "But Katie did it."

Sonia bit down on her lip. "I can't believe she spent the
past few years in a bunker. She must have been terrified."

"Sounds like Finn gave her some freedom after Henry
was born. She was likely so conditioned by then—what do
they call it, Stockholm syndrome or something—that Finn
never imagined she would try to escape."

Sonia wiped her bound hands over her eyes. "I wish she
could have known that Henry was safe before she died."

"All this time I thought it was Tom who'd abused him,"
Ray said. "I feel sick to my stomach every time I think about
the things that I accused my brother of. He was only trying
to help Henry escape. That's why he hid him in the loft bed

—in case Finn came by. He was probably planning to take him to our mother's place—he had nowhere else to go." He hesitated before adding softly. "He might even have told Henry he was his real dad so he would feel safe with him."

Sonia smiled sadly at him. "Your brother was a good man. He died a hero."

Ray pressed his lips together tightly. "He shouldn't have died at all. If I hadn't been so angry with him, he might have confided in me. But he hadn't seen me in twenty years, and he didn't trust me. Not that I blame him—I was from the outside world that had only ever let him down. It's my fault he's dead."

"No, Finn killed him," Sonia said firmly. "All we can do to honor Tom now is fight to stay alive. We can start by finding something to cut these ties with."

Ray gave an absent nod, eying a blanket just out of reach in the corner of the floor. If he lay on his back and extended his hands over his head, he might be able to grab a corner. Maybe there would be something useful underneath it. He wriggled into position and stretched out on the dirt floor. It took several attempts, but he finally succeeded in grasping the edge of the blanket between his fingers. Grunting, he tugged it toward him, revealing a small blue notebook.

"That must be Katie's," Sonia muttered, her voice breaking.

"I can't reach it," Ray said, sitting back up. "Anyway, it's not going to help us get out of here. I was hoping for some tools or a knife." He frowned in concentration, trying for several minutes to free his feet, before turning his attention to his hands. After a few minutes, he gave up, his wrists too raw to keep at it. There was no point in trying to dig out the iron ring either—no doubt Finn had some heavy-duty anchor securing it in place.

Frustrated, he eyed the hardback notebook lying just out of reach. Maybe he could tear off the cover and use it as leverage to force the zip tie over his wrists somehow. Holding one end of the blanket, he threw it over the book and, after several tries, gradually managed to tug it toward him. Sonia reached for it and opened it, flicking through pages of accomplished sketches—everything from beach scenes to birthday parties.

"This is heartbreaking," Sonia said in a hoarse whisper. "This was how Katie showed Henry the outside world."

"We're wasting time," Ray chided. "We need to focus on getting out of here."

Sonia frowned, turning the book sideways to examine a drawing. "Hey! Check it out! It's a picture of this room."

Trying to mask his irritation, Ray glanced at the sketch. It was an amateurish attempt, obviously Henry's handiwork, but one small detail caught his attention. Beneath the iron ring was a handful of tiny dashes—too exact to have been drawn by a four-year-old. His eye traveled across the page to the clumsy attempt at a door. Right below the lock was another small dash. Ray gasped as Finn's words flashed to mind.

Turns out Katie was a lot more resourceful than I gave her credit for.

He tapped a finger excitedly on the dashes. "Those are nails! Katie buried them to hide them from Finn! She's drawn one below the lock to show what they are—probably for Henry's sake, in case anything ever happened to her."

His eyes locked with Sonia's, and a flicker of hope passed between them.

"Hurry!" Ray said urgently. "We don't have much time."

Rivulets of sweat ran down his back as he worked, digging like a rabid dog for a bone. He struggled to loosen the dirt around the ring until his cramped fingers began to bleed.

"It's no use," Sonia sobbed, kicking at the ring in frustration.

"Don't give up, yet!" Ray urged. "It's our only chance." Wincing, he drove his bloodied fingers deeper into the dirt —yelping when the tip of his finger touched something sharp. "I've got something!" he gasped.

Scrabbling at the dirt, he uncovered a handful of three-inch rusty nails, wrapped in a scrap of paper.

"What is it?" Sonia asked.

Ray carefully unfurled the slip of paper and read it aloud. "Remember us: Katie Rose Lambert, born June 02, 1999, and Henry Jackson Lambert, born April 04, 2017."

Ray glanced over at Sonia's sorrow-stricken face.

"She was too young to die," she whispered.

"I wish we could have saved her," Ray said. He gestured to the nails. "It looks like she might have saved us."

Sonia brushed the tears from her lashes. "How? We can't pick the lock if we can't reach the door."

"No, but we can use the nails as a weapon. If we can't walk out of here, we'll have to fight our way out."

"But Finn has a gun," Sonia said dubiously.

"That's why we'll have to use the element of surprise," Ray replied. "We'll conceal the nails in our fingers—kind of like the brass knuckles prisoners use—and then when one of us gets close enough to him, we go for his neck. Maybe I'll get a chance when he gives me the paperwork to sign."

"You mean ... kill him," Sonia said breathlessly.

Ray scooted closer and fixed an earnest gaze on her. "Listen to me, Sonia. We have two small children who are depending on us. If Finn kills us, they'll both be at his mercy. You need to be prepared to do whatever it takes to protect them from this monster."

A light seemed to go on in Sonia's head and she nodded. "All right, I'll do it—whatever it takes."

TIME DRAGGED on and the light was beginning to fade, but eventually the heavy tread of footsteps signaled Finn's return to the cabin. Sonia immediately lay down on her side and tucked her hands between her legs, feigning sleep. Ray pulled his knees to his chest, heart thumping as he waited for the key to turn in the lock. Moments later, the door creaked inward and Finn's imposing frame filled the doorway. In one hand, he held a lantern which he set on the small table in the corner of the room, before striding over to them. "I'm sure you two had a nice chat while I was gone. Time to get down to business now." He reached inside his jacket and pulled out a pen and some paperwork. "Sign here," he barked, thrusting it under Ray's nose.

"You know this won't hold up," Ray said, glancing at the documents. "You need a notary to witness this."

"Let me worry about the technicalities," Finn replied with a sly grin. "I have an ex-military buddy who owes me a favor."

Ray slid a glance at Sonia who was pretending to stir in her sleep. Gripping the pen awkwardly between his fingers, he signed the form Finn held out in front of him.

"Much obliged," Finn sneered, slipping the paperwork back into his pocket. He kicked Sonia with his boot, and she yelped, her eyes popping open. Cowering from him, she pulled herself into a sitting position.

"It's time you and I had a little talk in private," Finn said, leaning over to cut her feet free from the iron ring. The minute he did, she fell on her knees in front of him, sobbing dramatically.

"Please let me go, Finn. Jessica needs me. I swear I won't breathe a word of this to anyone. Do what you want to Ray. Just let me go back home to our baby."

Shock decimated through Ray's brain. He slowed his breathing, trying to think through the fog of fatigue and confusion closing in on him like a dark hood—the prelude to his execution. What was Sonia doing? His trust in everyone had been eroded. Why should he hope it would be any different now? The dreadful thought that she was selling him out hung there for an elongated moment. If he was going to survive this ordeal, it wouldn't be by relying on anyone else. He tried to stem the relentless surge of panic shooting through his veins as he worked feverishly to retrieve the nails from his sleeve and position them between his fingers.

Finn reached down and seized Sonia by the hair. As he hauled her to her feet, she flew at him like a wildcat, plunging the nails between her fingers into his neck. Blind-sided by the attack, he staggered backward, roaring in pain, his hands reaching for his neck, spurting blood.

Hope and determination fused as one, powering Ray into action. In a burst of speed, he grabbed Finn by the ankle and toppled him. Struggling to gain the upper hand, Ray yanked the gun from Finn's holster and aimed it at him, adrenalin pulsing through his veins. "Stay down, or I'll shoot."

Groaning, Finn rolled onto his side and made a feeble attempt to get to his knees. He tried to say something, but the only thing that came from his throat was a dying gurgle.

Lost in her thoughts, Sonia stirred the pot of chicken chowder she was making for Sunday brunch. It was one of her mother's old recipes—a feel-good staple from her childhood. She had invited Ray and Henry to join them, knowing they wouldn't be around for too many more weekends. The nostalgic aroma wafting into her nostrils brought a smile to her lips as she recalled the many happy, carefree days she'd enjoyed as a kid.

She hadn't had a productive week of work since Finn's death—*since she had killed him.* What she had done hung over her at times like a dense cloud, invading her sleep at night, thwarting her ability to think straight by day. A tightly wound ball of grief and pain remained stubbornly lodged in her throat, the ever-present threat of tears like pepper in her eyes. *A classic case of PTSD,* her therapist had explained. The trauma of enduring years of abuse had resurfaced, demanding to be heard now that her abuser was dead.

In the early years of their marriage, Sonia had spent many a sleepless night worrying about Finn stepping on an IED, or dying under a barrage of enemy fire, or laying down his life in some equally heroic fashion. Never in a million years had she imagined he would die at her own hand—anything but a hero.

Killing someone, especially the man you had promised to *love and cherish until death do you part,* was proving to be no easy thing to live with. Ray, on the other hand, had been mercifully released from the terrible burden of believing he had killed his brother. She was happy for him, of course. But every time Sonia went to sleep and woke up again, the stark reality of her situation remained unchanged—Finn was dead, and she had killed him.

It wasn't that she didn't think he deserved to die for the reprehensible things he had done. She could scarcely comprehend that the man she had been married to, the father of her beautiful daughter, had conducted such a vile, secret life and successfully hidden it from her and the rest of the world for almost a decade.

The full extent of his crimes had sent shock waves through their close-knit community. As it turned out, Katie Lambert wasn't the only girl he had abducted. The police had found three additional drivers' licenses in his cabin belonging to missing girls from as far away as Pennsylvania, triggering a full-blown investigation by the FBI. A massive search of the area had been underway for months, but the most they could realistically hope to recover at this point were remains.

The doorbell rang, and her mother called to her from the family room, "Sonia! Ray and Henry are here. I'll get the door."

She turned down the gas ring to simmer and hurriedly wiped her hands on her linen apron just as Henry burst into the kitchen. "I made this for you," he announced, waving a drawing of a smiling woman with elongated fingers dancing in a field of flowers beneath a cheery sun. "I had to color you purple because the puppy ate my brown crayon and my dad said we didn't have time to go to the store to buy any more."

"I love it!" Sonia exclaimed, beaming at Henry as she embraced him. *My dad.* He said it with such pride that it melted Sonia's heart. He'd blossomed into quite the little talker over the past few weeks—even Jessica was finding it hard to get a word in edgewise. Henry was still pale from years of captivity, and small for his age, but Evelyn was doing her level best to fatten him up with an endless supply of casseroles and baked goods, which he eagerly devoured. He looked and acted like a completely different kid with his new haircut and chirpy demeanor. Even his big, brown eyes, so like his young mother's, had lost their air of sadness.

Only from his profile could Sonia detect any resemblance at all to Finn—not enough for anyone to pick up on. That would remain her and Ray's secret, at least until Henry was grown. Ray had kept Katie's sketchbook, in case he decided to tell Henry the truth one day. It was evidence that should probably have been turned over to the police, but with Finn dead, it hardly mattered.

"Jessica's waiting for you in her room. She has a new Lego set she wants you to help her with," Sonia said, ruffling Henry's hair affectionately before releasing him to run off down the hallway. A part of her wished Celia could have met him—the grandchild she'd always wanted—but it would have been disingenuous to have kept the truth of his real parentage from her. It was hard enough keeping it from her own mother, but Evelyn couldn't be trusted not to let it slip.

The consequences of CPS getting involved in the situation didn't bear thinking about. Henry needed a father, and Ray needed a family—an equation with a simple solution as far as Sonia was concerned. Ray had run from love for far too long. Now he would discover just how much love he had to give. Her instincts about him had been right—he was a good man. He would be a great father, sensitive and caring, and able to understand Henry's needs in a way few others could.

"I can't believe the change in Henry in a few short months," Sonia said, when Ray appeared in the kitchen with Evelyn's arm tucked into his.

"He talks non-stop from the minute he gets up in the morning," Ray said, peering into the pot on the stove. "That sure smells good."

"It's a chicken chowder recipe from my childhood," Sonia replied. "Mom always made the best chowder."

"We're going old-fashioned all the way today—apple pie and homemade vanilla ice cream for dessert," Evelyn chimed in, dragging him over to show him the freshly baked pie she had left cooling on the counter. "The quickest way to a man's heart is my pie crust," she added, with a wink. "I'll leave you two to catch up. I'm going to check on the kids."

Sonia caught Ray's eye and gave a wry grin, shaking her head as she set a pitcher of lemonade on the table. It was no secret Evelyn had done a one-eighty and was now on a mission to marry off her daughter to the eligible bachelor-next-door. Unfortunately for Evelyn, she was barking up the wrong tree. Ray was planning to put the house up for sale and move back to Virginia with Henry.

He was ready to put this chapter of his life with its haunting memories behind him now that he'd fully recovered from his accident—an accident the police were now looking at as suspicious given Finn's attempts to get his hands on Celia's money.

Ray's friends and neighbors back in Richmond were

eager to meet Henry—purportedly a nephew he was in the process of adopting. It would be a fresh start for Henry in a Kindergarten class where no one knew his history. The further he was from Booneville, the less chance of anyone discovering the truth.

Sonia harbored some measure of regret at not being able to tell Jessica that she really did have the little brother she'd always longed for. But Jessica and Henry, more than anyone, had to be protected from the awful truth. It was more than they could handle at their impressionable ages. That was something she and Ray agreed on. It still turned her stomach to think of what Henry had suffered through— the bunker he had lived in, and the terrible things he'd been forced to witness: Finn choking his mother, tethering her to an iron ring like an animal—the *never tell them* things.

"How did the paint job in Celia's kitchen turn out?" Sonia asked, opening the dishwasher and lifting out some clean glasses.

"You were right about the color choice," Ray said with a chuckle. "It looks fantastic, brightened the whole place up. I should have known better than to question your impeccable judgment."

Sonia had spent the past several weekends helping Ray redecorate and stage Celia's house after he'd gone through and tossed out all the junk that couldn't be donated. In fact, it had inspired her to do the same. She'd even gone so far as to empty out the storage tubs in the attic that hadn't been opened since Finn left. Apart from a small box of items she was saving for Jessica to go through at some future date, she had gotten rid of every other memory of Finn, including her "fairytale" wedding dress and album.

It had been hard to incinerate the dream, but the truth was it had only ever been a dream. Finn was never the man she thought she'd married. She had sat down with his superior officer and an FBI agent only last week and been shocked to learn there had been rumors of several previous incidents of sexual harassment before the alleged assault that cost Finn his military career. The first incident had taken place only six months into their marriage. A shudder ran across her shoulders as she set the glasses on the table. At one point, she'd been afraid the stranger next door might be a serial killer—turns out she'd been married to one.

"Are you okay?" Ray inquired, pulling out a chair at the kitchen table for her.

She shrugged as she sank down in it. "As well as can be expected. I'm still in shock over all the additional assault allegations the FBI told me about last week. I mean, I always knew Finn was a bully, but even after we divorced, I tried to focus on the good. I wanted Jessica to be proud of her father. She thought he was a war hero—serving his country on covert missions. Turns out even that was a lie." She gave a hollow laugh. "You know, Tom was the real hero. He died fighting a war worth fighting—he saved a child."

Ray gave a pensive nod. "I like that. It's a good way to remember him. It's been hard not being able to hold a service for him."

"At least you can be proud of him," Sonia said, pouring them each a lemonade. "I have only shame over who Finn was—not to mention over what I did to him. I keep second-guessing my actions."

"You did the right thing, Sonia. You have nothing to regret," Ray assured her. "The shock of it all is only just beginning to sink in. You need to be patient with yourself. Isn't that what you told me after my accident? It's going to take time to process everything."

Sonia took a sip of her lemonade. "You sound like my

therapist. He keeps telling me I need to compartmentalize what I did. Accept that I acted in self-defense."

"He's right. What you did was every bit as heroic as what Tom did."

"And what you're doing is noble," Sonia said, fixing a steady gaze on him. "Taking on Finn's child."

"As far as I'm concerned, I've been given a gift. Henry's given me a whole new lease on life," Ray said, his voice laden with emotion. "It's a chance to see the world through the eyes of a child—something I never had. And it helps that I understand the pain of neglect and abuse. I think I can be the dad Henry needs."

"I know you can," Sonia said, smiling at him. "He's a great kid. Jessica is really going to miss him."

And I'm going to miss you.

She couldn't bring herself to say it. They were both too damaged. Too hurt. Too wounded. And two broken people don't make a whole.

But brokenness didn't have to be their final destination.

True north lay in the hope of a new tomorrow.

And the sun always rises.

~

RIGHT BEHIND YOU

Ready for another thrilling read with shocking twists and a mind-blowing murder plot? Check out my psychological thriller *Right Behind You* on Amazon! Releasing December 2021.

- A gripping tale of explosive secrets with a jaw-dropping twist!

-

Do you enjoy reading across genres? I also write young adult science fiction and fantasy thrillers. You can find out more about those titles at **www.normahinkens.com.**

A QUICK FAVOR

Dear Reader,

I hope you enjoyed reading *Never Tell Them* as much as I enjoyed writing it. Thank you for taking the time to check out my books and I would appreciate it from the bottom of my heart if you would leave a review, long or short, on Amazon as it makes a HUGE difference in helping new readers find the series. Thank you!

To be the first to hear about my upcoming book releases, sales, and fun giveaways, sign up for my newsletter at **www.normahinkens.com** and follow me on Twitter, Instagram and Facebook. Feel free to email me at norma@normahinkens.com with any feedback or comments. I LOVE hearing from readers. YOU are the reason I keep going through the tough times.

All my best,
Norma

BIOGRAPHY

NYT and USA Today bestselling author Norma Hinkens writes twisty psychological suspense thrillers, as well as fast-paced science fiction and fantasy about spunky heroines and epic adventures in dangerous worlds. She's also a travel junkie, legend lover, and idea wrangler, in no particular order. She grew up in Ireland, land of make-believe and the original little green man.

Find out more about her books on her website.
www.normahinkens.com

Follow her on Facebook for funnies, giveaways, cool stuff & more!